I0662342

You're Still There

Jamie O. Colt

You're Still There

Jamie O. Colt

For my dear friend...who, had she ever learned these books existed, would have been shocked and then hilariously thrilled.

I can still hear your laughter. I miss you.

Playlist

"To Someone From A Warm Climate (Uiscefhuaraithe)" by Hozier
"Yoü and I" by Lady Gaga
"Rain" by Sleep Token
"when the party's over" by Billie Eilish
"I Want You to Want Me" by Letters to Cleo
"Wait For Me" by Kings of Leon
"Gimme All Your Love" by Alabama Shakes
"You Should Probably Leave" by Chris Stapleton
"Conversion" by Khruangbin, Leon Bridges
"All I Wanted" by Paramore
"By and By" by Caamp
"Aneurysm" by Nirvana
"Fade Into You" by Mazzy Star
"Believe" by Mumford & Sons
"Push" by Matchbox Twenty
"Layla" by Eric Clapton
"Fear and Friday's" by Zach Bryan
"Alone" by Heart
"Wanna Be Loved" by The Red Clay Strays
"The End" by Kings of Leon

I wish I could say
That the river of my arms have found the ocean
I wish I could say the cold lake water of my heart
Well, Christ, it's boilin' over
But it happened easy, darlin'
Natural as another leg around you in the bed frame

- Hozier

Prologue

Elsi:

N orma yells from the living room for the second time that I need to hurry up. I sigh and pull the scrap of receipt from the back of the book, saving my page before setting it down next to me on the bed. I've been dressed and ready for a while but was hoping for a miracle that she would forget I promised to come with her and leave without me.

Not. Likely.

"Coming!" I glance in my full length mirror. My just-barely-strawberry blonde hair is falling across my shoulders in unplanned waves, as it always does. The black corduroy overall skirt I'm wearing covers very little of my legs. I lock eyes with my reflection and think briefly that I should have shaved them and then watch myself shrug. My eyes look pretty with mascara on, I should wear it more often. It makes my light brown eyes a little less boring. Looking at my gray short sleeve top, I consider a sweater but decide against it since it's been pretty warm for late April in Southern Vermont and I don't want to have to carry it. My canvas sneakers are already on so I really have no other reason for not heading out to meet Norma. I lean forward toward the mirror and pull my glossed lips back from my teeth to make sure none of my dinner is still there even though I brushed them after eating.

You're just stalling, Elsi. I sigh loudly one more time, really just for my own benefit, and head out my bedroom door.

"Finally!" Norma says to me, glancing up from her cellphone.

"Fuck off," I toss back at her.

She holds up her middle finger with a big smile and I follow her out the front door. Norma's black hair is pin straight, tied up in a high ponytail that swings as she leads me down the front steps. Her makeup with signature red lipstick is flawless. A flowy white tank top falls around her waist and ends just barely above her tiny denim shorts, showing a sliver of her flat stomach. She's several inches taller than me, at almost six feet tall, thin, and toned with legs that go on for miles. I'm not technically short for a woman at 5'4", but she makes me feel it. We're total opposites. Our height. Our hair. Her pale skin is a few shades lighter than my naturally tan complexion and where she is thin, I have curves. My shoulders are broader, my bra is a few sizes larger, and my waist starts narrow but then flairs out to my hips and thick thighs. To top it all off, she is unbelievably outgoing and I am a homebody.

Despite our extrovert/introvert differences, she is the most important person in my life. My best friend. My right hand woman. My soul sister. We've been roommates all four years, When we met it was an automatic connection. I was nauseously nervous to move to a new state, where I knew absolutely no one. I had to move on my own so I was kind of an anxious wreck taking a plane for the first time, collecting my bags, getting a ride to the college, and then having to find where to get my room assignment. So by the time I was standing in front of my dorm room door, I was physically shaking from exhaustion and tension. And then I walked into the room. Norma looked at me with a beaming smile, asked if I was Elsi, and then wrapped me in the biggest, warmest hug. I needed it so badly, and the fact that she could tell from one glance at me, had me clinging to her like a life raft and since that moment, we've been nearly inseparable.

Tonight, we're headed, me begrudgingly, to a party a few roads over at an apartment of Norma's teammates. Norma is obnoxiously popular at our college. Partially because she's on the basketball team but mostly because she is breathtakingly beautiful, and kind, and fun. The party is being thrown by some of the girls who played with her on the basketball team. They're celebrating their neighbors, the baseball team, after their big win last night. Norma's season ended in early spring but the sports teams at Cort University are all pretty close. It's a jock thing. And I totally get it but I opted not to play my coveted softball while attending college and have instead dedicated my time to my classes and my job, which pays for said classes. Any time I have outside of that I try to spend reading but Norma doesn't feel that is time well spent. She feels that the last month of our college careers should be used to party and have fun before we're thrown into the real world. My idea for our last month in college is to fucking chill before we have to be responsible. But I never win these arguments.

"So am I going to know anyone here?" I ask as we stop at a crosswalk and wait for the signal. This is a college town on a Friday night, so the roads are packed with cars and the sidewalks are packed with people.

She gives me a side eye, "Yes, El. You're going to know a bunch of people...like you always do. It's going to be fine once we get there."

I groan.

"You know what I think you need?"

"Hm?"

"A good, meaningless, sexy as hell hookup."

I grab her hand as we cross the street, "Nor-"

She laces her fingers through mine as she interrupts my unenthusiastic reply, "No, seriously, it's been far too long and maybe that will help you!"

"But maybe it won't."

"Even if it doesn't help, it's still getting laid and *that* is a win, my friend."

I can't help but laugh at her. She's right that I'll have a good time once we're there. I'll stick with her or one of our other friends, have a drink, and loosen up. And I appreciate her trying to help me get over this weird funk I've been in lately.

Really it's been the last few months. I know I should be happy. I have a great best friend, we have a group of kind, fun people we hang out with regularly, I love my major, my job is pretty entertaining, and we're about to graduate and move on to bigger and better things.

But I look around knowing all this and just feel...not much of anything.

I've been turning Norma down for nights out since the semester started at the end of January but she wouldn't take no for an answer this time. So I'm going out tonight in the hopes that maybe I get myself out of this weird phase and back to my usual self. And maybe getting laid *will* help but I'm really not looking for that tonight. Plus, that's not really my thing. Like at all. I'm in my head far too much for something like that.

As we turn the corner of the block and walk up the stone walkway to the party, people are everywhere and some are already yelling greetings to Norma. She keeps her hand in mine as she hollers back, not stopping until we're inside the house. The apartment is really a duplex, one side is rented by some girls on the basketball team and the other side is rented by guys on the baseball team. The baseball side of the house is dark, probably because they're all at the party.

As we walk into the house, which is throbbing with music coming from somewhere, she pulls her hand from mine and throws her arm over my shoulder, squeezing me into her and kissing the side of my head, "I love you and listen, you know I'll leave when you want."

I give her an honest grin, "I know, babe."

She looks around the living room, probably for our friends.

"Think Will will finally crack?" I ask, leaning in close so she'll hear me. She's been pining over a guy from the baseball team for over six months now and he flirts with her, but he's yet to actually ask her out.

She rolls her eyes and I leave it at that, knowing she's losing hope by the gallon every minute we get closer to graduation.

I point toward where I know the drinks are, "Can we find a drink before you run off to socialize?"

She squeals an agreement and I follow her through the living room and into the kitchen where it seems just about everyone is gathered.

I'm not sure how long ago we got here but I've had a couple beers and way too much conversation. I'm sitting at the kitchen counter with some of the girls I know from the basketball team or from classes. It's pretty hard to hear over the music blasting from the living room and the other conversations happening.

This house is completely packed with people, like it's almost impossible to move through the room. It's all just very exhausting.

"Anyone want another?!" I yell to my friends in the hearing vicinity. A few nod to me and I slide off the stool I've been parked on. I elbow my way to the fridge for the beers and on the way, keep an eye out for where Norma may have ended up.

I make it back to the group and hand out drinks before shouting, "Going to try to find Nor!" They shoot me good luck and I grab my beer off the counter, taking a sip before I start elbowing through the crowd to find my lady. This is insane. How do people do this every week? *Multiple* times a week?

It usually isn't hard to figure out where Norma is, I just follow the music. So I push my way toward the thumping bass, into the living room, and sure enough, she's dancing her sweet ass off, surrounded by a few of her teammates and some of the baseball players.

Being friends with Norma has kept me in the know of who's who of the athletes. I also go to plenty of home games throughout the year just to ease the itch of wishing I was playing something. I know the people surrounding her, even if I haven't talked to them much. She has her arm draped across the shoulder of one of her teammates and she sings along to the song, her ponytail sways behind her as she moves to the beat.

Some random people and what seems to be the rest of the baseball team are scattered around the room on couches, the floor, or along the wall. How any of them can hear each other for conversation is beyond me.

As I scan the faces, one guy catches my eye. Well, he *always* catches my eye. Nate Croman. We've been in a few classes together each year, we're both business majors, and he's one of the starting baseball players. He has a bit of a reputation for being a complete dickhead but I've never really seen that. Maybe it is true, but I know that at least 10% of him is a good guy. I've witnessed him help our classmates on multiple occasions and I know during our sophomore year, he met our elderly Pre-Calculus professor at his office before each class in order to carry his books for him. I used to work a shift before that class and I got done about 30 minutes early so instead of going to my dorm, I'd grab something to eat and wait in the empty classroom. I was surprised when about two weeks in, Nate came through the door with all of our professor's necessities. I stopped being surprised within another two weeks but never said anything about it either.

I've barely spoken to him in the four years we've been orbiting each other but he is the *exact* vision of all my dirty dreams. If someone were to ask me what my type was, I'd describe Nate Croman. He is tall, so unbelievably tall, with hair so blonde that it almost looks white. It's slightly too long and sticks up all over the place. I know he runs his fingers through it often and probably messes it up on purpose but boy, does it work for him. His cheekbones are gorgeous, his jawline is sharp, his nose is narrow and only slightly crooked, probably from being broken once or twice. In his black tshirt I can see tattoos covering one arm and just barely peeking up above his shirt's neckline. He lounges on the couch with a beer hanging loosely from his hand, he has large hands with long strong fingers, and he looks like he could not give less of a shit about any of the people in this room. He looks *bored*.

God, the things I'd let him do to me.

In real time though, I just quickly glance through the people around Norma as I approach her. None of them seem to take too much notice of me and that is just fine. But when she sees me, she throws her hands in the air and shrieks, "Did you get laid yet?"

I close my eyes and take a breath, "*Jesus*, Norm. No, and could you not scream that?"

She laughs as I glance around to make sure no one heard her over the music. I catch Nate's gaze, there's a curious look on his face. Did he hear her? Does he think I've never had sex? Because I have! Once. I look away from him and back to her.

"What's this?" she pulls my beer from my hand and takes a sip, "We need something better than this."

"No, Norma, I'm-"

"SHOTS!" She cuts me off with a scream and everyone within three feet of us cheers. Everyone but me and Nate.

I groan loudly since no one can hear me anyway.

I've had two shots of tequila and decide to quit on the beer at this point. Water is my new best friend. Norma is sitting on my lap on the couch, mumbling in my ear about how I just need to get up and pick a guy to fuck. Real wholesome, ain't she?

"I'm not just going to pick some guy, Norma Belle."

"Oh, shut up and do it. I've seen *at least* three different guys approach you tonight. We never have to speak of it again if you don't want to, but just let yourself be carefree for *once*."

"I'm carefree!" I insist. Three guys have definitely not approached me for anything but a quick hello. I think?

She throws her head back laughing and I try to hold her somewhat up. "Carefree, my ass," she says. "You overthink everything, you're always working and studying and worrying about doing the wrong thing and being embarrassed or whatever but there is nothing to be embarrassed about, baby girl! You're smoking hot! You should get some."

Well, *she* certainly isn't holding back. Maybe it would be nice to hook up with someone. That rush of adrenaline that comes from it, maybe it will help me feel better. Or maybe that's just complete nonsense. Hooking up with a stranger just isn't something I do. The thought of it makes me antsy and uncomfortable. How would I even initiate a thing like that?

"I'll think about it while I pee." I push her off my lap and she lets out a playful screech.

"Elsi, baby."

"Hm?" I turn back to her.

"Just do it. Just go for it." She says all of this leaning toward me with her eyes completely closed. I'm going to have to take her home pretty soon. It's a damn good thing I trust all these idiots around her.

Once in the bathroom, I lean back against the door and let out a huge breath. The quiet feels really fucking nice. I pee and then stare at myself in the mirror for a few minutes trying to absorb the solitude into my bones and blood before having to go back out there. Norma's words keep replaying in my head but I just don't know if I can do it. Can I do it? What's the harm really? We graduate in a month and then I never have to see any of these people again. I can totally pick a random guy and just hook up with him. I don't even need to have sex with him, we can just make out. Yeah. Yeah, a make out session I can probably do.

My resolve set, I open the bathroom door but instead of heading back to the party, I look down the dark, seemingly abandoned hallway to my left and go that way instead. I'm not entirely sure why but it's quieter and the quiet just kind of draws me in. I don't bother peeking into any rooms because that always seems dangerous, so I pass a couple doors and then follow the hallway around a turn that leads to an exterior door. The back door I'm guessing. I don't go outside though, I just lean back against the wall and close my eyes.

Who am I kidding? I'll never be that person who's brave enough to proposition someone. Ugh. I should get Norma home anyway. Just another second of quiet and then I'll go get her.

An insane creaking noise breaks my daydreams. I jump, my heart pounding, my nerves going haywire, and when my eyes shoot open, I see a man walking through the door from outside. The scent of cigarettes following behind him.

"Oh, shit, sorry," he says, realizing that he scared the absolute crap out of me. Probably from the crazy gasping noise I made.

As he steps into the light of the hallway, I see Nate Croman's stupidly perfect face and just stare at him for a second. Probably a second too long and reply, "No, no, that's okay. I just kind of zoned out."

He nods and pops a mint in his mouth. He holds the container up to me, gesturing to ask if I want one. As if this is a normal occurrence for us to be within two feet of each other. And I'm surprised to see my hand reach out toward him. He cups the back of it with his, steadying it as he taps the container down to let some fall out. His hand is almost twice the size of mine and it's surprisingly warm.

"Party too much?" he asks. His voice is just as sexy as the rest of him. It's deep and melodic and makes me tingle.

As I shamelessly take in his face, I realize his eyes are green. I always thought they were hazel. I admire them, framed by long eyelashes, as he slides the mint container back in his pocket. "Yeah," I breathe out a laugh, "something like that."

When he glances up to meet my gaze, he gives me a tiny smirk and I can just barely see his white, straight teeth. Butterflies start to flutter about in my chest. Will I ever fantasize about another man like the way I do Nate? I can practically hear Norma telling me to just fucking go for it. I pop the mint in my mouth and step closer to Nate. We graduate in less than a month. I can be brave. He had bent over to give me the mint and he's standing straight now, towering over me. I can totally be brave. His hair hangs down across his forehead as he looks down at me with not much of any emotion on his face.

"I think I'm just gonna-" I begin to say and stop myself. I feel one second of hesitation but you know what? Fuck it. I want to be able to say I did this when I'm old and gray. So I throw caution to the wind and decide on a risky and probably embarrassing chance, reaching up to grab his neck and pull Nate fucking Croman's face to mine and slam our lips together.

My stomach immediately flames hot and does a few flips. I push up on my tippy toes to press into him farther. Only about a millisecond after crashing my mouth to his though, I panic and pull away, dropping back down onto the heels of my feet. Nate is looking at me with what seems to be a mixture of confusion and desire and before I can even think of what to say, he bends down and presses our lips back together, one of his big hands sliding around my waist and pulling me closer to him. What. Is. Happening?

I go with it because it's Nate Croman, who I've fantasized about for years, and I've had a few drinks and feel the liquid courage pumping through me. His lips are soft and when he opens his mouth, I mimic the motion so that our tongues meet. My stomach bottoms out. He tastes minty and just a tad like cigarettes. My brain is spinning and I'm hot, my whole body is hot. His hand presses into my lower back, and I take another step into him, my chest against his. I feel so tiny pressed up against his large frame. And why is that so fucking hot?

I'm in a whirlwind of desperate freaking need as his mouth moves against mine and I take his lower lip between my teeth. A bang from one of the rooms startles me and Nate breaks our kiss, looking around. Reality crashes down on me. Followed very, very closely by a huge wave of embarrassment.

"Oh, God," I whisper in complete panic, he whips his head back to me. "Shit, I'm sorry. I can't believe I just kissed Nate Croman," I realize I'm talking about him *to him* and apologize again. "I'm sorry." I squeeze my eyes shut, hoping when I open them this isn't happening. "I'm El-"

"I know who you are, Elsi," he chuckles a little.

Oh. I open my eyes again. He knows who I am?

He grabs a strand of my hair and tucks it behind my ear. Another bang from one of the rooms makes me jump again. He jerks his head toward the back door, "Come on."

Grabbing my hand, he pulls me with him outside. It's dark out here, the sun having set a while ago, but the lights from the windows provide a dull glow that still lets me make out his handsome features. He walks me backwards so my back is to the brick of the house, with one hand on the wall next to me. The bricks are cold. It feels good, like it's grounding me, clearing my head.

"This doesn't seem like something you usually do," he gestures between us. "No judgment at all. I just rarely see you at these things anymore and I don't think I've ever..." he trails off.

Seen me hook up with someone.

I laugh, a quick genuine laugh and he smirks in response. I shake my head, "This is not something I *ever* do."

He doesn't reply. I think he knows there's more to it and is giving me a second.

"I didn't want to come tonight but Norma..." I shrug. "I've been in a weird place lately. Well for months now. Nothing's wrong but..." I feel emotion start to clog my throat. "I saw you come through that door and I just-" my voice cracks. I stop.

He waits. His green eyes are intense as they try to read me.

I take a steadying breath, and look away from him, down at his Vans. "I just wanted to feel *something*."

He stays quiet but when I look back up, he leans in towards me. His cheek brushes mine and I can feel his breath on my ear as he whispers, "I can help you with that."

I don't move at first when his fingers grip my jaw, his palm pressing into my throat, and his lips connecting with mine. I only move when our mouths open and tongues meet again. My heart feels heavy as it beats. I grip onto his tshirt, pulling him closer. This is a dream. I cannot believe this is happening. He takes another step closer and his thighs press against mine. I'm pretty sure I groan into his mouth when I feel his erection on my hip. Is there anything sexier than knowing you're desired?

He pulls his lips from mine. "If you want me to stop, I need you to tell me."

I just stare at him for a second. Why would I want him to stop? And then I realize that he's waiting for me to respond.

"Okay," I say, my voice sounding hoarse.

He holds eye contact for another second and then nods, "Okay."

His lips are back on mine, his hand still pressed against my throat and jaw. It's possessive and sexy as hell. His free hand finds my thigh and his fingers tickle as he glides them up towards the bottom of my skirt, sliding under and landing on my ass. He squeezes and my breathing is becoming ragged. He doesn't wait long though before his fingers travel back down my thigh and between my legs. He's moving achingly slow and the anticipation is killing me. For another moment or two I continue to think I'm dreaming but the chills spreading across my body and his tongue on mine convince me it's actually happening. He hooks a finger into my thong and pulls it aside. I'm trembling from nerves and desperate need.

"Relax, Elsi," he encourages and I spread my legs further apart. When his fingertips graze my clit, I audibly inhale and I can feel him smile against my lips in response. As his fingers slide easily along my clit, he kisses down my neck. I bite his earlobe and he returns the gesture by biting where my neck meets my shoulder, making my knees shake.

I've never felt like this before, like I'm not sure it's really happening but I'm so desperate for more. His fingers slide back toward my entrance and when I think I might go crazy from need, he pushes two inside of me and moans.

He moans.

Oh God, this feels good. His fingers stretch me perfectly and I'm not sure I can continue to stand much longer. I can't focus on kissing him anymore and he isn't bothering. He pushes in and out of me in a steady rhythm and then he uses his thumb to continue the circles on my clit. I think I might die. I can feel his erection digging into my hip. He's everywhere. Holding my jaw and pressing on my throat and his mouth is on mine and his fingers are inside me. I whimper.

"*Fuck*," he breathes out against my lips.

He knows exactly how to touch me and I've daydreamed about this so many times but it's somehow better. My body is moving on its own now in motion with his hand and that encourages him. He moves a little faster and his tongue is back in my mouth. It's all too much. I feel the coil tightening inside of me as he curls his fingers and hits a spot that makes me see stars. I let out a pathetic little moan.

"*Yeah*, that's it," he mumbles into my mouth.

My hands slide up around his neck and hold him to me. His thumb hits my nerves just in the right spot and I come undone. I cry into his mouth through heavy breaths and whole body shakes. He keeps the motion steady, letting me ride out the orgasm.

As I come down off the wave, he pulls his fingers out of me, then fixes my underwear and skirt. We're both breathing heavily and he rests his forehead on mine.

"That..." I start to say but don't know how to finish. Instead I just slide my hands into his hair and bring his lips to mine again in a much softer kiss than before. He responds by tugging me off the wall and wrapping his arms around my waist, pulling me tight against him. One of his hands slides to my ass, allowing him to press his erection into my waist.

If I thought I wanted Nate before all of this, it has nothing on my craving for him right fucking now. My tongue reaches out for his again and our kiss returns to something along the lines of desperation. His hips buck into me. I need more.

I pull slightly away, my bravery somehow thriving, and ask, "Is there somewhere we can go?"

His eyes are burning heat and he nods exactly as I hear my name being called from inside the house.

We both still. I'm hoping beyond hope that Norma hasn't decided that this is the moment to find me and head home.

"Elsi! El!"

"Fuck," I whine and drop my head to Nate's chest.

"It's okay," he says quietly with a chuckle.

"Her timing sucks. She probably wants to go. I-" I cut myself off because I don't particularly want to leave. The one freaking time I don't want to leave. I could just tell her no but I also don't want her to walk home alone. I look back up at him, "I'm sorry."

He shakes his head. "There's nothing to be sorry for."

"ELSI!"

He gently cups my cheeks and his gaze dances across my face, like he's taking in every single detail. Then he presses one last soft kiss to my lips and takes a step back, "I'll be seeing you, Elsi."

I breathe out a disappointed sigh. "Out here, Norma!" I yell, looking into Nate's perfectly sexy face. I just know I'm really going to regret this ending. He takes a few more steps back. "Thank you," I whisper to him but he just gives me that quick smirk again.

As Norma opens the back door and steps out, Nate disappears around the side of the house.

Chapter One

Elsi - Five years later:

Norma yells to someone on her end and I rip the phone away from my ear.

"*Shit*, Norma!" I bark, not masking my annoyance since this is the third time in about five minutes that she's done this to me.

"Oh, sorry. Anyway, can you stop and grab the cake? It should be ready by 6 and it's already paid for."

"Yes, of course." I already told her once that I could grab it but she didn't hear me over her own yelling. "Who are you screaming at anyway?"

"Oh, just my co-worker. She's in the other room."

"You didn't think to walk out and have an indoor volume type conversation?"

"I did think of that, but then I didn't do it. Don't be a bitch, El," she laughs into the phone.

"I'll see you at 7, right?"

"Yes, I'll be there already. Thank you!"

I hear papers shuffling and know that's my cue to hang up before she starts screaming again. "See you then. Love you."

"Love you," she replies and the line goes dead.

I toss my phone onto the stack of papers I'm currently trying to organize on my desk. I have end of year paperwork I need to file within the next few weeks and everything is in shambles, as is common here. Other than my typical job duties, for the past two years I have been trying to muddle through the absolute shitshow of a filing system that basically didn't exist before me. Sometimes it really sucks to be an organization freak, but that's also part of my appeal as an employee. I'll do my work and also get the documents and accounts filed in an organized and easy to figure out way.

Working at EmpowerNest has been the most fulfilling job I've ever done. It's a nonprofit organization that houses single mothers as well as providing programs for educational and career opportunities within and around the Boston area. While it is my dream job, the records were such a freaking mess when I arrived, that I'm not really sure how anything actually got done beforehand. But the other employees are wonderful and other than the filing nightmares, I truly love what my job entails. I'm basically an event planner but an event planner whose events change the lives of the women who reside and benefit from EmpowerNest's offerings. I get to organize the college and career fairs, some of the workshops, and my favorite, the fundraising events to help support the awesome work this organization does.

Do I get paid a lot?

Absolutely not.

But do I get paid enough to live in Boston?

Yes.

Do I completely and totally love the work I do?

Double yes.

Even with the headache of the mountains and mountains of paperwork that very often cover my entire desk, I would not trade working here for much of anything. Not only is the work I do important and gratifying, the people I work with are amazing, and the women who benefit from the services are hardworking and dedicated mothers who want what's best for their children. It is really a dream come true.

Now if only I could find my desk before I leave for dinner in about 35 minutes.

At 6:45, I have the cake in hand and am heading the three blocks to the bar Norma chose for Will's birthday dinner. As I'm trying to navigate the sidewalk without tripping, my cellphone rings. I shift the box haphazardly to one hand and reach into my coat pocket. It's Scott.

"Hey!"

"Hi, honey," Scott says in his typical cheerful tone. "This a good time?"

He always asks me that when he calls and I almost roll my eyes, "Of course. I'm just walking to the bar, cake in hand."

"Oh good. I was hoping to catch you and say hi before you got there. Work was okay?"

Scott, my mildly older boyfriend of 35, is a commercial airline pilot. We've been together since January and things are going well but his schedule is pretty inconsistent so he often misses a lot of this stuff. It is what it is. He's kind and sweet and good to me and pretty darn handsome too. Especially in that airline pilot uniform.

"Yeah, it was okay. A bit hectic after being off yesterday, but all good and now I can enjoy the weekend."

"I wish I was home to visit."

I smile, "Me too. Where are you exactly?"

"Denver. From here I fly to Vegas, back to Denver, and then home."

"Great. We still on for dinner Monday night?"

"Absolutely. You let me know where to meet you and I'll be there."

"Sure," He always lets me pick dinner. Which at first was nice but now it almost seems like a chore. Sometimes I want to be surprised or just simply not have to make a decision.

We talk for a few more minutes about his flights and about Thanksgiving yesterday, which he spent with his mother in New York and I spent with Norma and Will, and then I tell him I'm about to walk into the bar.

"Tell Will I said happy birthday, okay?"

"You got it. Talk soon. Fly safe."

"Night, Elsi," and he hangs up. I drop my phone back in my pocket and smile to myself as I step up to the door.

Norma yells my name the second I walk in and I scan the people at the bar until I finally spot her walking toward me. A smile immediately breaks across my face, as if I didn't see her all day yesterday, or just about every day for the past nine years. I'm always happy to see my lady.

"Who the hell are all these people?!" I ask her as I get close, pushing carefully through the crowd holding the cake box up above my shoulders. We come to this bar pretty often and it's rarely so busy.

She leans forward and gives me a kiss on the cheek before taking the box. She's wearing a pale pink silky blouse tucked into a black pencil skirt with black knee high boots. Her black hair is pin straight, falling past her shoulders and her lips are red as always.

"Not a clue. Wish they'd all fuck off. Let me see if they can store this in the back and we can get you some wine."

I follow her to the side of the bar and one of the bartenders, who we know fairly well at this point, comes over seeing her with the box. She asks if they have a fridge to put it in and Antoine is happy to help, asking whose birthday it is and if he can sing along when the time comes. I can't help but smile at the enthusiasm.

"Stay here, I'll put it in the back and then take your drink orders." He points at me, "You look like you need something ASAP." He walks off into the back without another word.

I turn to Norma with a look of disbelief, "I *look* like I need a drink?! What is that supposed to mean?!"

She laughs but shrugs, "Who knows but if he's not going to make us wait to order, then I'm not going to argue." She gestures to the bar which is insanely packed with people.

"Where's the birthday boy?" I ask her over the noise.

"He got a table over there. A little more room," she points to a table away from the bar. There are about a dozen people sitting around Will. He turns 28 today, so Norma planned for us all to get some drinks tonight. But of course it's Black Friday and most people have had the long weekend, so it's completely insane.

"Who's here?"

She links her free arm through mine, "The usual. Frank, Charlie, Sarah, Alina, and a few guys from work."

Looking at the table, I see Will throwing his head back at something one of the guys must have said. Sarah and Alina are leaning into each other, smiles on their faces as they talk animatedly.

Norma and Will have been together since graduation night of college. Norma had been crushing on him for a long time and the idiot waited until the very last second to ask to kiss her, which she enthusiastically agreed to. Luckily for the both of them, Will had already planned to move to Boston too. Norma and I got an apartment and started working at our entry-level jobs as she and Will started really dating. He had a great job offer out of college so he made good money from the get-go. He proposed about a year after that and she abandoned me, with my undying approval, as they moved in together. Then about two years ago, I got to be maid of honor at their wedding and ugly cry as they swore to love each other forever. They're really, truly great together and Will is the only man to ever come close to deserving Norma.

"I should warn you though," she starts, grabbing my arm gently. I look at her confused. She makes a face like her news is awkward, "It's probably a non-issue, but Nate Croman is here."

I look back to the table and sure enough, Nate's face comes into view as one of the other guys shifts to grab his drink. He talks casually to Frank, one of our closest friends. My stomach does a weird swoop as I lay eyes on him. A completely unexpected blast from the past. I was so sure, like beyond sure, that I would never lay eyes on him again.

"Nate Croman," I say and then turn away from him before I'm caught.

"Yeah. Weird, right? But he has stayed in contact with Will over the years and I guess his California company has a branch in Boston and they sent him here for like six months or something to work on a project. Apparently he got here at the beginning of the month but Will, the jackass, didn't mention anything about him until this morning when he told me he'd be coming tonight."

I'm not quite sure what to make of this. I haven't seen Nate Croman in person since a week or so before our graduation from college. After our hookup at the party, I only saw him a handful of times, where I always pretended I didn't see him, and then we graduated and I moved with Norma to Boston.

Looking at him now after all this time, that faded and ancient attraction fizzles. I don't know him anymore. In all honesty, I never knew him, but I'd have to be blind not to see how gorgeous he still is. Is he somehow *hotter*? He's truly a man now. None of that boyhood is left in his face. He's all muscle and masculinity. His hair is still so blonde it's almost white, but instead of being too long and sticking up in every direction, it is neatly cut and combed. He's wearing what I'm guessing are his work clothes, a black button up, a black tie, and a black suit jacket. His suit fits him really, really well, showing off his broad shoulders and muscular arms. I'd wager it was custom tailored and cost him a fortune. I can only assume that hidden by the table are black suit pants and black shoes. He has one hand curled around a bottle of beer.

"Okay, ladies. What can I get you?" Antoine comes back over and helps me pull my gaze from Nate.

"Prosecco, please," Norma smiles as she orders.

"I'll have a pinot grigio. Thanks!"

He hustles off to get us our glasses and I can't help but glance back over to the table I'm about to head to. "Nate Croman," I say again with a disbelieving sigh.

"He's still pretty hot," Norma says with a nod beside me.

"So fucking hot, Norm. Like what the actual fuck?" I honestly don't know how I feel about this. Our hookup was a blip. It was a 30 minute thing in the span of my entire 27 years, so why is this even something I'm muddled over? But I know the truth that even though we only hooked up the one time, I wanted way freaking more than what I got, and I had been borderline obsessed with the man for at least the three years leading up to that night. So in reality, he was a big deal to me but *I* was a blip to him.

Our friendly bartender brings us our drinks, "You girls let me know when you need that cake and my perfect vocals."

Laughing, we thank him, and Norma asks him to put our drinks on Will's tab.

"Ready?" she asks.

I shake my head, take a few sips of my wine, look at her with a cringy face, and then nod.

She takes a step toward the table and I follow, quickly glancing down at my outfit. I'm in a black fitted blouse which is tucked into cut off plaid trousers of black and gray. Oh jeez, I haven't looked at my hair in hours. I run my hand along the top of my head hoping there are minimal fly-aways. Then internally shrug that there's no way to change anything now and immediately chastise myself for even wishing that I was dressed differently. For what? None of my friends will second guess my work clothes.

"Scott flying tonight?" Norma asks just as we reach the table.

Scott, yeah. God, I'm an asshole!

"Yeah, I'll see him Monday night for dinner. He'll be in town for like four hours or something stupid like that."

Before Norma can respond, Will looks up and spots me and I shout, "Birthday boy!" Throwing my free hand up, I bounce around the side of the table so I can wrap my arms around his neck. Will is a handsome man. He's well over six feet tall, which is good for Norma, who's also a giant. He has black hair he keeps neatly trimmed on the sides and a little longer on top. His eyes are an insane ice blue. Tonight he's dressed casually, having been off today, wearing jeans and an olive green cable knit sweater that I'm sure Norma bought for him.

He hugs me tight, "Hey, darling!"

"How's it feel being old as shit?" I tease, catching sight of him rolling his eyes.

"Joke wasn't funny yesterday *or* this morning and it ain't funny now," he laughs, nudging me with his elbow.

"You love my jokes, Will," I wink.

Will and I have a great relationship. I completely and absolutely consider him my brother. If I'm being painfully honest, I'm way closer to him than my actual brother. We tease and pick on each other relentlessly. He lets me vent to him. He's my apartment's unofficial handyman. He understands my quirks that no one until Norma ever did. I trust him completely. And he treats my best friend like a princess. He and Norma are family.

"Take a seat. Nor, come sit!" He calls behind me.

I sit next to Will, Norma sitting on my other side. I can feel him reach his arm around me to grab Norma. Reading his mind, I press forward into the table as he pulls her towards him. They meet behind me and I hear the sound of a kiss, a whisper, and a giggle.

I shake my head with a smile and greet the table, getting a choir of responses. I specifically don't look in Nate's direction. I'm not sure why, but I don't want him to know I realize he's here. Or maybe he'll think I don't even remember him. Actually, I'd be surprised if he remembered *me*.

Sarah and Alina both say hi and reach across the table to grip my hand. I give them a bright smile.

"How'd your exam go?" I ask Sarah, my voice carrying over the music. Sarah is tall like Norma, with shocking red hair, and green eyes. She's a native to Boston, sweet, and incredibly outgoing. She's about to graduate with her Master's degree in education and has been taking all of her certification exams. Her last one was this week and then she should be certified to teach once she graduates next month. She worked as an accountant for a few years after she graduated college, which is how we met her. She worked at the same bank as Norma. But a couple years ago she decided to go back to school to be a math teacher. She said she wanted more interaction which makes sense because other than Norma, she's the biggest people person I know.

She smiles, "I think it was pretty good! Just hoping the results come quickly, so I can relax."

I wave my hand at her, "I'm sure you crushed it!"

She shrugs in her typical modest way and Alina changes the subject to some gossip from her job that we've all been eating up for the past couple weeks, living vicariously through her. Alina is shorter than me, only about 5'2" and a firecracker. Her hair is perfectly dyed a golden brown and highlighted every month, her nails are always immaculate, and her makeup is tutorial worthy. She's loud and proud and often the life of the party. She works as a paralegal at a well known law firm in Boston but the absolutely insane drama that goes on in her office is so freaking entertaining. She has a really good way of keeping entirely out of everything but still getting every last detail about what's going on. I know basically all of the names of the people she works with but haven't actually met anyone.

"Wait! Wait! I thought Marina was the one dating John?" Norma borderline shrieks.

"Girl, she was! She got right in Angelica's face about not being good enough for Bobby and how he needs a woman like her and John was literally in the next room and heard everything!"

"There's no way!" I say in disbelief.

"So John comes out and asks Marina to repeat what she said. She hesitated for like two seconds and then repeated it! Told John that Bobby is who she wants to be with and walks right out of the office."

"So is she with Bobby now?"

Alina shakes her head, "No!"

Norma and Sarah gasp.

Alina continues, "He told her that he's always had a thing for her but he doesn't want to ruin their friendship by dating."

"What a fucking copout!" Sarah interjects.

"Of course it is! He's not into her *at all* but I think he felt guilty or something after she went off in front of the whole office about him."

"This is insane. So what did John do?" Norma asks.

Alina shrugs, "Went on with his business like absolutely nothing had happened."

Sarah shakes her head, "This is unreal."

We all laugh at the ridiculous stories and drama that has no impact on us whatsoever. Maybe that's what makes it so entertaining.

I lean back in my seat and take another sip of wine. As the night has gone on, we've rearranged our seating a few times to mingle but now the girls and I are all clustered together along one corner of the table. Will sits on the opposite side of Norma so he can still touch her, but he talks with his friends.

Nate gets up, catching my eye, and I watch him stand. His black suit is fitted so well to him and when he turns away from the table, I enjoy the muscular shape of his shoulders and arms. I keep myself from sighing at the nostalgic memory of him having me pressed up against the house all those years ago. I would have done a lot of things to make that man feel good. But that was over five years ago now and there's no reason he even remembers who I am.

I nudge Norma with my shoulder, "Should we get the cake?"

"Oh! Yeah, totally." She pulls on Will's arm to get his attention and says something to him when he leans towards her. He nods and kisses her cheek.

We make our way back to the bar and Antoine comes bustling over and asks what he can help us with.

"Well, certainly another round of these," she gestures to our glasses and then turns and points to Will, "and another gin and tonic for that sexy man."

"Whatever you want, you got, girl!" he tells Norma and turns to get those drinks made.

When he comes back over, I tell him we're also ready for the birthday cake.

"*Finally!*" he claps and turns around yelling, "It's time Betty!" to the other bartender and disappearing into the back room.

Norma looks at me with shock on her face and I laugh with her, our foreheads coming together.

Antoine comes out of the back with the cake in his hands. He sets it down in front of Norma and then reaches down, pulling a lighter out of some hiding spot and sliding it in front of me. I light the big candles of a '2' and '8' and then ask Norma, Antoine, and Betty if they're ready.

"Ready!" Norma says, slipping her fingers under the cake's cardboard and lifting it slowly off the bar. As she walks over to the table where everyone else is seated, I keep my hands braced around her, a glass in each, to attempt to catch her if she loses her footing. She isn't entirely sober at this point.

"One-two-three-four!" Norma shouts and we all join her in singing 'Happy Birthday' to Will who looks at each of us with a smile and then locks his gaze on his wife as she loudly and enthusiastically sings to him. I can't help but laugh through the song, looking away from Norma and catching sight of Antoine and Betty doing a full Broadway production behind me.

As we sing the last "Happy Birthday to you,' I glance around the group of friends gathered and I catch Nate's gaze. His eyes are locked on me, like I've had his attention for a while, and I am immediately conscious of my heart thudding in my chest. His expression gives nothing away as he looks back at me.

In my peripheral, Will is leaning forward and blowing the candles out. As everyone cheers and laughs, my eyes rip away from Nate's. I'm still aware of him though. Aware that he claps but doesn't smile and I know he didn't sing. I can't help it when my eyes flick back to his. He continues to watch me, this time with a sort of curious look on his face.

Norma breaks my attention by stepping back and bumping into me. I turn toward her and lean in, gripping around her waist. "I'll see if they have a knife and plates and stuff."

When I get back to the bar, Antoine is ready with the things I need. "You're like a mindreader."

"Don't I know it," he says with a raise of his eyebrows. I return to the table to cut the cake and Frank helps me pass out slices to everyone.

We eat, have a few more drinks, and then all go our separate ways. I specifically don't look toward Nate again. I stand outside with Sarah and Alina, who live together, as we all wait for our rideshares. Will and Norma live close enough to Charlie that he gives them a ride home.

Once back in my apartment, I take off everything but my underwear and lay in my bed, thinking through the night. I had a blast with the girls like always and Will definitely felt celebrated. But my mind keeps going back to Nate. We didn't speak and it's not like there's anything to say. I don't even know the man. But what's repeatedly going through my head is the way he made me feel that night all those years ago. I haven't thought about him in a long time. I'm not sure when I thought about him last honestly. But seeing him tonight, I remember how his hands felt on my skin and the way my heart beat and how desperate I was for him to never stop touching me.

Have I *ever* felt like that again?

Since graduating college I've been with a handful of guys and a few of them were fairly serious boyfriends but when is the last time I felt like I might absolutely combust from desire? Like I might not survive if the man in front of me didn't touch me? And now that I was thinking about it, I wasn't sure I'd ever felt that aside from that one single night with Nate back in college. And the real shitty part of this realization is the fact that we didn't even have sex. He just fingered me against a brick wall.

I lay my head back against my headboard and sigh. Guilt washing over me for the umpteenth time tonight.

I shouldn't be thinking this way when I have a boyfriend. A nice man who treats me well. But even though Scott's wonderful and handsome, he's never truly got my blood pumping. We've had sex plenty of times and it was...fine. No, that's not fair. It was good. He was always attentive before he got off and a girl can appreciate that. But I don't go out to restaurants with him and wish his hands were on me. I've never felt that mind numbing desire where my fingers and toes tingle with the memory of it. Our relationship is safe and-

Shit.

It's boring. It's safe and boring.

Shit. Fuck. Dammit. I'm bored with my relationship with Scott.

Chapter Two

Nate:

E lsi. Fucking. Abbot.

Chapter Three

Elsi:

"Norma," I pull my feet up underneath me onto her couch and curl into myself. "I think I'm going to break up with Scott."

"What? Why?" she asks, her head whipping away from the TV. "Did something happen Monday night?"

"No," I shake my head, remembering dinner with Scott the other day. "No, everything was fine."

She cocks her head to the side, waiting for me to continue.

I groan. "It was *fine*. I'm bored!" I confess, dropping my head back on the couch.

"That's fair."

I let my head loll to the side and look at her, "Fair?"

She twists up her lips and nods, "I like Scott a lot. He's super smart and kind and gets along well with everyone but the dude is kinda *blah.*"

I squeeze my eyes shut, "Why didn't you tell me?"

She shrugs, "You were into him and he was kind to you. What would I have said?"

I muddle this over. "Yeah, alright. I'm going to break up with him."

She reaches over and squeezes my knee, "What made you realize all of a sudden that he's not the guy for you though? Just last week you were brainstorming Christmas presents for him."

I make a whining noise, like a child, knowing this was coming, "Please don't judge me or read into this because it's not something to be read into."

Her eyebrows come together, "Oookay..."

"Seeing Nate," I start and pause, expecting her to say something or scream or jump off the couch but she just waits patiently, her face giving nothing away. "It really doesn't truly have anything to do with him. But seeing him, I remembered how he made me feel. We only hooked up that one time, but Norma, I have *never* been turned on like that before or since and I just want to feel that again. That desperation and just raw fucking need. You know? I don't want a relationship because it's easy. I want to *feel* something."

She barks out a small laugh, "That's hardly asking too much, baby girl. You have to feel something for your partner. You have to want them."

I take that for the honest truth, knowing that her and Will have found that in each other.

"Do you think you'd want to reconnect with Nate? I can't help but assume we're going to see more of him."

I shake my head, "No, this isn't really about him. I don't even know the man. And honestly, he's kind of intimidating."

Norma gives me a naughty smirk, "Maybe that's part of the appeal."

I laugh, "Oh, it definitely is!"

"So when are you going to tell Scott?"

"We're having dinner again tomorrow. I suppose it's as good a time as any."

My stomach is in knots, wondering when the right time to break the news to Scott will present itself. We ordered dinner in to his apartment and are sitting at the table scooping Chinese food onto our plates. I'm glad we're at his place so I can sneak out easily once I break the news. I wonder how he's going to react. He's a super chill guy but it's not like I've broken up with him before to know how he might respond to it.

We have light conversation through the meal and afterwards, I grab our plates and offer to wash them. He sits back in his chair, "Thanks, El."

Scott is incredibly handsome. He keeps his brown hair buzzed short, a style he kept since being in the military for a few years in his early twenties. His eyes are a deep brown, warm and friendly. He's wearing a henley and jeans, the henley hugs his arms nicely. The thing I find the most attractive about him though are his hands. They're strong and worn, like he uses them often. They're very masculine and pretty sexy and it makes me feel conflicted that when he touches me with them, I don't melt into a puddle.

Ugh.

My whole life I have been chasing a need to be the most important person in someone's life. Which I suppose isn't that unusual, even if there's a flaw in it. Being the most important person to someone else maybe isn't a great or healthy goal but at least it's something I'm aware of. Right? My parents have always been super involved in our community since my dad is the town's preacher. They're wonderful parents. They're loving and supportive and always showed up for me and my brother, Elijah, but I was always competing for their attention with not only Elijah but the *town*. They always knew everyone and loved everyone and were involved in everything. They always acknowledged my accomplishments but it was always followed up with a quick topic change to something happening with Elijah who followed in my father's footsteps or Sally at the Town Hall or Peter who worked as a secretary at the church or Martha who taught with my mother. All people who also needed my parents. I was always sharing them.

When I went to college and met Norma, it was the first time in my life where I felt that I had someone who I was just as important to. She immediately became my person. We were attached at the hip and we told each other everything. I knew that I was just as important to her as she was to me and it healed some inner part of me that I didn't realize was broken. And because of that, she'll always be my person. Then she found Will.

I have never, for one second, been resentful about Norma finding Will and falling in love so quickly. If anything, I'm grateful she found someone who actually deserves her. But soon after they started dating, I knew that my place as her most important person was going to be overtaken, as it should. A person's life partner *should* be the most important one in their life. She is still available to me whenever I need her, and honestly, Will is too, but I'm back with that need. It's led me from relationship to relationship but I haven't found it yet. Maybe the fact that I'm looking for it is what the problem is but I don't think it's too much to ask to be important to someone else. To feel like they need me in their life just as much as I need them. That I come first, before anyone else. But I just can't find it and sometimes I'm terrified that I never will.

Scott is definitely into me and he's attentive and loyal but does he need me? I doubt it. If he does, I don't feel it. And I certainly don't feel how I should toward him either. I see him so sporadically and it barely affects me when he's gone for long periods of time. There's nothing wrong with our relationship per se, but that doesn't mean it's right. So maybe it's best this ends now because it's not a love connection. It's just an easy connection.

I finish the few dishes, after dragging it out, and sit down across from Scott at the table, knowing that I'm not the person for him but still sad that it hasn't worked out.

Here goes nothing.

"So, I've been doing some thinking lately...about us." I don't pause, I don't want to give him time to interrupt me and make me lose my nerve. He shifts in his seat, leaning forward to show me he is listening. "I really like you Scott, and I think you're maybe the kindest, most thoughtful man I've ever known but-"

He finishes for me, "But this isn't working?"

I just look back at him for a moment and he gives me a knowing nod.

"It isn't working," I confirm with a deflated breath. "I'm not even sure why it isn't working but I just know."

A small smile appears on his face, one of acceptance and I feel relieved, like maybe he has these same feelings. "I know what you mean. I like you a lot too, Elsi, but sometimes it just isn't quite enough."

I reach across the table and grab his hand, he squeezes my fingers. "It's going to sound cliche but I honestly hope I still get to see you here and there."

"I'm sure we'll bump into each other," his thumb slides across my knuckles.

"I'm sorry, Scott," I pull my hand from his gently and stand up.

"Yeah," he stands too. "I know, Elsi."

I head to the door and put on my boots and coat before gathering my purse. He steps towards me and I understand the gesture and wrap him in a tight hug, my arms going around his waist. When I pull back he leans down and presses a quick, soft kiss to my lips. A goodbye kiss, I suppose.

"Get home safe," he reaches past me and pulls his door open.

"Night, Scott."

When the door closes behind me, I feel a huge weight lifted from my shoulders. God, I was so nervous to do that but he took it incredibly well. I think he must have felt the same way. He seemed to almost be expecting it.

The following night, Norma insists we meet up to talk about the breakup. I'm sure she just wants to make sure I'm okay and that it went well even though I've already told her about four times that it went smoothly. But I get it and so I agreed. We planned to meet at a bar we love that's perfectly halfway between our apartments. It's small and cozy and the bartenders are fairly familiar with us. I'm about a half hour early but figure I'll grab us a spot to sit and maybe read my book to pass the time.

I walk inside and am grateful for the warmth that washes over me. It's frigid in Boston in early December. I look around at the seating along the walls and notice a few empty spots. They have these super comfortable armchairs seated around low circular tables and that's always where we like to sit.

I walk over to the bar to order myself something to drink and eye up an empty table with two comfy chairs next to it. As I wait for the bartender to finish up the drinks he's currently making, I look around at the other people seated at the bar. It's Friday night, so there are a decent amount of people scattered about.

My eyes scan the crowd and stop just to the right of me, where they catch on the back of a tall, well dressed, and very blonde man. *I'm sure it isn't him.* The second I hear his voice though, I know with certainty that it's Nate Croman sitting three seats away from me, facing a pretty and petite blonde woman in a stunning red dress. How is this possible?

"I'm here temporarily from San Francisco," his voice is deep, pouring over me like dark chocolate, thick and smooth. It is exactly how I remember it. He has this way of speaking that is slow and methodical and lets you know how completely sure of himself he is. It's downright sexy.

"Wow, big change." I can tell by the girl's voice that she's trying to sound impressed, or trying *to* impress.

"I'm from the Northeast," he says dismissively, looking past her as he speaks.

"What is California like? I'd love to go there," her fingers land on his bicep, drawing his attention back to her, and I turn away, not wanting her or him to catch me looking.

I really wish the bartender would finish up those damn drinks.

"It's alright. Good weather, music, food."

"Mm, I'd love less winter," she croons.

"Right. Uh, excuse me," Nate says to the woman and out of my peripheral vision, I see him climb off his bar stool and walk in my direction.

I brace myself and try to look surprised when he speaks to me. Honestly, not that hard though since I am genuinely surprised that he'd come over to me. He apparently does remember me from college.

"Should show more cleavage if you want the bartender's attention," he says as he stops next to me. I can't tell if it's a joke or not but my defenses go up.

"Classy."

"I thought so," raising his hand casually, he gets the attention of the bartender and after the man slides the newly made drinks to the patrons in front of him, he comes quickly over to us. I glare at Nate, unamused, but he just gestures to me and says, "She would like a..."

"Pinot grigio, please."

The bartender nods, "Anything for you, man?"

"Yeah, Basil Hayden. Thanks."

"What's a Basil Hayden?" I ask skeptically as the bartender turns away from us.

"Bourbon."

I tsk, "Figures."

Glancing up at him, I catch his eye as he looks down at me. "What figures?" He says it with no emotion. None. How does he do that?

"Big fancy businessman orders a top shelf bourbon, *while*, might I add, a pretty woman in a red dress ogles his bicep."

"Oof," he breathes out, touching his hand to his chest to feign injury. "You jealous, Elsi?"

I scoff, "Hardly."

He leans down on his forearms, making us a little more level, the man is so freaking tall. "I was surprised to see you the other night."

I shrug, trying to seem unbothered by this conversation, "You shouldn't have been. I spend all of my time with Will and Norma."

He tilts his head in understanding, "I remember you and Norma being close in college and I saw you in the wedding photos, so I guess I really shouldn't have been."

"Here you are," the bartender says, placing our drinks down in front of us.

"Thank you!" I hold out my credit card to him, "You can leave the tab open."

"Sure," he nods.

I drop a $5 bill on the bar and walk away from Nate, not giving him a second glance. I don't know that talking to him is such a good idea. I don't want to fall into a weird timewarp of obsession from five years ago. I find a table along the windows and sink into one of the beloved armchairs before checking my phone. Norma probably won't be here for another 20 minutes at least. So that gives me time to chill and drink my wine before ordering her one and myself another.

I'm sipping my wine, debating if I want to take my book out of my purse and read for the next 20 minutes, when Nate fucking Croman helps himself to the seat across from me at the little table I found.

"That seat is taken."

"Did I do something to piss you off, Elsi? Because it seems like you're sunshine and fucking rainbows to everyone in this city but me."

Oh.

I deflate at that. I guess I did put up a ton of walls the moment I saw him and am being a bitch to him with really no cause whatsoever. I let out a breath, "Yeah, shit, you're right. And no, you haven't done anything."

He seems accepting of my somewhat apology and leans back in the chair. "Why'd you avoid me at Will's birthday?"

"I didn't," I say with honesty. I had no reason to speak to him, that isn't avoidance.

"You did," he insists. "You also avoided me for over a month after that night in college."

"That was a long time ago," I shake my head, trying to hide the shock that he'd even bring that up. "It was just a hook up, Nate. I was surprised that you even knew my name back then *almost* as much as you remembering me now," I confess.

"I remember you. I knew plenty about you back then and you weren't shy to share that night either." His eyes burn into mine as he takes a sip of his drink.

What is happening right now? Why is he bringing this shit up five years later?

I groan, residual embarrassment washing over me. "I hate that I shared that stuff with you that night. I wish I could take it back. It made me vulnerable."

The way he is leaning back in his chair, you'd think he owned the entire bar.

"And now it makes me your prey," I add without thinking.

His green eyes stay focused on mine, "I've never thought of you as prey before...but I will now if you'd like." I see the smallest evidence of a smirk before he hides it by taking a sip of his drink, "You know, I think of our time together pretty often. Almost as much as I think about what might have happened if we weren't interrupted."

I clench my thighs together at the very sudden and unexpected change in tone. I've been thinking of that night a lot lately and am regretting now that I've gotten off to the memories a time or two. So even though the reaction I'm having now makes sense, it is completely unwelcome. I straighten up, willing myself not to allow him to read my face, "Let me summarize it for you: You'd have fucked me and then forgotten me."

His eyes continue to stare daggers into mine, but otherwise he looks unaffected, almost bored, "Maybe."

"We weren't even friends then, Nate. We've talked more tonight than we ever did in college."

"I'd have talked to you in college if I thought you'd entertain the idea. I figured you had no interest and that assumption was confirmed when you blew me off after I got you off."

My eyes widen and I fight looking around to make sure no one heard. "That wasn't-"

"Hey, El!" Norma's voice comes from my left, stopping me mid protest. I hadn't seen her walk in. She zeroes in on my visitor, "Oh! Hi, Nate. It's good to see you." She glances at me quickly and, knowing her the way I do, it says a *lot*. What is he doing sitting here? What are we talking about? What the actual fuck is happening?

"Yeah, you too. I just ran into Elsi and sat down to say hi. I'll leave you ladies to it though," he stands up out of the chair and holds it for Norma to take.

She smiles up at him, "Thanks, Nate. We can't interest you in joining us?"

If I was able to kick her without him seeing, I would have.

"No, you have your girl's night. I'll be seeing you two." His gaze lands on me and stays for a second before he turns and walks back over to the bar. He walks with an air of unbothered confidence. His posture perfect, his face unreadable. He doesn't sit back down by the blonde, instead walking to the far side, taking a seat in a newly vacated stool. One where he is in direct eyeline of us.

"What the fuck was that?" Norma says, being sure to keep her face neutral which I appreciate.

"I don't even know. Hang on, let me get us drinks."

Once I'm sitting back down after carefully avoiding meeting Nate's eye at the bar, I fill her in on the conversation. She's eating it up.

"Girl, he wants you *bad*!" She nearly shouts and I scrunch up my nose at the proclamation.

"He does not. It's like he just wants to terrorize me or something. He likes to watch me squirm."

"He certainly likes to watch you. He's barely taken his eyes off of you since I got here."

On impulse, I turn my head and glance at the bar and sure enough I catch his eye over the rim of his glass as he takes a sip of his bourbon. A flash of heat ripples through me and I ignore it as I turn away from him.

"There is literal smoke rising from the eyefucking you two are having. It's hot!"

"He was just flirting it up with some blonde at the bar before you got here. I'm just a conquest. Unfinished business from his college days. He saw me at Will's birthday and now has some sort of mission to get under my skin before heading back to California."

"Maybe you should let him," she says coyly as she sips her drink.

I give her my best deadpan look and repeat what I said to him only a few minutes ago, "Let him fuck me and forget me?"

"I doubt he'd forget you. He hasn't yet. But Elsi, you wanted that man *bad* in college and he's somehow hotter and available and seemingly into you. And you're single now so what harm could be done from a little fling?"

I don't respond right away because my instinct is that the harm would be me feeling something, like I did back then, and then it being ripped away. "I'm not going to let him use me."

"Well, of course not. I wouldn't be okay with that either but if it's a mutual understanding then it isn't using. A one night stand," she shrugs, "maybe a few nights."

"I don't know. Can we talk about something else?" I ask.

She gives me a sharp nod, "Done! Tell me about what happened with Scott."

We spend the next hour talking about Scott and our plans for the next month of the holiday season. At some point Nate must have left and I didn't notice, which is perfectly okay with me. I don't know how I feel about that incredibly random and unexpected conversation. Did he really know about me back then? What did he know? And does he still think about me? As the questions flip through my brain, so does my skepticism, assuring me that this is all a game to him.

Chapter Four

Elsi:

"**E**lsi, please come!"

"Norma Belle, you do realize that this is like the fourth time in three weeks that you've wanted me to go out. It's like you don't even know me anymore!" I whisper in a harsh tone as I walk through the career fair currently taking place at a local community center. It's the last one for the year and I'm relieved it's finally underway. There are a ton of people walking around, most of whom are a part of EmpowerNest's outreach, and each booth has people huddled around. It's going great.

"Elsi," she groans in her typical bratty voice. "Please. We don't have to stay long but Will told the guys he'd go and I would skip it too but it's that new place you know I've been dying to go to. You'll love it too, it's all steampunk and funky inside. You can pretend you're living in one of your books!"

"I'd rather be *reading* one of my books in my pajamas with a glass of wine!" This has been a long day and I've been looking forward to just going home afterwards.

"You can do that all day tomorrow and Sunday, which I know you're planning on anyway. Please, Elsi!"

I sigh because I know I'm going to cave. I always cave to Norma. I don't even have to actually say anything. She knows by my sigh that I intend to go.

"Yay! Okay, great! I'll see you at 7!"

When I get to the bar, I'm a little annoyed at how gorgeous it is inside. I was spitefully hoping it'd suck but it's pretty awesome. It's definitely a steampunk vibe like Norma said. There's exposed brick everywhere, iron beams, metal wheels and cogs along the walls, Edison bulbs everywhere you look, giving the place a dim lighting. The seating is all wood and faux leather. It's really truly a fictional world, so I'm immediately less annoyed with Norma for making me come. Her hand grips my arm and she pulls me towards the bar where we hop onto two empty seats. The bartender comes over to bring us menus. He's probably average height and thin with a mustache that is twirled up on the ends and some old time aviation goggles dangling around his neck. Honestly, besides the get-up, he's pretty cute. His eyes are slate blue and his mahogany colored hair is neatly combed to the side.

"Good evening, ladies. My name is Mickey. Let me know what I can get you," he leaves the menus in front of us with a smile before swiping some empty glasses off the bar.

All of their drinks have weird names and seem to be serious mixologist stuff with smoke and foam and crazy colors. I decide on a drink called the Lord Cyrus which, based on the description, is basically a French 75.

"What are you thinking?" I ask Norma, laying my head down on her shoulder as she continues skimming the options.

"I think the Witherdale Fashioned," she points to a drink that's made with bourbon, honey simple syrup, and orange.

"Oh, that looks tasty!"

"Have you two decided?" Mickey asks, looking between us.

"I'll take the Lord Cyrus and she'll have the Witherdale Fashioned."

"Ah, great choices. The Lord Cyrus has been my favorite lately."

When he steps off to make our drinks, Norma leans in, "He's cute! In spite of the 'stache."

I jerk my head in a sharp nod, "Oh, absolutely." I take my eyes off Mickey, whose short sleeve shirt hugs his muscled arms well, and look around, "When's Will going to be here?"

She glances to the door, "He said he was getting done around 6:30 tonight, so it should be any time."

"Who is he meeting here?"

"Frank, Charlie, Nate, and a couple guys Nate knows, I think," she shrugs.

"Convenient you forgot to mention Nate coming," I eye her, wanting her to know that I am genuinely annoyed and she definitely picks up on it.

"If I told you, you wouldn't have come. We don't even need to sit with them. We'll do our own thing here," she waves her hands above the bar top in front of us. "We can spend our time getting you in good with Mickey so he takes you home and you can cut his mustache off in his sleep after he fucks you senseless."

I let out a bark of laughter but it's interrupted by a voice from over my shoulder.

"Seems I showed up at a good time. Who's getting fucked senseless?"

I know it's Nate behind me before I even look and the slight widening of Norma's eyes confirms it but she recovers immediately, a naughty smile on her lips. Much to my horror she admits, "Oh, Elsi. By the bartender. I hope, anyway."

I just stare daggers at her and then mouth *What the fuck?* But all she does is smile back, like absolutely nothing is wrong.

"You into that look, Elsi?" Nate asks and I spin in my chair to finally see him. He's dressed in his typical completely blacked out suit and it looks infuriatingly delicious on him as usual. "The mustache and the goggles?" He gestures around his neck, his face stoic and uncaring.

Mickey starts to make his way over before I bother to answer. "For you, ladies."

"Thank you!" Norma and I both say. My drink is purple and bubbly and looks yummy.

"Want me to keep a tab running?" he asks us, his gaze very briefly catching on Nate and then back to me.

"Please. That'd be great," Norma confirms, handing him her card.

"Do you need a second?" Mickey asks Nate who shakes his head.

"Bourbon. Neat. Whatever is top shelf."

Mickey nods and walks off without a word.

"You two joining us tonight?" Nate asks, leaning on the bar casually.

"Nah, girls' night at the bar," Norma nearly shouts as she slaps her hands on the bar top, mimicking a drum roll.

"Here you are, man," Mickey says, sliding the drink towards Nate's hand.

Nate hands over his card, "You can leave mine open too."

Taking the card, Mickey walks back toward the register.

"Well, enjoy your night, ladies," Nate nods at us and wanders back over towards the other guys he must be with.

Norma gives me a knowing look, which I'm positive has everything to do with Nate but I sidestep it by bringing up work. She knows exactly what I'm doing but doesn't argue.

"So how long has this place been open?" I ask Mickey when he brings us our second round and the dinner we ordered.

"A few months. It was a little slow at the start but once word got out, we've been pretty busy. You haven't been here before?"

"No, first time."

"My brother actually owns the place. I started here a few times a week to help him out when he opened but kind of love it, so I stuck around."

"So what did you do before this?" Norma leans in and asks him.

"Oh, this is just a side gig. I work full time as a middle school guidance counselor"

"Oh, wow!" I can't help but exclaim. "I wouldn't have pegged that." I'm more intrigued by him now for whatever reason.

"It's the mustache, right?" He gestures to his face and I respond with a laugh.

"Sounds miserable," Norma says with a grimace.

"Sometimes," he chuckles, "but the kids are awesome."

Swoon. "How long have you been doing that?"

"Five years. What do you do?" he asks me and then glances around the bar to make sure no one needs him for anything.

"I'm a project manager for a nonprofit."

"Oh damn, noble as hell. What kind of stuff do you do?"

"Event planning mostly but also sort of oversee a lot of what goes on."

"That's badass."

"I work as a bank manager in case you were wondering," Norma chimes in with a teasing look and then takes a bite of her chicken marsala.

I swat her with the back of my hand.

"Just wanted to make sure you two knew I was still here," she laughs.

Mickey gives me a bright smile, not bothering to deny her comment, and then looks around the bar, "I'll be right back."

"He's into you, babe," Norma leans in and whispers.

I shrug coyly, "He's cute." I turn in my seat then and find where Will and the other guys are hanging out. There's about eight of them, some I don't recognize, and I scan their faces until I find Nate's. He's leaning back in his seat, one hand reaching forward and wrapped gently around his glass. One of his friends is talking to him and he's responding with what seems like boredom. His face is not showing any sign that he's even really invested in the conversation. For whatever reason though, he turns his attention toward me and our eyes meet. A flame erupts in my chest. My cheeks heat at being caught looking at him but I don't look away. He gives me the tiniest little smirk. It's a cocky, knowing smile. Without changing my facial expression, I look away from him and turn back toward Norma.

Norma and I spend much of the next hour finishing our dinner and talking with Mickey when he has a moment to chat. He's very obviously flirting with me and I am leaning into it. Shamelessly. Especially as the drinks keep coming.

"I have to run to the bathroom," I tell Norma while he's off helping other customers.

"Don't be too long or Mickey will miss you."

"He's into me, right?" I ask for confirmation.

"Oh, hell yes. He's into you."

I follow the signs for the bathroom down a set of stairs and to the left along a dim and fairly creepy hallway. I take a few breaths of the quiet air and then touch up my lipstick in the mirror before heading back out. As I walk back down the hallway towards the stairs, an arm reaches out and gently grabs my hand, pulling me. My adrenaline spikes at the unexpected movement and I get ready to start screaming but I catch sight of Nate and my fear turns to annoyance.

"What are you doing, Nate?" I basically shriek, the fear still pumping through my veins.

Once he's fully pulled me into the dark alcove he's standing in, he steps into me and I retreat on instinct, until my back is pressed up against the wall. His hands are on either side of me, boxing me in. He crowds my space, getting so close but not quite close enough that we're touching.

I look up at him, hoping he sees defiance in my gaze and ask again, "What are you doing, Nate?"

He watches me with that typical expression of stoicism on his face. He leans down so that our noses are just barely touching, I can smell bourbon. "You ever been fucked before, Elsi?"

Immediately the anger spikes. I raise my hands and push on his chest but he doesn't budge. He has no right to ask me that. Pissed off, I spit out, "Yes. Of course I have, you asshole."

He stays still. His eyes take in my face, glancing to my nose, lips, back to my eyes. "No, you haven't."

I want to protest but he steps marginally closer, still not touching me. I hear my breath getting heavier, feel my heart pounding harder. I can't decide if I'm scared or pissed off or turned on and maybe the combination is what makes the wetness pool between my thighs.

He continues, "You might have gotten laid before, Elsi...but I don't think you've ever been fucked. Not properly. Not like I'd do to you."

Like he'd do to me. My eyes shut without my permission and a sharp throb of heat goes through my body. Straight to my core. A tiny whimper escapes my lips. I open my eyes and watch his pupils dilate. He's not moving, except for the tiniest fluttering of his jaw muscle.

"Be a good girl and don't go home with him," he says, shocking me out of the trance I was in, and stepping away.

Good girl? Oh boy...

I don't say or do anything as he turns around and leaves me in the alcove. I can't even decide if I'm offended or pleased by him asking me not to sleep with the damn bartender. Well, he didn't really *ask.*

When I calm my racing heart and head back upstairs to Norma, Nate is again sitting over by the guys like nothing happened.

"You okay?" Norma asks, her eyebrows coming together in concern.

I sigh as I sit in the bar stool, "Yeah. Nate cornered me downstairs."

"Did he do something?!" She sits up straighter, ready to spring into action.

"No," I shake my head. "No, he- Well, he cornered me in order to whisper filthy shit in my ear. He's a dick."

She squints her eyes questioningly, I can tell she's amused and trying not to smile, "How filthy?"

"*Filthy*, Nor, and I was super fucking blindsided but didn't even hate it, which pisses me off more. He had no fucking right and it made me feel a lot of things but hate wasn't one of them."

She blows out a dramatic breath, "He's got it bad."

"But I still just think he's messing with me. Like it's a game."

"You really think so?"

"Yeah, I feel like he sees me as some weak little joke. That he'll mess around with my head for a few weeks to get a laugh and then just move on."

She twists her lips, "Jeez, El. Maybe you should just avoid him then, if that's what you think."

"Too bad you keep making me come out and he's apparently a part of Will's freaking friend group now."

She defends Will without a hesitation, "They were always friends."

"I know. I just liked it better when Nate was Will's friend from across the country."

She laughs at that and I cannot help but turn my gaze towards where Nate and the other guys are sitting. I find Nate watching me. Again. My heart flutters and I can't tell if it's from our hallway encounter or if it is just from this moment catching him. Either way, my body throbs with heat and I shift in my seat. His gaze stays locked on mine but he must notice my discomfort because he gives me the cockiest little grin and then raises his glass to his lips.

I pull my attention from him, back to Norma. "I think I'm calling it a night."

She nods in agreement, "I'm with you. I think I've had one too many of these Witherdales. Poor Mickey though. I think he thought he had a shot."

I frown, "Yeah, my bad on that one."

"I'll pay the tab. Order yourself a car and I'll walk you out."

As she pays Mickey, he tries to keep me engaged in the conversation but I keep my responses to general politeness, hoping he will get the hint.

"I'm here every Friday. Maybe I'll see you again?" he asks hopefully with a timid smile. He really is pretty handsome. Too bad my mind is overloaded by the cocky businessman about 20 feet away. Who I'm sure is watching this interaction.

I give him what I'm hoping is a kind smile, "Yeah, sure. We love it here."

Norma chimes in with agreements and takes the conversation back over until he wanders off to help other patrons.

"Let me say goodnight to Will and we can walk out. My ride is like four minutes away." I loop my arm through Norma's as we walk over to the guys. How can I say goodnight to everyone except Nate? I don't even want to look at him and what will probably be a stupidly satisfied grin because he thinks I listened to him by not going home with Mickey. But I just wasn't up for it. I need my bed and two solid days of silence at home.

"You leaving?" Will shouts, a clear indication that he has had plenty to drink tonight.

I give him a big smile because I love tipsy Will, "Yes, dear. It's past my bedtime."

"Did you order a ride?"

"She did. I'll walk her out," Norma says.

"Nonsense. It's too cold for you out there. I'll walk her and keep her safe," Will postures up like he's a valiant knight and I can't help the giggle that escapes. So fucking nerdy, I love it.

"Thank you, kind sir. I certainly accept."

He offers me his arm and I take it before turning to the rest of the group, looking at Frank and Charlie but then giving a general sweep of the other guys, "Bye, everyone!"

I hear goodbyes as Norma leans in to wrap her arms tightly around me, "Love you, El. Text me when you're home."

"Love you, and I will. Same for you, please." I let her go and my traitorous eyes fall on Nate who watches me for a second before tipping his glass slightly in my direction. He then looks away, moving on with his night and my resolve is set that this is a game for him. He doesn't *actually* care what I do.

Will walks me out of the bar and down the steps to the street. "What's the name of your driver?"

I check my phone, "It should be a black Highlander and the driver is Misha."

"I bet this is it," he gestures to a car a little ways down the block and I follow his lead. He opens the back door and leans in, "Misha?"

"Yes. Elsi?"

"Yeah," Will confirms and then steps back to allow me to climb into the back seat. "Be safe. Text Norma when you're home." He says this loud and I'm sure it's so the driver knows that he'll be expecting to hear from me in about 15 minutes. I smile at his protectiveness.

"Thanks, Will. Night."

Chapter Five

Nate:

I wasn't planning to corner Elsi in that hallway but I saw her walk away from that ridiculous bartender and I just couldn't help myself. The idea of her going home with him, with anyone who isn't me, made me irrationally murderous.

I was so fucking blindsided seeing her again at Will's party. I wanted her immediately. But it's nothing compared to now. Now that I've pressed her up against that wall and she made that breathy little moaning sound. It was the prettiest thing I've ever heard. It immediately sent me into the memory of touching her in college. And now I'm determined to hear it again. I'll do whatever it takes to hear it and work even more out of her.

God, I bet she sounds so beautiful when she's being fucked.

Chapter Six

Elsi:

"**W**ill is going rogue and inviting us all to his company Christmas party."

I roll my eyes, though she can't see me, "So same as the past three years? We conveniently show up to the party and no one bothers to check a guest list?"

Norma laughs through the phone, "Yes, exactly. Perks of working in a huge company, I guess."

"Who else is unofficially being invited?" I ask as I walk toward the break room.

She hums, "I have to call Sarah and Alina. Will was going to text the guys."

I'm not sure if 'the guys' only entails the usual Frank and Charlie or what but I'm not going to ask if Nate will be there. It doesn't matter if he is.

"Alright. It's Friday night?" I pin my cellphone between my ear and shoulder so I can pour myself another cup of coffee.

"Yeah, at 7."

"I'll come to your place after work so we can get ready and ride over together."

I hear her keyboard clicking away, "Deal. Let me know what you're going to wear. I bought a new dress but am unsure about it. I'll send you a pic."

"Alright, I'll do an inventory of what I've got and send you options," I agree.

"Love you," she makes a smooching sound.

"Love you too, babe."

"You're sure this dress isn't too much?" I ask Norma as I stand in front of her full length mirror. The dress is a fucking knockout if I'm being honest. It's a deep teal satin material with spaghetti straps. It's tight on my chest, showing off some cleavage, and form-fitting the rest of the way down to midcalf. I have to wear those annoying boob stickers with it though since the satin shows off every line and bump. I paired it with some strappy black heels.

Norma comes out of her bathroom and howls, "*Damn*, girl. It's perfect."

"So not too much?"

She shakes her head, "I'd say it's just enough."

I take another look and sigh, feeling marginally exposed. I certainly fill the dress out more than she would, being bustier and having far more curves. But it really does look great. She, however, is still in her underwear. "Alright. Where's your dress?"

"Getting into it now!" She runs back into her bathroom and comes out a few minutes later to have me zip up the back.

I do a dramatic whistle as she turns around, "Now this dress is killer. Love the velvet, babe."

"Me too! I saw it a few weeks ago in the store and had to grab it." She takes a turn looking at herself in the mirror. The dress is black with off the shoulder long sleeves and a sweetheart neckline. It's tight to her thighs and then flows out around her.

"Will is going to *die*," I tell her over her shoulder.

"That's what I'm hoping for," she smirks.

"Just make sure he doesn't rip it later. It's too pretty to ruin."

The event is high-class and way too fancy for my tastes but I have fun every year pretending to belong there and drinking expensive champagne and eating delicious food. When we arrive, Norma and I walk arm in arm and Will guides us with his hand on Norma's back. As usual, no one is at the door checking names of people, so we stroll in and head over to the coat check. The event is in the main banquet hall which has hundreds of people scattered around tables, both sitting and standing. There is a live orchestra in one corner playing Christmas songs and servers walking around with trays of champagne and hors d'oeuvres. Will stops a man carrying champagne and passes one to me and Norma.

"Thanks, babe," she smiles.

There's a bar along the side wall and he walks us that way. I scan the crowd not recognizing anyone. Sarah and Alina couldn't make it tonight but I know Charlie, Frank, and Nate will be here. I didn't ask Norma about Nate, but she told me earlier, probably realizing I was refusing to ask but wanting me to be prepared.

I don't see him yet though, so I relax as I take a sip of my drink and check out the trays of food as they're paraded past us.

I lean toward Norma, "You think they have karaoke around here somewhere?"

She lets out a bark of laughter, "God, if only."

"These people couldn't handle it."

"Oh, absolutely not. There would be a lot of clutched pearls," she jokes.

I giggle as I take another sip of my champagne.

"Hey, guys!"

Norma and I turn to see Charlie marching over to the bar, looking handsome and trendy as always with his sandy blonde hair styled nicely to the side and wearing a tailored brown suit and penny loafers.

"Hey! No date tonight?" Norma asks.

He shrugs, "Nah, flying solo. Frank here yet?"

"We haven't seen him," I shake my head.

"Hey, man," Will says to Charlie as he turns from the bar.

"Mingle with any bosses yet?" Charlie asks. He works for the same company as Will, so he, unlike me, actually belongs at this party.

"Nope. Hoping to get a drink or two in me before having to make small talk."

Every year, Will steals Norma from me for a while in order to be cordial and impress his bosses. It's a bonus that his wife is an absolute fucking knockout, and lord knows, the dress she's in tonight will certainly help.

"There's Frank and Nate now," Will gestures behind me and Charlie with his drink.

I turn around and spot the guys. Frank looks wonderful with his hair pulled back into a short ponytail and wearing a navy blue suit and brown dress shoes. But Nate knocks the wind out of me with his standard all black attire, fitted perfectly to his body, his hair combed nicely to the side, and an air of confidence that should be illegal. No one should be allowed to look so fuckable in a suit. I pretend to barely notice him.

"Ladies," Frank says, giving Norma and I each a little hug. "Douchebags," he says, bumping fists with Will and Charlie.

"What's good tonight?" he asks, waving his hand toward the bar.

"Everything," Charlie lifts his glass, "It's open."

"Tits!" Frank cheers quietly and closes the space between him and the bartop.

"Hey, Nate," Norma says with a subtle nudge to my arm.

He doesn't respond, just nods his head at her. His eyes flick to me briefly before he follows Frank to the bar.

I look at Norma out of the corner of my eye and she makes a funny face which causes me to laugh. I shrug through the disappointment settling in my bones, I guess we're back to him not knowing me. That's probably for the best I try to remind myself. I don't actually want him to continue these mind games with me. It's better if we just exist in the same spaces. Nothing more.

One of Will's bosses walks up to us at that moment. I can see on Will's face that he was hoping for a few more drinks before this happened. And since the man walked up to us, we're all kind of forced to stand here. I'm not sure about the others but I hope he doesn't figure out Frank, Nate, and I are party crashers and ask us to leave. But my fears are for nothing because about three minutes into his conversation with Will, Nate and Charlie wander over and are both greeted by name.

"Good to see you, Mr. Fischer," Nate says, shaking his hand.

"Glad you could make it to the party, Croman. We've been enjoying working with you this past month."

"Oh, my pleasure, sir. Thank you for the invite. It's one hell of a party."

"Yes, we do go a bit overboard every year. I hope you enjoy yourself." Mr. Fischer's eyes travel to me and I know that he is assuming I'm with Nate, but of course I can't correct him.

The guys go back to their small talk, Nate now included, and Norma looks at me with a puzzled face and mouths *What?!* But I'm just as blindsided as she is so I shrug and shake my head. I had no idea Nate worked with Will.

After the boys do their required chat, they ease up knowing that part of the evening is over and done with. Will gets swept into a conversation at the bar with Charlie, Frank, and some other guy I don't know, leaving Norma and I alone with Nate.

She takes no time before asking, "How do you know Will's fancy boss?"

"His company has been doing some business with ours and I've been a middle man. That's why they sent me here for a few months."

"Huh," Norma huffs, clearly annoyed. "Will didn't mention it."

"Just boring work shit," he shrugs.

"Nor!" Will calls from the bar and when we look over he gestures for us to join them.

As we take a step over, a strong and rather large hand lands gently on my lower back, guiding me through the crowd to the bar. The feeling of it there gives me the chills but in the best possible way. Here we go again.

Maybe I need a minute.

"Going for a pee," I whisper to Norma. "Which way do you think it is?"

She turns from Will and spins in a circle looking for doorways.

Frank on my opposite side chimes in, "I think it's out by the entrance. There was a hallway heading behind the coat check. I think it's back there."

"Thanks." I set my drink on the bar and lean to Norma, "I'll be right back."

"Kay."

I find the bathroom exactly where Frank had said. I take a few deep breaths in the quiet, looking at myself in the mirror. There's been a lot of talking and music and people and Nate. I just need a second to regroup. I make sure my dress isn't crooked or wrinkled, reapply my lipstick, take a few more deep breaths, and then head back out to the party.

I only make it a few steps out of the bathroom when Nate appears out of a doorway and grips my bicep, pulling me gently into what seems to be the employee entrance to the coat check. I stumble through the door, my arm completely engulfed by his hand.

"How do you find these places?" I ask exasperated, looking around to make sure no one is here. I try to ignore my rapid heartbeat.

"Luck," he shrugs and then steps into me. I stand my ground, not letting him back me up like last time but it doesn't deter him in the slightest. His hands land gently on my forearms and I feel chills run up my spine. He surrounds me, stepping so close, and leaning down to whisper to me, "You look beautiful tonight." His nose glides along mine and I close my eyes at the tingling that goes through me.

"Thank you," I breathe out.

"This dress just might kill me," he breathes out, like he's in pain. His fingers begin to travel, running down the satin along my thigh. The feel of his strong hands only blocked by a thin strip of fabric has me feeling like putty.

I don't respond because what is there to say? Please rip the dress off me? Please don't corner me again? My mind isn't sure what it wants. Actually, my mind knows exactly that this is a terrible, terrible idea. It's the rest of me that's wanting his hands on every single inch of my skin.

His hand flattens against my hip and glides along to the small of my back, pulling me marginally closer to him. I look up into his eyes, trying to figure out his game plan. His nose is still against mine and I can feel his breath on my face. He's just so close.

"Nate-" I start to say with no plan as to where I was headed. Should I tell him to leave me alone? Should I tell him to take me home?

"Elsi?" Norma's voice sounds from the hallway.

My spine stiffens but Nate leans even closer and when he speaks his lips brush against mine, "I'll be thinking of you in this dress later. And then I'll be thinking about how it'd look on my bedroom floor."

A rush of heated breath escapes my mouth and my thighs squeeze together at the throbbing that comes from his words and the ghost of his lips on mine.

"Elsi!" the call comes again.

Nate steps back without my having to ask and gives me room to stand up straight. I should check to make sure my dress isn't disheveled but I can't trust myself to stay in this room with him for one more second. So without another glance at him, I walk out and find Norma in the hallway outside the bathroom door.

"Here, Nor," I call to her and she whips her head around to look at me. I feel drunk. Swoony. Unsteady.

"What are you-" she starts to ask but I cut her off with a shake of my head and gesture behind me. She looks past me and I'm sure Nate must come out of the room because her eyes widen.

"Norma," he says in casual greeting and then walks away from us, heading back to the party.

"What the fuck?!" She whisper screams so no one else can hear, almost running to me. "What the actual fuck, Elsi?!"

I just shake my head, feeling kind of deflated, "He just cornered me again. Nothing happened."

"What'd he say?"

I can feel the heat grow in my cheeks, "That he liked my dress."

She deadpans, "Right."

Chapter Seven

Nate:

A fter the Christmas party for Malden & Sons, I head to a local bar with a few of my work buddies. We all got the invite to the Christmas party for being liaisons for the company. I intended to skip it but then I heard Will mention that Elsi would be there and I can't seem to keep myself away from the woman. She's like a vacuum or a magnet or gravity and I am powerless against it.

I'm half convinced she doesn't even like me but she looks at me with those big, beautiful, innocent eyes and I get sucked in. I can't control it.

And if I don't get my dick inside of her soon, I feel like I may die. Seriously. It's all I can think about. In meetings, at the gym, at home. Always.

Misael finds us a high top table near the bar. I've never been here, but the others seem to know it well. I asked Will, Frank, and Charlie if they wanted to join us but they all passed. I can't really blame them, it's already past midnight but I feel jittery after being near Elsi all night and I knew I wouldn't sleep right away.

"Man, Blackburn's wife is fucking bangin'. How'd he bag that?" Alvin asks from next to me once we've all got our drinks and sat back in our seats. He's the only one I know well, having been sent here from California with me.

"They met in college. Been together since then," I answer.

"Damn. Good for him, the fucker."

"I don't know," Craig chimes in from across the table. "I think that friend of hers was the real eye candy tonight." I feel my body tense even though he's not wrong. Elsi in that dress was almost painful to look at. She's fucking sexy. Her dress hugged every single part of her perfect, curvy little body. Her round ass and thick, toned thighs were fucking torturing me. She definitely had no bra or underwear on because they'd have shown through the fabric, which was so thin that it was like I was actually touching her when I cornered her in the coat closet. I bet her perky breasts would overflow my hands. She's tiny compared to me even though I suppose she's got to be average height for a woman. But wearing those heels, I didn't have to lean down as much in order to press into her. She wore her hair up which showed off her neck and shoulders and I wanted to run my fingers and tongue along her skin there. Fuck, she's incredible. But for some insane reason, I don't want anyone else to have noticed her.

Alvin laughs loudly, forcing it out, "Better watch it, Craig. I think our boy, Nate, has some claim on that one."

Craig's eyes shoot to meet mine, "That so?"

I don't have a claim on her but the idea of anyone else touching her makes my skin crawl so instead of denying it, I say, "That's so."

"You fucking her?" Craig asks, brash as he seems to always be. "Bet she's tight as hell. Probably filthy too with that good girl act of hers," the laugh Craig lets out makes anger travel up my spine.

"How about you shut the fuck up, Craig?" I bark and the other guys look at me with confused curiosity.

Alvin leans forward, his face questioning, "You actually like this chick?" The disbelief I see on his face is plain as day. Unable to believe I might actually *like* a woman. Though what he knows of me from California gives him all the reason to believe such a thing.

I scoff, not willing to get into this right now. I take a gulp of my drink, "If any of you even think about touching her, I'll fucking kill you." I assume my tone is enough for them to know I'm serious, because they all lean away from me an inch or so and Misael immediately changes the subject to work shit.

Good. That'll definitely keep them away from her.

Chapter Eight

Elsi:

The end of the year at EmpowerNest is generally pretty breezy. We don't schedule any events for the second half of December or usually in January either so we can finalize documents for the year and start fresh. It's nice because it allows me time to Christmas shop and relax and not stress too much during the holiday season.

I'm setting up my mat at my weekly yoga class when Norma strolls in with her gym bag. "Joining you today," she says as she drops her stuff next to mine.

"I see that," I give her a kiss on the cheek. She doesn't often come to yoga. She's more of a cycling girl, wanting the fast paced environment. "What's the occasion?"

"Holiday stress," she takes a sip from her water bottle, "and Alice is out this week." Alice runs her cycling class.

"Ah, I see. Well I love it when you come."

She feigns flipping her hair over her shoulder, it's actually tied in a bun on the top of her head, "I know. Coffee after?"

"Yes, please!" I'll never ever turn down a coffee even when it's 5pm on a Monday.

The yoga instructor, Adam, comes in and starts setting up at the front of the class. He's a short, Hispanic man with a deep and accented voice that immediately calms you. We get into our positions and I will my mind to be empty so I can relax and enjoy this. No thinking about work or Christmas presents or Nate. As Adam begins the session, I go through the motions, letting his soothing voice wash over me as I focus on my breathing. He walks through the room encouraging us and repositioning people whenever necessary. By the end of class, I'm sticky with sweat and feeling energized and refreshed.

"I always forget how much I love his classes," Norma sighs beside me as she leans back on one hand and drinks from her water bottle.

I let out a slow breath, "He's seriously the best."

We pack up our stuff and head out of the gym, heading next door to the privately owned coffee shop that we frequent. We order and I pay as Norma grabs us a small table by one of the front windows.

"Did you decide on Will's Christmas present yet?" I ask as I put our coffees down on the table, knowing she's been going back and forth for a while on what she wants to get him.

"Yeah, I think I'm going to get him those MMA tickets. We'll have to fly to Vegas but he'll be so excited." Will is a huge fan of professional mixed martial arts. He watches it almost weekly and has always wanted to go to a fight night. He'll be ecstatic.

"He'll love that, Nor. Plus, you can make some fancy dinner reservations."

"Oh, I've already been looking at some great spots where we can eat."

"Where will you stay?"

"Well, I think we have to stay at one of the big name hotels since we've never been. Maybe the Bellagio or The Venetian or something."

"Hm," I hum enthusiastically though a sip of coffee, "Definitely the Bellagio."

"Done!" She agrees with a hand slapping the table. "Did you send out your parents' gifts yet?"

"No, I have to do that this week. I just got Elijah's this weekend, some new book on the Civil War that he'll probably like." My brother is really hard for me to shop for since we aren't that close but I do know that he's a big history buff and this book has gotten a lot of good reviews since coming out last month. I just hope he doesn't have it yet. But it's somehow already the week before Christmas so I need to get the package out tomorrow in order for it to definitely get to them in time.

We switch to some work stuff that she's been stressed about and talk through that for the next hour before she checks her phone and sees it's about dinner time. She invites me to her place, as always, but I opt to go home instead and eat a salad while I watch some mindless TV for a few hours.

"Okay, but I'll see you Friday night, right?"

I sputter out an exasperated breath through my lips. We're going out. Again.

"That's a yes," she rolls her eyes at me. "Love you."

We grab our empty cups off the table and put them in the proper basket before kissing cheeks and walking out the door, going in our separate directions.

That Friday I, of course, end up going out to that same bar we went to for Will's birthday because Norma is a bully and I can't say no to her. And I also somehow end up at a table with Nate. Alone. How does this keep happening? And why can't I seem to remove myself from these situations? My traitorous brain isn't even upset about being alone with him. It's excited. And so is the rest of me.

Nate hasn't said much since Charlie got up and left us alone at the table. He just quietly sips his drink, glancing around the room.

I think of the Nate I sort-of-but-not-really knew in college. He used to be the center of the party, all attention on him even though he seemingly did not give a single shit about anything or anyone. Often even being dismissive and rude to people. Now he seems content to be on the sidelines, quietly taking in the atmosphere. "You're different, you know."

His eyes meet mine. "I don't think so." He shifts back in his seat, "But maybe. Things change over time."

I take a sip of my drink and before I can say anything else he asks, "What was I like back then?"

"Popular. Cocky. Bored. You had a reputation for being kind of a dick."

He grins and jerks his head, apparently amused by my description of college Nate. He doesn't bother to deny any of it. "And what am I like now?"

I look down at his hands, relaxed and strong. Then I can't help but glance at his lips before returning my focus to his eyes. "Pushy. Quiet. But you still seem bored most of the time."

He chuckles. "I'm not bored right now," he gives me one of those minuscule smirks that annoyingly make me feel something like...special. "You're different too."

"Yeah, I am," I nod in agreement but my curiosity makes me ask, "But why do you think so?"

He takes a second to look me over, appraise me, take inventory of Elsi now versus Elsi then. "More confident. More outgoing. More beautiful. Still unnecessarily kind to everyone though."

I can't help the smile that spreads across my face and I can see the corner of his mouth beginning to rise again before he stops it.

"The way you were that night," I can tell he knows that I mean *that night* in college when we hooked up. "You were so...sweet. You weren't what I expected then and certainly not how you are now."

He tilts his head and shrugs, "A fluke. I wanted to throw you to the ground and fuck you silly but that wasn't what you needed."

I fight to keep my face neutral as my insides jerk at his blatant comment. "I guess it wasn't."

I keep my eyes on him as he sips his drink and I hear the glass tap back down on the table, "But you wanted me to take you back to my room."

It's not a question but I answer anyway, "Yes."

He leans forward slightly, dropping his voice, even though I know no one is listening, "Would you have wanted me to fuck you?"

I debate for only one second and settle on the truth, "Yes." And then I sheepishly add, "*Silly*."

He doesn't smile but I see a little muscle work in his jaw and a feeling of accomplishment spreads through me as I grin back at him.

After that we fall into a silence and I glance around the bar, spotting Norma sitting alone with Will and leaning in to whisper something in his ear. He turns his face and captures her lips. His hand reaches up, cupping her neck. I love how much he loves her. A jerk in my stomach reminds me that I want that. I want that so much.

Charlie comes back over with a new drink in hand and strikes up a conversation with Nate about MMA. These men and their professional fighting. I take this as a good moment to sneak away and head over to the bar to get a new drink.

When the bartender slides me the glass, my watch vibrates. I fish my phone out of my bag and open it. With a squeeze of my insides, I quickly glance over my shoulder at Nate who is in the middle of saying something to Charlie. I look back to my phone.

> **Unknown: I'm not done with you yet tonight.**

My heart thumps in my chest, knowing it's Nate and having no idea how he got my number. I take a big gulp of my gin and tonic before responding.

> **Me: I'm not scared of you Nate Croman.**

I fight the urge to turn around and see his reaction. My phone lights up.

> **Nate: Sure you are baby. But you shouldn't be.**

And before I can think about him calling me baby or how to even respond, another message comes in.

> **Nate: I just want to make you feel good.**

My thighs squeeze together, fighting the desire that's twisting through me. I will not be a horny mess as I sit at the bar alone. I won't.

"You okay?"

I jump at Norma's voice so close to me.

"Sorry!" she says with a laugh.

"I'm okay," I say and then I tilt my phone in her direction and let her read what Nate wrote.

She lets out a low breath, "Jeez, girl. Not very subtle, huh?"

"Not subtle at all."

She lowers her voice, "Are you going to let him fuck you?"

I look at her and then close my eyes as I nod. "Yep," I say dramatically, popping the *p*.

"Good," she clicks her glass against mine. "There's too much tension in you lately. You need a good release. And I'd bet money that man is good in bed."

As usual, I am grateful for Norma. For a friend who tells me exactly what she thinks and passes absolutely zero judgement on the decisions I make. Who could ask for more in a bestie?

Will wanders over and joins us, standing behind Norma's bar stool. "How are my two favorite girls?"

"Kind of hungry," I admit and look around the bar top for a menu.

"I could eat," he agrees and reaches behind the bar and grabs some. "Babe?"

"Sure!" Norma agrees, holding her hand out for one of the menus.

We order food from the bartender a few minutes later.

"El, I'll be over tomorrow to check your shower faucet," Will says over Norma's shoulder.

My shower head has been leaking lately and I mentioned it to him last week. "Thank you. Do you need stuff from the hardware store? I can meet you there first."

He shrugs, "I have to check out what the issue is first. If we need to, we'll run out after I get there. I'll be by after the gym, probably like 11 or so."

"That's perfect. Thanks, Will. I owe you one."

He waves his hand dismissively. Will is a bonafide handy man, he can fix just about anything. He's been on call for my apartment's wear and tear for the past five years, since Norma and I lived together, and he never asks for anything in return. I make a mental note to run out to the market in the morning so I can make him some snacks when he comes over.

The bartender delivers our food and Will takes the seat next to Norma so we can dig in. I ordered the lobster ravioli, which is my guilty pleasure at this bar. Once we're done eating, Will wanders off to talk to the guys and I'm full and sleepy and ready to leave.

"I'm ready to go home," I lean over and tell Norma.

"Okay, babe," she gives me a sweet smile, knowing I've been ready to go since I arrived here. "You still coming for dinner tomorrow?"

There's a new murder mystery movie that she, Will, and I have been dying to watch. "Yes, what are you making me?"

"Was thinking some sort of soup."

"Perfect. I'll bring some wine."

"You going to order a car?"

"Nah, it's not too cold tonight." I only live like five blocks from here. I might as well save the money.

"Do you want us to walk you?"

"No," I shake my head. I glance at my watch and see it's only 9:37. "It's not even that late. I'll be okay. I'll see you tomorrow." I lean over and give her a kiss on the temple.

"Night babe. Text me when you get home."

I say goodnight to Will and glance around quickly wanting a glimpse of Nate but not spotting him. On my way to the front, I make a quick detour to the bathroom.

As I'm heading back out towards the front, wrapping my coat tight around me, I shouldn't be surprised when an arm reaches out and grabs me, pulling me into what seems to be a janitor's closet. Because, of course, Nate needs to accost me before the night is over. I'm off balance as he pulls me into the room, closes the door behind me, and then presses me against the wall. My unzipped jacket leaves my chest against the cold bricks. His front is against my back and he's holding each of my hands in his, down by my thighs. I can barely move. Annoyance flares through me. Followed closely by flaming desire.

"Jesus Christ, Nate! You can't keep cornering me like this everywhere we go!" I'm borderline shrieking as I try to push off the wall to no avail.

"The Lord's name in vain, Elsi," he tsks, stepping in closer so his thighs are pressed to the back of mine. "Shame on you."

"Fuck off."

"Mm," he hums in amusement. "I thought you were a good girl."

I will not admit for any amount of money the feeling I get in that moment when he calls me a good girl. I won't do it. I also don't respond to him.

"I've been thinking," he says, his lips grazing the shell of my ear and giving me chills.

I shiver.

"Have you?" I ask, my tone unimpressed. Almost bored. Though I'm anything but bored. I try to jerk one of my hands from his grip but his hold is too tight.

"I've never fucked anyone without a condom before," he starts and my whole body stiffens, wanting to hear more despite knowing better, "but that's what I'm going to do to you, Elsi. I can't stop thinking about it. I've fucking *dreamt* about slipping into you raw. Your tight, warm little pussy stretching around me."

My nerves are fucking live wires. No one has ever spoken to me like this. So unfiltered and needy. It's working exactly how he was hoping it would. I am turned the fuck on. God, I want him. And no one has ever needed me badly enough to corner me in a bar closet. It feels *good* to be desired. His tongue is against my ear and I can't really help the reflex of leaning back into him. I can feel his muscular body against me, responding to my movement, and the unmistakable feel of his hard cock digging into my lower back.

"I'm going to make it so good for you." He leans further into me and kisses along my neck, below my ear. Quickly forgetting that I'm trying to be cold towards him, I drop my head back onto his shoulder to give him better access. His mouth on me is unbelievable. I know I should stop this, we're in a bar closet for goodness sake, but things that feel this good cannot possibly be bad for you, right?

He lets my hands go and I brace them on the wall in front of me. Pulling me back into him, he spins us around, so he's the one leaning back against the wall instead. He keeps me pressed to him in the process, one hand cupping my breast, and when his teeth graze my neck, I hear myself gasp. My whole body comes alive under his attention and I need more friction, so I grip his thighs and push my ass back into him and grind on his erection, loving the fact that he so obviously wants me too.

He breathes out and it's somewhere between a laugh and a moan, "I knew you'd be a dirty little thing for me."

"Nate," I almost cry with desire. I'm becoming a desperately needy mess. This is exactly the feeling I've been searching for. It's everything.

"Tell me what you need, Elsi," his breath on my skin causes my eyes to close.

"I don't-" my brain cannot function properly, too drunk with lust. I scramble for words, for anything to help ease the ache. "Just touch me."

His hands immediately begin to shift. Fingers find my neck and jaw, tilting my head to the side to give him better access to press his lips along my skin. His other hand finds the clasp on my dress pants and with minimal effort, he's sliding under the fabric, along my skin and finding my center. The warmth of his hand as his fingers touch my clit makes me gasp.

He moans at the sound, the vibrations are fucking wonderful against my neck.

He strokes my clit back and forth and I shamelessly widen my stance before he finds my entrance and slides a finger inside. *Yes. Yes. Yes.* Still needing more, I begin moving my hips, riding his hand as he works in and out of me. He reads my mind and presses the heel of his palm firmly against my clit. A second finger slides inside of me. Holy shit.

I can feel his hard cock as I rub my ass against him and I know he's enjoying this too.

"Such a good girl, Elsi," he assures me. His voice steady despite his heavy breaths.

I can feel my walls clench his fingers at his words. His praise is a fucking drug.

I reach up and slide my fingers into his hair, he responds by closing his teeth on the shell of my ear and grinding his hand into my clit.

The coil of pleasure is getting tighter and my hips move frantically, chasing release. Nate presses open mouth kisses along my jaw and stops with his cheek brushing mine, his lips just a breath away.

"Let me feel you cum," he encourages me.

I wish his lips were on mine, they're right there, but he doesn't close the distance. He pushes his fingers into me again and curls them forward and I feel my knees buckle as the orgasm rips through me. Nate's hold on me is firm though and he keeps me pressed to him as I break apart around him. My fingers pull at his hair and I cry into the small space of the room.

I melt even further into his grip as my body stops throbbing, feeling weak and spent. He doesn't let me go, even as his hand slides from my center.

"Fucking perfect," he breathes. "*Jesus*, you're fucking perfect."

A squeezing sensation grips my heart briefly and leads to warmth spreading through my chest and down my arms. I think this confirms my suspicion of having a praise kink...at least coming from this man. Who knew?

His hand shifts from my lower stomach and then all I see is his forearm across my vision as he brings his hand to his mouth. I tilt my head and catch his eye just as his lips open and his fingers slide in. He keeps eye contact as he licks my cum off his skin. Enthusiastically. With pleasure.

I shift slightly and am reminded that he is hard. Probably painfully so.

"Nate, I-"

He seems to anticipate my concern and brushes me off, "Not now."

"But-"

"The first time you make me cum, Elsi, it will be inside you."

His confidence might normally annoy me but I feel my pussy clench again, like it has a mind of its own and cannot wait for that to happen. Instead of relaying my absolute okayness with this plan, I say, "You seem sure."

"I am," he says and lets me go so I can step away from him. I turn around to face him and his hands go back to my dress pants but this time, he reclasps them for me and then straightens my blouse. I fight the smile that threatens to spread at his thoughtfulness.

Once he seemingly decides that I am presentable again, he reaches for his own pants and shifts them a bit, probably to accommodate his erection. But now there's a weird silence and I don't know where to go from here. Deciding to make my escape, I take a step away.

"I'll see you," I say, my voice oddly quiet, "I guess."

He gives me his classic half smirk, "You'll see me."

With a sharp nod, I open the door and leave the closet. A fucking janitor's closet. *Real classy, Elsi.*

Chapter Nine

Elsi:

"**M**erry Christmas!" I holler as I push open the Blackburns' front door. "Merry Christmas!" the two yell to me from the kitchen.

I kick the door closed behind me and lug my bags to the living room, plopping them next to the couch. Their Christmas tree is fat and short, completely full of lights and ornaments from over the years, a lighted star on top, and few presents underneath. It's a perfect sight for Christmas morning. The rest of their living room is filled with garland and lights and Christmas decor that feels comfortable and homey. This is what my Christmases have been for the past five years and it's perfect and familiar.

Before coming over, I did a video call with my parents and Elijah. I had received their presents in the mail a few days ago and they sat under my tree waiting to be opened. My mom's smiling and very close up face greeted me when I called and they propped her phone up so I could see everyone as we all opened our presents. My parents loved everything I sent, especially my dad when he unwrapped the new barbecue rotisserie that I had shipped to him. My mama laughed at the dishtowels I sent that were adorned with ridiculous pictures of farm animals. Elijah grunted a thank you for the book. He sent me a pair of slippers. In the wrong size. I gave him a big smile and told him they were great. I unwrapped my parents' gifts next, all perfectly wrapped by my mother. They sent me books, some of which I might even read, new pajamas, an adorable pair of sunglasses, and a gift card for the airline I usually use to book flights home. All very thoughtful and special. I couldn't help it when the tears started to form as I opened the gifts that they put so much time and money into. I miss them so much, especially on Christmas, and I thanked them a million times. We stayed on the phone for a while after that, just drinking coffee and chatting and talking about our plans before they had to hang up in order to get ready for their respective church services.

The smell of bacon gets stronger as I walk around the corner and into the Blackburns' open kitchen. Will and Norma are in matching buffalo plaid pajamas. There is Christmas music playing softly from the TV on the counter and Will is frying the bacon that smells delicious while Norma fills a glass with orange juice and champagne before holding it out for me.

I give a dramatic sigh, "Thanks, babe."

"Merry Christmas," she says again, holding up her own glass for us to clink them together.

We spend the rest of the morning eating, exchanging presents, and watching *White Christmas.* Will freaked out when he opened his gift from Norma with their trip to Vegas all planned out and tickets to the MMA fight. He keeps reopening the box and looking at the tickets. It's adorable. I gifted him a new tshirt with his favorite professional fighter on it. Totally tacky and he absolutely loves it. For Norma, I got a gift card to a restaurant she mentioned wanting to try while they were in Las Vegas, along with a pair of earrings I found at a craft fair last month that will look perfect on her. Will gave me a gift card for my favorite bookstore, which he gives me every year and I greatly appreciate every time. Norma got me an adorable new pair of ankle boots and a beautiful painting done by a local artist that I adore. It's watercolor, probably 6x8 in size, and is of an empty park with a willow tree off to the side but serving as the focal point. It's incredible and I can't wait to hang it up tomorrow.

Around midday, after we put out some lunch snacks, Will insists we continue our silly tradition of playing a round of Monopoly. The stupid game takes hours but the champagne keeps our spirits up as he completely bankrupts each of us and rules the board.

"Fun as always to be completely destroyed in this fucking game," I groan sarcastically and he raises his glass towards me in a cheers motion.

"I need to start dinner," Norma announces and I take the opportunity to follow her to the kitchen. Will takes over putting the game away and then moves to the couch to turn on football.

As Norma starts chopping the asparagus, she asks me about Nate and I shrug, telling her I haven't heard from him since our last night out at the bar. She makes an unimpressed face with one eyebrow raised. She knows exactly what went down in that damn janitor's closet.

"I thought for sure after that I'd see him again right away but I haven't heard from him. I don't know though, maybe it's for the best."

"I'm surprised at how wishy-washy he's being. Not what I expected from Croman."

"Yeah, I'm not so interested in these games he's playing but-" I shrug.

She looks up from the cutting board but doesn't say anything.

"He makes me feel something," my shoulders droop like it's a heavy weight to admit it.

"That fucker,' she says, pointing her knife threateningly with a smile.

"A complete bastard," I agree.

I help Norma with the mashed potatoes and start making the gravy when she pulls the prime rib from the oven, which smells heavenly. While Norma tosses a salad together and I whisk the gravy, a knock sounds from the foyer.

Norma pauses, "Will?"

"No clue!" Will calls from the living room, understanding her question of who it could be at the door. "I'll get it!"

I turn the burner off and lift up the gravy boat so I can fill it with the finished gravy.

"Look who I found!" Will calls and I glance over my shoulder mid pour and see Nate. And then I spill the steaming hot gravy onto my hand holding the gravy boat.

"Shit!" I blurt as Norma greets Nate.

"You okay, El?" Will asks, rushing around to come to my aid.

"Spilled gravy!" I say, putting the saucepan and gravy boat back down. I turn and rush to the sink to rinse the gravy off, glad it wasn't hot enough to really burn me, though it still stings. Will wipes up the gravy I spilled along the counter. I turn back to grab a dish towel and squeeze my eyes tightly shut to brace myself before I look at Nate properly, "Hey Nate! I didn't know you were coming."

He's not in his usual all black business attire and my eyes dance across him, taking in his outfit. It brings me back to our college days and how he'd look when I'd spot him from across the room. He's wearing jeans that fit him just right, showing off his strong thighs and probably his ass, which I'll double check later. And on top, he's wearing a black hoodie with some logo in white on his left peck. His blonde hair is not gelled into place, but looks freshly washed and hanging loosely across his forehead. Honestly, he has never looked sexier.

He looks to Will and Norma, "Sorry for not texting but my plans were cancelled last minute and I remembered Will's invite to dinner."

Norma glances quickly in my direction without either man noticing before saying, "Of course it's okay! We made an ungodly amount of food."

"Thank you," he gives her a polite smile, "I didn't come empty handed." He holds up a paper bag and puts it on the counter where it clinks identifying it as some kind of alcohol.

Will reaches into the bag, "Ah, the good stuff." He pulls out a bottle of some sort of brown liquor, probably bourbon knowing Nate.

"Champagne too. Elsi had mentioned you guys hammer the bubbly on Christmas."

I'm surprised that he remembered that passing comment.

"We do!" Norma laughs. "Thank you! Fill me up, William." She slides her glass towards him on the counter.

"Anything for you, baby girl." He grabs the bottle and begins to work it open.

I turn back towards the gravy and properly fill the serving dish this time.

"How was your Christmas, Nate?" Norma asks behind me.

"Great. Quiet."

I wonder if that means he's been alone at his apartment all day. What did he do? The thought bums me out. He could have been here with us. With me. But

I quietly sigh at myself, falling back into the pattern of thinking we're something when we certainly are not. We don't even know each other.

I open the cabinet with the plates and bowls and pull out another setting for Nate. I grab the stack and some silverware and carry it over to the attached dining room. Norma has the table set beautifully. There is a golden table runner with a handful of candles lit across the space. Each setting has a large dinner plate, a smaller bread plate, and a small salad bowl. On the side is an emerald green napkin with the silverware on top. She has pretty water glasses out for each of us and some of the food is already placed around the table.

Norma fills Nate in on our day and Will chimes in to explain the absolute beating he gave us in Monopoly which Nate politely chuckles at. The guys then get distracted by the football game that has now taken over the kitchen TV.

It hits me then how I must look at this moment. I haven't looked at myself since this morning because I certainly wasn't expecting to see anyone but Norma and Will, least of all Nate. I finish setting up his spot at the table and then casually make my way toward the bathroom. I close the door behind me and groan at my reflection. I started the day with my hair in a bun at the top of my head, which probably looked cute about eight hours ago, but now it is near my ear and fly-aways frame my face, sticking out in every direction. I didn't bother putting any makeup on this morning but the faint pink in my cheeks from the hours of champagne gives me some color. My pajamas are loose and shapeless but at least they're festive with their red and white candy canes. There's not much for me to do in the way of improvements, other than try to tame my hair. I pull it out of the elastic, run my fingers through it a few times, and then retie it into a neat bun back where it started at the top of my head. Washing my face won't hurt either, so I do that quickly, pat myself dry with the hand towel, and make my way back out to the kitchen. I catch Norma's eye immediately and she gives me a wink and an "OK" sign with her thumb and pointer finger.

When Norma puts the last serving dish on the table, she announces that we can all sit to eat. She and Will circle around to the far side of the table and take seats next to each other. I pull out the chair across from Norma and that of course, leaves the seat next to me for Nate. This is fine. Everything is normal.

Feeling like I'm the only one who's uncomfortable by this sudden change, I take a subtle deep breath, and try to talk myself into chilling out. This wouldn't be weird if it were Frankie or Charlie so it doesn't need to be weird since it's Nate. Though, to be fair, Frank and Charlie haven't finger fucked me in a janitor's closet.

Everything is normal.

"This looks awesome, Norma," Nate compliments.

"Thank you! Elsi helped big time. Luckily she's a good cook too," she gives me another wink. "I'd have never been able to do this on my own."

"And I am complete shit in the kitchen," Will chimes in.

Norma's eyebrows raise, "True."

I wonder briefly how often Nate eats a home cooked meal. Maybe he cooks.

"Do you cook?" I ask without really thinking about it.

His eyes shift to meet mine and I will my cheeks not to warm.

"A bit. Just essentials."

Norma puts prime rib on Will's plate as she suggests, "Like..."

"Hm," he thinks for a second, "Eggs, steak, spaghetti, sandwiches..." He shrugs, implying that's about it.

After that, we finish filling our plates, cheers to another Merry Christmas, and then dig into our food while a silence falls between us, only broken by the Christmas music quietly playing from the kitchen.

Even after we finish eating, we remain at the dining room table and continue to talk and drink and eat dessert. While I was feeling awkward at first, I've fallen into an easy comfort as we all enjoy each other's company. Nate has always been this otherworldly being to me, he seemed so far out of my reach, but he's just...normal. At least way more normal when it's just the four of us. He jokes and talks about his job, telling funny stories. He tells Norma all about California. He even smiles a few times.

"So, remind me, who's coming to the New Year's Eve party?" Will asks, his voice carrying a slight slur, suggestive of the numerous bourbons he's had over the past couple hours since eating dinner.

"Do you listen to *nothing* I say?" Norma teases in a too-loud voice, leaning in toward Will. Her smile is wide and her cheeks bright red.

"Of course I do, I just want to hear you say it again," he says confidently and I laugh at his bullshit. "Who might I expect to see at such an event?" Will keeps his eyes closed for the entire question and I giggle again. I suppose I've had a lot to drink too since everything my friends do seems to be hilarious.

"Me and you, Elsi, Charlie, Frank, and their plus ones. The ladies from the bank and you said you invited a few guys from the office."

"Alina and Sarah are doing a spa thing," I say before he can ask where they will be. They booked a three day spa retreat.

"You're coming too, Nate?" Norma asks.

"Yeah, of course," he confirms and my stomach does an excited little bubble.

"You got a date for the night, El?" Will asks and I see a subtle shift from Norma, and assume she's squeezing his thigh under the table. I haven't spoken to him at all about this weird thing with Nate, but I'm sure Norma has filled him in.

"Nope," I say as casually as I can. I briefly hope he'll ask Nate the same question but he doesn't and I'm too much of a coward to do it myself.

Norma recommends watching another Christmas movie so we migrate to the living room where she drapes herself across Will on their loveseat which leaves me and Nate on the couch. I purposely sit on one end to leave space between us but he sits exactly in the middle, leaving only about a foot of empty space. His closeness makes it a little hard to focus on the movie but I manage to zone in, letting the Christmas magic wash over me and I relax back into the couch.

Only about 20 minutes into the movie though, Norma sighs, "I'm going to take my husband to bed. You guys take your time." She stands. "Nate, you're more than welcome to stay if you'd like. All I have to offer is the couch, but it's pretty comfortable."

"Thanks, Norma. I'll head home in a bit though. Thank you again for dinner."

"My pleasure." Norma comes over and leans down to kiss my check.

"Night, babe. I'll lock up."

"Thanks, El," she turns back to Will who's definitely asleep. "Come on, honey." She reaches down and grabs his arm.

"I'm not even tired," he says, his eyes barely open.

"I know, Will. I'm tired though. Take me to bed."

He stands up with a surprising burst of energy, "Yes, ma'am!" He throws his arm over her shoulder and they turn towards their bedroom.

"Merry Christmas, guys!" Norma calls over her shoulder before closing the door behind them.

I glance at Nate and he gives me a small smile before I turn back to the TV and continue watching the movie. We sit like that for a moment but I'm not really watching anymore, my mind is running a mile a minute. I wonder why he's staying. And God, I hope he kisses me before he leaves. I feel like a jittery teenager waiting to have her first kiss. My thoughts dance across the memories of our few times together and snag on that first night, five years ago, when he surprised me by kissing me back after my moment of rare bravery.

"You guys do this every year?" Nate asks, interrupting my daydreams.

"Yeah," I say, turning to look at him. This is what we do every year. Norma and Will are my people. My family. "We have a tradition. We get brunch out on Christmas Eve, go home for naps, church, and then dinner at my place. I made stuffed sole last night. I always do some sort of seafood. Then they host Christmas day which includes Will destroying us in Monopoly, lots of drinking, Christmas movies, and dinner."

"That's nice. Dinner was great."

"Norma's a wonderful cook. Do you have Christmas traditions?"

He squints his eyes like he's thinking hard, "None."

"None?" I ask in disbelief.

"Nah," he shrugs. "Santa became a myth pretty early for me so that kinda ruined the magic of it. I still got presents and stuff but usually just laid on the couch watching movies all day. Oh! Actually I do have a tradition, I watch *Die Hard* every Christmas."

I smile in spite of the fact that his Christmas tradition is legitimately being alone and watching a Bruce Willis movie. "I love *Die Hard*." Which is true but it's also all I can think of saying in response to his maybe unintentional confession.

"The best," he agrees.

We fall into another round of comfortable silence. Nate laughs at a scene in the movie and I glance at him. He is so comfortable, so at ease, his smile genuine and relaxed. He looks so young in this moment.

"Nate?" I find myself saying.

"Hm?" He turns to look at me.

I steel my nerves to ask him something I've been wondering for over five years, "Why did you kiss me back that night in college?"

Giving me his full attention, he takes a minute to think about his response. "Well, aside from the obvious?"

"That I was tipsy and started it?"

He chuckles, it's a bright sound. "That you were an incredibly sexy woman who took me completely by surprise when I thought you had no idea who I was."

"What? Everyone knew who you were."

He shrugs, "Most people, maybe, but I didn't think you cared enough to know."

"Oh my God, Nate, I was-" I cut myself off before I embarass myself and tell him how totally obsessed with him I used to be. "I knew who you were. But I'm sure you had girls lined up."

"Well, I didn't particularly care for any of the other girls. You were in a ton of my classes and I was always so fascinated by how much you seemed to absorb. You basically never said anything. But every once in a while you'd raise your hand or share something during group work or whatever and it would be this crazy profound and insightful comment. I was always super fascinated by you and thought you were incredibly hot but I figured you were way, way too good to be hanging around me."

I scoff, not believing for one moment that he noticed me in college, "Ridiculous. I was just an introverted nerd who was usually too scared to speak in front of others."

"Doesn't matter. You kissed me and I fell into it, obviously. But when you told me how you felt that night it was the first time anyone real had ever admitted to a feeling like that. That numbness. I thought I was the only one that ever felt that."

"Of course not." I'm surprised he latched onto that or even remembers it.

"Well now I know. But back then it wasn't something that was ever brought up, until you did."

"I guess it was a weird thing to say in the moment," I make a face.

"I don't think so. It was honest. Do you still feel like that sometimes?"

It's a vulnerable question but I don't hesitate to say, "Yes. I never really even know why."

"Yeah," he nods, "me too."

What a crazy confession from this man who has so many walls and barriers around him.

"God, when you told me that..." He breathes out a laugh, "I so badly wanted to be the one to make you feel something."

I smile, "You definitely did."

"But not enough for you to talk to me again."

"To be fair, I was exceedingly embarrassed, and I thought you'd rather I just pretend it didn't happen."

"Quite the opposite," he shifts closer to me and leans forward slightly. In a near whisper he continues, "It was the hottest moment I had ever experienced. The sounds you made when I slipped my fingers inside of you. How fucking *tight* you were." He leans closer, his green eyes sparkling, "Were you a virgin then?"

I feel like I'm frozen in place but manage to shake my head. He watches my mouth as I respond, "I had had sex once before."

"Hm," he hums, taking up more of my space. "I wanted to fuck you then almost as badly as I want to fuck you now."

My whole body clenches at his words. Always such filthy words.

I don't move as he closes the distance between us. His forehead connects with mine and my eyes fall closed. If he doesn't kiss me, I might cry. I haven't felt his lips on mine properly for over five years and lately that's all I have been able to think about. More than anything else he says he wants to do to me, I just want to feel his mouth on mine.

I can hear him inhale softly and then he moves slightly so his lips brush mine. Barely. Chills start at my neck and travel down my spine. The anticipation of this. Have I ever wanted anything more?

A hand lands on the side of my neck, his thumb pressing up into my jaw and I lift my head a little before his lips are there. Soft but firm. I hear him inhale sharply through his nose. My heart rate spikes. And I gently kiss him back. We sit like that for just a second and then his lips are parting and I mimic the motion so that our tongues meet. A satisfied moan escapes my mouth and he responds enthusiastically, his tongue working faster over mine, his body shifting closer to me. We're in an awkward position, both of us twisting to kiss each other and he seems to think so too because he pushes forward, turning his whole body as I lay back and he follows me. My head lands on a pillow and without breaking our kiss, Nate ends up laying across me on the couch. I can feel his thighs and his hard stomach against mine. His arms frame around my face. My hands drift up to his shoulders and then around to his back and pull him more firmly against me.

Our tongues are hungry, our breath coming quickly. This is what I've been missing in my life. This *need*. God, I've never wanted someone as badly as I want him right now. But we're on a couch in the middle of my best friend's apartment and now isn't the time. But I know he wants me too from his hard cock digging into my upper thigh and his desire for me makes warmth pool between my legs. I shift them apart to try to ease some of the friction but he makes it worse, moving his body to allow his cock to line up with my center. I can feel his hardness through my pajama bottoms and his jeans.

I'm becoming a desperate, whimpering mess underneath him. My fingers dig into his shoulder muscles and just when I think we need to stop before it becomes too much, he rocks himself against me, his cock grinding against my clit.

I breathe in sharply but hear him groan over that. He pulls his lips from mine before kissing my cheek and then across my jaw and down my neck. His mouth is everywhere.

"You feel so good underneath me, Elsi."

My brain falters and I don't respond. *Can't.* Because at that moment he rocks against me again.

"I can't wait to be inside you," his voice quivers with need.

I breathe out another whimper and try to protest, "*Nate-*"

"*Fuck.* I know," he rocks against me one more time and groans. "I know."

He stops his motion against my desperate center and returns his lips to kiss me slower, more gently, before he eventually pushes up and pulls his lips away. He stays hovering over me though, looking down at me.

His lips are darker now, lips I don't want to stop kissing me, and I reach up and run my fingers along them.

His eyes shut and he whispers, "What are you doing to me, Elsi?"

I feel breathless and...sexy, desired, wanted, *needed.*

"I should go." He presses another kiss to my lips, this one gentle and sweet, before pulling himself off me and the couch.

I follow him to the door and I want to ask him when I'll see him again. I want to ask him what this means to him. I say nothing though as he leans down and kisses me again, his tongue urgent against mine for a brief second before he is pulling away, whispering goodnight, walking through the door, and shutting it behind him.

Chapter Ten

Nate:

I had no plans today. Not a single one and I was okay with that. I had intended to spend Christmas at home watching movies, eating take out, and relaxing. But too often my thoughts drifted to Elsi. I wondered what she was doing. I pictured her with Will and Norma, her head tilted back in a laugh, which happens so often when she's with them. I thought about how her pussy squeezed the life out of my fingers last week. I remembered how her mouth felt against mine all those years ago and questioned if it'd feel the same now. And then I found myself pulling jeans and a hoodie on, bagging up the fresh bottles of bourbon and champagne I bought yesterday, and heading to Blackburn's place.

And when they welcomed me in, I lied about plans being cancelled. I swallowed hard at the sight of Elsi in her holiday pajamas with her hair a mess and her cheeks beautifully pink. Just being near her was intoxicating, especially once she relaxed into the night and was just her true, honest self. I wasn't planning to kiss her. I wanted to show her that I thought of her as a friend and not just someone I lusted after but then we were talking and I was leaning in and she was glancing at my lips.

Fuck.

The kiss was better than my memories. Better than my fantasies. Her perfect body was so soft and willing underneath me and it took more self control than I thought I could possibly have to peel myself away from her. I'll see her for New Year's Eve and I'm determined to have her. God, I hope she lets me have her.

Chapter Eleven

Elsi:

N orma and Will's party is in full swing. The apartment is crammed with friends and coworkers. There is music playing and the TV shows the people packed in Times Square in New York City. Norma leans over me, sitting on the arm of her couch as we talk about her Las Vegas trip plans with Will. They're going mid January and she just finished booking everything and is beyond excited.

"Did you get the dinner reservations you wanted?" I got her the gift card for the top spot she wanted to go to but since then she's found a couple more she wants to try out.

"Yes!" she claps enthusiastically.

"All three?"

"Yep! One for lunch and two for dinner. It's a food trip for me for sure."

"I just saw some crazy bar they have there on social media. I'll send you the video if I can find it again. It was one of those hidden bars that you need a password for."

She nods as she sips her drink, "Yes! Oh, that'd be super cool."

"You'll feel so sneaky and posh," I say with a tone of importance.

She laughs, "You can always come with us, you know."

"Babe," I deadpan, "I'm already a third wheel in our everyday lives. I hardly need to be a third wheel while on vacation."

"Maybe you could bring someone," she says, jerking her chin subtly behind me. I turn around and see Nate coming through their apartment door. My stomach does that weird swooping thing that it has grown accustomed to doing whenever I see him again. I wasn't sure if he was coming or not, considering the party started over an hour and a half ago. It's already 10:30pm. He looks sexy in a plain black long sleeve shirt that hugs his arms. His tattoos just barely peek over the hem of his neckline. I wonder how much of him is covered in tattoos now, if he's added more since college. His jeans always fit him really well, showing his muscular thighs. His hair is not slicked to the side like usual, but looks soft as it falls around his forehead. Like it was on Christmas.

I turn back to Norma and raise an eyebrow, "You think you're *so* funny."

She sticks her tongue out at me. "Let's go talk to our men," she stands up and grabs my hand so that I follow her.

I whisper aggressively as we walk across the apartment, "I hardly would categorize Nate as mine, Norma Belle."

"Whatever," she rolls her eyes.

"Hey, baby," Will greets Norma as we walk up, wrapping his arm around her waist.

She kisses his cheek, "Hey, Nate. Glad you could make it."

"Yeah," he gives her a polite grin. "I wouldn't miss it. Thanks for the invite." He turns his attention to me and nods, "Elsi."

"Hey," I give him a small smile. "Can I get you something to drink?"

"Thanks, I brought some bourbon. Can I just get a glass? Will, you want some?"

I turn to the cabinet as Will picks up the bottle Nate must have brought, "Hell yeah, this is my favorite."

"I know, that was the point," Nate quips.

I grab the guys two glasses and fill Will's with ice. "You take yours neat, right?" I ask Nate as I hand him the empty one.

His eyebrows raise marginally, "I do, yeah. Thank you."

"There's tons of food, obviously. So help yourself," Norma says to Nate.

I lean toward Will, "By the way, I made you an extra dish of buffalo chicken dip. It's in a container hidden in the back of the fridge." It's his guilty pleasure and I've taken to making extra to leave him a side dish that he doesn't have to share.

"You're a fucking saint, El," he says, clinking his glass against mine.

By 11:45, we've mingled with everyone and have settled back in the kitchen, leaning against the counter and telling stories from college. Nate breathes out a laugh through his nose as Will tells of a time they were at an away game and got lost in the town at 2am and were too drunk to find their way back to the hotel. They ended up sleeping on the grass in the local park and were found in the morning by their coach who made them do laps at 7am until a third of the team was throwing up.

"Sometimes I think Coach hated us," Nate says. He's standing next to me and his hand is propped on the counter behind me so that his arm rubs against my back when either of us move.

Will shrugs, "We won too much for him to truly hate us."

"Two minutes!" Frank yells from the living room.

Norma squeals in excitement and grabs Will's arm before dragging him to the living room so they can see the TV. I catch Nate's eye as I laugh at my peppy friend skipping away. He leans down to whisper in my ear, "You look great."

I look down at my outfit, black leggings and a fitted plum colored sweater. "You're just trying to get a New Year's kiss," I joke, nudging him with my shoulder.

"I'm getting a New Year's kiss, Elsi, and that doesn't change a thing about how sexy you look."

"Always so sure of yourself," I roll my eyes at his confidence as my blood heats. "Come on."

Nate follows me to the living room and stands behind me as I stop next to Norma. She turns to me and smiles, bouncing on the balls of her feet. As the countdown starts, Nate steps up next to me. My eyes meet his and I smile but he doesn't return it, just locks his eyes with mine.

"TEN!" Everyone in the living room screams. The excitement of a new year, of a restart, making the room jittery and ecstatic.

When we get to "FIVE", I feel Nate's hand on my back between my shoulder blades.

I look at him again as I shout, "FOUR!"

He doesn't count down with everyone else.

"THREE!"

His hand runs up to the back of my neck, his fingers digging gently into my skin.

"TWO!"

He grips me in a way that encourages my whole body to turn so I'm facing him. I think I can hear my heart over the screams and cheers of the room.

"ONE!"

He leans down and presses his lips to mine as everyone yells, "HAPPY NEW YEAR!" and "Auld Lang Syne" starts to play. I melt into him. My free hand gripping the front of his shirt pulling him into me further. His tongue reaches out to search for mine and I'm so fucking willing to oblige, letting our mouths explore each other. It's not a long kiss but it does serious damage to my brain function. I feel woozy and aflame as he pulls away slightly, whispering against my lips, "Happy New Year, Elsi."

"Happy New Year," I smile up at him and this time he returns it. My insides burn.

I turn to hug Norma and Will, shout to Frankie and Charlie, and feel the excitement absorbing into my skin. The adrenaline makes my blood sing. I wrap my fingers around Nate's arm and give him a tug, pulling him through the kitchen and toward the hallway.

As I push open the guest bedroom, where I always sleep, Nate grabs me when I'm only half way into the room and slams his mouth down on mine. He guides me the rest of the way through the door and as it closes, he pushes me against it, crowding my space, his mouth never leaving mine. My fingers wrap into his hair. The kiss is urgent and as his tongue glides along mine, I feel the sensation through my entire body. I feel my limbs go rubbery and moan into his mouth.

"You feel so good, baby." His fingers dig into my scalp, tilting my head to deepen the kiss. His other hand cups the side of my breast before traveling down my side and landing on my ass, pulling me into him. I can feel his erection on my pelvis and my breath catches. My mind is foggy. I can't get close enough to him. His hands are everywhere. The kiss is becoming sloppy and desperate, our teeth knock.

Nate moves his mouth from mine and it travels down my neck and back up to below my ear, where he whispers, "What the fuck are you doing to me?" An echo of the same question from Christmas. The desire and need is throbbing through me but before I can respond, his mouth is on mine again, slower this time. My fingers and toes tingle and then he pulls away, pressing our foreheads together. "Come home with me."

I'm breathing heavily and my chest squeezes. My eyes meet his green ones, searching and hopeful.

"Please, Elsi. I need to be inside you," his fingers flex into my hip.

"Okay." My voice is so quiet that I'm not sure he could even hear it.

"Yeah?" He sounds almost surprised.

"Ye-" but before I can finish the word, he's kissing me again.

"Let's go," he says urgently and pulls me away from the door so he can open it.

We say goodbye to everyone at the party and Norma gives me a hug and a "Fucking finally," before I gather my stuff and follow Nate out the front door. I'm fairly certain it was the quickest goodbye in history.

The drive to his apartment is quiet but his hand is warm on my thigh. High on my thigh. Slowly boiling my blood.

He pulls into a parking garage not too far from the Blackburn apartment, and we take an elevator up to the fourth floor. It's one of those nice elevators, where the metal is still shiny and it smells like cleaning supplies. From that and the hallway alone, I can tell this is an expensive place. The hallway floors are polished hardwood and the walls a pretty deep green. The lights on the walls are elaborate iron sconces. He stops at the third door on the right and pushes in the key.

Holy shit.

Nate makes money. This apartment is gorgeous. There's a brick wall along one side with black shelving which doesn't hold much but a few books. The rest of the walls are a dark gray. His furniture is all black leather. The curtains on the windows are pulled back and he has views of the street and neighboring buildings.

He reaches to help me out of my jacket and I let him pull it off my shoulders. Catching sight of his sparkling clean kitchen, I take a step to check it out but he grabs my arm and pulls me back towards him, "I'll give you a tour in the morning."

Then he's kissing me again. His arms immediately circle around me and draw me into him. He's so much bigger than I am, his hard chest and muscled arms totally envelop me. It makes me feel feminine and delicate. When his tongue glides against mine I can hear myself whimper. He inhales sharply in response and his fingers grip into my hair, tilting my head back so he can kiss me deeper. Harder.

I breathe out a nervous laugh against his mouth and he wastes no time, bending down and lifting me up by the back of my thighs. I yelp at the unexpected movement and wrap myself around him before returning my mouth to his.

I can't see where we're going but we end up on his bed. He stops and leans forward, laying me down and without letting me go, he follows and sprawls on top of me, his knees between mine, his hands still palming my thighs. I am not a fan of the space he's allowing between us though, so I unwrap my arms from his neck and slide them around to his back, pulling him down on top of me. He resists at first, until he moves one arm next to my head and props himself up on it. Without dropping all of his weight onto me, he comes down and I can feel his hard body against mine, pressing into me in all of the right places.

The hand still on my thigh, pulls my leg around him so his hard cock can settle between my legs. It's a complete tease that we're fully clothed but, like Christmas night on the couch, when he begins to rock his hips, the friction against my clit makes me gasp.

"I have been dreaming of the sounds you make for five fucking years." He pushes back off me and kneels.

He pulls me sweater off and bends down to plant a kiss on my exposed stomach, giving me the chills. When he sits back up he's smiling, it makes me melt. He looks so youthful and carefree when he smiles. His eyes narrow and his white teeth show. I love to see it.

I will myself not to be self-conscious as he pulls my bra and leggings off and kneels above me looking down at my mostly naked body. His fingers brush against the small tattoo on my upper thigh, right below my undie line. A little daisy. My birth month flower. I got it a week after graduating college and thought I was so badass.

"You're so beautiful, Elsi." Before I can feel embarrassed by the comment, he reaches behind his head and grips his shirt before he pulls it over his head and throws it to the side of the bed. And now it's my turn to marvel. The man is *fit*. The tattoos I remember glimpsing in college are drool worthy and he's added to them. A lot. They go across his chest and ribs, touching the base of his neck, and down each of his arms. His dress shirts completely cover them and I absolutely forgot how sexy they are. But before I can get the chance to inspect them, he crushes me again with his weight, his mouth becoming more and more desperate against mine and the warmth from his skin seeping into me. As his tongue continues to explore my mouth, one hand glides along my stomach and up to my breast, squeezing and teasing me. My breath is becoming frantic, like I'm forgetting to breathe all together.

"Are you on birth control?"

"Yes." I confirm easily and he groans. I expected this. I remember his comment from the other day about not using a condom with me. The memory makes the heat inside of me burn even hotter. I've never had sex without a condom even though I've been on birth control since I was 18. But I won't be telling him no, I already know it. I also know he'd listen if I asked him to put one on. But for some reason, I completely trust him. And I want to feel him.

He pulls off of me again and I'm getting really tired of the anticipation. The air feels cold where he was just pressed against me. His gaze takes in my face, breasts, stomach, and lands on my panties where he hooks his fingers and pulls them down in one swoop. I giggle, definitely from nerves again, as I lift each leg so he can slide them off and he smiles up at me. Another real smile to add to my collection. I get that weird pinching feeling in my chest as he runs his hands along my calves and grips my knees, guiding my legs apart gently. I've never had a man put me on display like this before, with all the lights on in his room, and it's a little embarrassing but the heat in his gaze chases those thoughts away.

His eyes flick back to catch mine and he holds my gaze as he leans forward and settles his face between my thighs. My breath stutters just as his tongue reaches out and flattens against my clit. Bliss explodes in my brain and he hums in approval and begins to devour me, his tongue slow and methodical. One of his hands nudges against my entrance and as he pushes two fingers in, my back arches and my head falls back.

"Oh God," I breathe out and Nate responds with a desperate groan that vibrates against my center.

"So wet. So fucking responsive," he praises.

A tightness starts low in my stomach and I know it won't take long for Nate to get me off. The anticipation alone had me close to combusting. And now he's working me like magic, every single movement feeling better than the last. His fingers push in and out of me slowly, curling as they go and I don't think I can take much more of this. I rock myself back and forth in rhythm with his motions as the edge creeps closer and closer. His tongue is providing the most perfect amount of pressure.

"I want to hear you cum," he encourages, "I want to hear all the pretty little sounds you make." Then his lips wrap around my clit and suck. And that's all I needed. My whole body jerks and I am crying out as the orgasm slams through me. My hips jerk off the bed, pressing against him for more, more, more. He's happy to oblige, making sounds of approval as he continues to push his fingers into me harder and harder, lengthening the orgasm.

"Nate!" I cry out, not sure if I want him to stop or if I want more.

He pulls his mouth from my clit. His fingers don't stop pushing into me though. His lips find mine and I can taste myself on him. His tongue greedy for more.

"I'm going to make you mine, Elsi. That's what you want, isn't it?"

"Please," I somehow get the word out through my gasping but God, yes. I want to be his.

He removes his fingers and sticks them in his mouth. I just lay there in a complete lusty daze, watching him lick himself clean of me. He crawls backward off the bed, and I get another view of his perfectly muscled arms, his tight chest, his sexy as hell *v*, as he unbuttons his jeans before pushing them down and stepping out of them. I notice the tattoos on his thighs briefly before taking in his cock. He's fucking huge. Of course. Precum glistens at his tip.

"Nate-" I say in disbelief.

He climbs back onto the bed and between my spread legs. He reaches between us and lines his cock up with my entrance. "You'll let me fuck my cum into you. Make me feel good. Right, Elsi?" he asks right before he begins pushing into me slowly.

"Yes," I say as I try to breathe deeply through the stretch.

I angle my hips to allow him to slide in easier and he pushes my legs further apart as he watches his cock disappearing inside me, humming in approval. He looks up at my face and leans down, bracketing my head with his arms and kisses me as he pushes in more and more. The feel of him is unbelievable. He's so big.

His hips meet mine and his head drops to my shoulder. "Christ- Fuck *me*," he says with a shudder. After a moment where he doesn't move at all, he pulls himself out a bit and rocks back in, letting me adjust to his size. It feels otherworldly, beyond anything I've ever experienced.

My eyes shut as he chooses an intoxicating rhythm. His fingers firm where he grips me like he wants to be even closer.

His breathing is becoming faster and I can feel his lips graze mine as he asks, "Who's inside you right now? Who's fucking you raw?"

"You are."

He makes a sound between a sigh and a groan, "That's right. How do I feel?"

"I'm so-" I gasp on his thrust. "I'm so full, Nate." His back muscles under my fingertips flex with each movement. I've never felt so fucking good.

"I know, baby," he gives me another quick kiss before pulling out again and pushing back in harder. He makes a trembling, breathy noise that is maybe the hottest thing I've ever heard. No man has ever been so undone by me before, it's intoxicating. "You feel...fucking incredible." His rhythm picks up pace, grinding into me harder and faster. He's ruthless and needy, bordering on frantic and I completely understand. How many times have I thought about this? But my imagination had nothing on reality.

Nate's fingers run through my hair and grip, pulling slightly so I look up at him and he kisses me again. Our teeth clash together from his desperate pace. His other hand palms my thigh again and shifts my leg to wrap around him, allowing him to somehow go even deeper.

"*Oh*," I breathe into his mouth.

"You're squeezing me fucking perfectly, Elsi. Such a good girl for me."

Holy *shit*, do I love him calling me that.

"Such a good girl," he says again between thrusts, "letting me fuck you like this."

The tension inside of me begins to build again as his pelvis nudges me over and over.

"You going to cum again? Soak me with this perfect pussy?" He reaches between us and begins to slowly circle my clit with his thumb.

"*Oh God-*"

He slams into me again and again. His hair falling down around his forehead, a complete mess like how I remember from college. He's never looked more handsome than he does at this moment. His guard down and completely unraveled by me.

I whimper just as the orgasm barrels through me. I'm crying out and it fuels him.

He moans my name. "Oh *fuck*. That's it." He loses his rhythm and kisses me sloppily, chasing his own release and with a groan, I can feel him swell and cum inside me.

When he stops, he drops his weight down onto me, his face pressed between my jaw and collarbone. He breathes hard against my ear. After a moment he gives a little chuckle, "Somehow, that was about a million times better than I ever imagined it being."

I giggle at his rare laugh and his breathlessness and twist my fingers into his hair.

"I'm never going to get enough of you," he confesses.

This causes me to stall. It's such an intimate and vulnerable thing to say that I'm almost positive he didn't mean to say it out loud. I don't respond, letting it wash over me.

After a few moments of comfortable silence while I play with his hair, he begins to shift back and slides out of me. He doesn't go far though, just sits back on his heels still kneeling between my legs and locks his eyes on my center. I can feel his cum there and know that's what he's watching. He takes a deep breath through his nose and then reaches out and runs his finger along my opening, running through the mess he made of me. I jerk slightly, still sensitive, but I don't otherwise move. I just watch him, feeling incredibly exposed but allowing him to continue.

He pulls his now wet fingers from my center and reaches over to run them along my lips, the scent of both of our cum hitting my nose. I don't move as he paints my lips with it or when he leans forward and kisses me. It's by far the most erotic moment of my life, our lips molding, our tongues gliding together, the taste of us in both our mouths.

He pulls back from me, a cocky smirk on his face.

I sigh contentedly, "We should clean up."

"No," he says, shifting to sit next to me on the bed, "I want my cum to stay on you."

I begin to think of the many reasons to protest but I don't say any of them. It feels dirty in the best kind of way to think of sleeping with Nate's cum still inside of me.

We climb under the covers and Nate situates me to have my back pressed against his chest. We touch from shoulders to feet and he drapes his arm across my stomach. Again, I'm surprised by the intimacy of it and I give myself a silent warning not to make anything more out of this than what it is.

"Goodnight, Elsi," he says into my hair.

In the morning, I wake up to fingers playing with my nipple and I squirm at the feeling, wetness already pooling between my thighs. Memories of the night before flash through my mind and I think about the cum still on my skin. Nate's fingers squeeze before slowly trailing down my stomach, so lightly that it tickles and I press backwards into his body. He doesn't say anything but I can feel his cock already hard on my ass. I shift just a little to allow him better access when he finds my clit. He exhales hard into my ear as he begins to slowly circle, causing my whole body to heat and more wetness to pool at my entrance. I can't help myself from gently rocking into his hand, the action causing me to rub against his cock. His fingers work me slowly so that the feeling is gradual to build but soon I'm a panting and whimpering mess.

He pulls his fingers away to shift himself, lifting my leg slightly. I realize what he's doing as he positions his cock against my pussy from behind. I lift my leg higher and drape it back over his, arching my back as he starts to push into me. He props himself up on his other arm. Then his fingers return to my clit while he so slowly moves in and out.

"So fucking tight." His breath hits my ear. It's the first thing he's said this morning and it sets me on fire.

Needing to touch him somehow, I grip the forearm that's circling my clit. He buries his face in my hair as he continues with his slow and mindblowingly deep thrusts. It's not long before I feel my orgasm cresting and my fingers dig into his forearm.

"Nate, I-" but I cut off as my body ripples and the pleasure pulses through me. It's more intense than the two last night and I hear myself moaning and whimpering incoherently.

He pulls his fingers from my clit and reaches up to grip my jaw, turning my face so he can capture my lips with his. The kiss is brutal and punishing and his thrusts become harder and faster until a groan escapes from deep in his throat and he spills inside of me. He doesn't stop the kiss though, his tongue exploring mine as his movements still, his fingers tight on my jaw holding me to him. Once he's had enough, he finishes the kiss with one last gentle peck and then lets my face go before pressing his forehead to my temple.

Taking a deep breath, he slowly pulls out of me before laying flat on his back. I flip over and drape myself across him, thinking it might be more intimacy than he wants but the thought flees my brain a moment later when his arm comes up to wrap around my back.

Looking up at his face, I think this must be the best start of a new year I've ever had.

Chapter Twelve

Nate:

I'm fucked.

I'm good and royally and completely fucked. I thought that finally having Elsi after years of wondering and fantasizing what it'd feel like to slip inside of her would end the uncertainty and let me bleed her from my system. But holy shit did I miscalculate.

When I woke up and she was in my arms...

Fuck. I've woken up to women in my bed plenty of times. But I've never woken up to Elsi in my bed. Her perfect body pressed against me. Her soft skin under my palms. The smell of her shampoo invading my nose, her hair against my face. I don't even know how to describe the feeling of it. I just don't.

Then she let me touch her again. And being inside of her is better than anything I've ever experienced.

Afterwards, I made her eggs while glancing up at her fucking perfect smiling face. She's just so beautiful. When I drove her back to her car, I kissed her goodbye and since then, I've gone barely five minutes without thinking of her. She was so fucking willing and enthusiastic and responsive to every single thing I did to her. The way she gripped my cock and cried out in pleasure when I was fully seated inside of her and how she didn't object when I told her to sleep with my cum between her legs. Jesus, I'm getting hard now thinking of it.

So now, I've effectively made myself addicted to this woman. I lost control of this situation and of course, the solution is to keep my distance from her, but what I'm actually going to do is fuck her again and again and again, until she tells me she's done with me.

Chapter Thirteen

Elsi:

"**B**abe, you're coming out."

"Norma. This is getting insane. We've gone out like twice a week every week for a damn month. I can't keep doing this. It's bad for my mental health. I'm hemorrhaging money. I need my home time. It's a Wednesday night. I need to sleep! I've felt like a zombie for weeks."

"I know," she whines into the phone. "I totally know but this is the last one for a while, I promise."

"Bullshit, Nor."

"The bar has a happy hour and oysters!" The bitch knows my weakness. "Please come and then I promise I won't ask you to go anywhere else for the rest of January."

"Norma," I groan.

"Nate will be there. Use it as an excuse to get laid again."

My stomach squeezes at the thought of him but I brush it off, "I don't need to get laid again. Plus, I think he probably considers this conquest complete and will probably leave me alone. Anyway, I'll come for the oysters but I'm not going out again until February. I'm holding you to it!"

"Well, his loss if that's the case. But yes! I can't wait to go. I'll send you the details."

"Mkay," I say, less than pleased. "I'll see you tonight."

The restaurant is way busier than I anticipated for a Wednesday night, so they really must have a great happy hour or something. When I walk through the door, the wave of warmth is welcomed and I see Norma at the bar with Will. She's in a gray dress that stops mid thigh, black tights, and knee high boots. Will's dressed in one of his gray suits for work and has his arm wrapped around her waist. As she laughs at something he says, he leans forward and presses his forehead to her temple and laughs with her. They're so in love and I so love that for them. I smile as I head their way, taking in the rest of the people around the bar. Nate is already here talking with Charlie but he doesn't see me and I pull my gaze away from him so we don't make eye contact if he does notice.

Norma looks over her shoulder and spots me. She spins out of Will's hold and raises her hands up. I do a bouncy little jog over to her and wrap my arms around her back as she squeezes around my neck.

"You're here!" she cries.

"Of course I'm here! I'm a complete push over. Hey, Will." Norma lets me go and I plant a kiss on Will's cheek in greeting.

"Hey, El. Do you know what you want?" he points to the bar. "Norma informed me that I am treating you tonight."

I give her a dirty look, "Completely unnecessary. Where's that fancy happy hour menu for me to pick from?"

I browse the options and ask the bartender for one of their fancy drinks, a gin and grapefruit one, and a dozen oysters. Norma throws her arm across my shoulder and leans in, "So I think you were wrong."

"About what?" I ask curiously. I'm not sure what we've been debating.

"Well, I saw the moment Nate noticed you."

I roll my eyes but feel my heart pumping in my chest and try not to read too much into it.

"And of course he basically showed no reaction because he only has one facial expression *but* since he saw you, he hasn't taken his eyes off you."

"Norma," I say with a tone that I hope says 'you're being unrealistic.'

"I mean, you do with that what you will, but I don't think you're just a conquest for him as you keep trying to tell me."

"Well, I'll believe that when evidence is provided to me of the contrary."

She laughs, "You're such a dork."

The bartender delivers our drinks and a ton of oysters and we pass the time consuming everything while we talk about work. Everyone mingles and I spend some time with Sarah and Charlie. Sarah got hired by a high school about 30 minutes away and starts in a few weeks. She's nervous about starting mid-year but she's also excited and I know she's going to be great. She has the patience of a saint while being firm but reasonable. She has the right heart for teaching.

When Sarah and Charlie wander off to get new drinks, Nate comes over and stands in front of me. "Nate," I say in greeting as casually and carelessly as I can muster.

"Elsi. How are you?"

"Oh, I'm just great. Having a nice time?"

"Sure. Drinks are good. The view is good."

"The view?" I ask, looking toward the windows but I just see the street outside.

"*You*, Elsi. I was being..." he waves his hand, "cute."

"Hm," I can't help the smile that spreads across my face. "Cute."

I see that tiny cocky grin that's so unanimous with Nate and then he masks it by taking a sip of his drink.

And I allow the alcohol to make me brazen and say what's been on my mind since getting here tonight, "So now that you've had me, I shouldn't expect to be pulled into janitor's closets anymore, right?"

I watch his face for a reaction but he gives nothing away. He leans forward, "Now that I've had you, you should *always* expect it. I haven't had nearly enough."

Heat burns through my stomach but I school my features and say, in my best attempt at a coy tone, "What makes you think I want more?"

He sighs, exhaling loudly, "Because we both had the best sex of our lives last week and I know you're not done with me yet either."

The best? *I* was the best for *him*? Something like relief and excitement rolls around in my stomach. I try to continue with the casual vibe though and raise an eyebrow, "Awfully cocky."

He takes a step closer to me. "I know what I want, Elsi."

"Hey, guys," Frank says, clapping his hand down on Nate's shoulder, not realizing the lusty conversation he's interrupting. Nate straightens up, stepping back to where he just was.

"Hey, Frankie. I was wondering where you were!" I say enthusiastically, maybe suspiciously so.

"Got stuck late at work. Beginning of year shit. How are things?"

Nate and I share the polite version of how we've been lately, focusing solely on work and not on our sexual escapades with each other.

"I've been meaning to ask how you've been making out with that silent auction project." Frank steps between me and Nate to put his empty water glass down on the bar.

I twist my lips to the side in defeat, "Really not great. I can't do the auction without a sponsor but none of the companies we've worked with in the past are available for at least six months. I was hoping to do it in March or April so the money could begin to be put to use by summer." I shake my head, "It is what it is, but I'm hoping for a miracle."

"What type of sponsor would you need?" Frank asks.

"Oh, it really doesn't matter but if the hope is to raise at least a few million, then we'd need the company to bankroll an event that could accommodate that type of fundraising. So like a venue, dinner, drinks, entertainment, and whatever else for super stinking rich people. And as usual, I'm being too enthusiastic and am planning beyond my means."

"Well," Frank says, putting his forearm on my shoulder and leaning in, "If I know you, and your complete inability to give up, I know you'll make it happen."

I smile at him, Frank is eternally optimistic and I love that about him. "Well, thanks Frank. I hope so too. I didn't get to ask last week how your Christmas was."

"Oh, it was great."

"Did you go somewhere?" Nate chimes in.

"My parent's out in Michigan. My brother still lives by them with my sister-in-law and my two nephews. I go back home every year. What about you, man? What'd you end up doing?"

Nate jerks his head toward me, "Spent the day at home and then had dinner at Will and Norma's."

Charlie's eyebrows raise, and I don't miss his glance in my direction. "Oh, sweet. Norma's a great cook."

"She is," I agree. I look around the bar for his date from New Year's Eve, "Where's your new girl?"

He waves his hand dismissively. "That was a one time thing."

Nate chuckles next to me as I roll my eyes.

"I'll be right back, guys," I say, figuring I can let them continue this conversation without me. I lean forward and put my empty glass on the bar and turn to head for the bathroom.

The sign for the restroom points down a wide hallway. I go in even though I don't actually need to pee and stand in front of the mirror, checking my eyeliner. After having a few moments of quiet, I wash my hands and head out the bathroom door.

There's a handful of doorways along the hallway and I'm on high alert from past experience. So I'm not totally surprised that as I pass a set of double doors, one opens and hands pull me in. I stumble to the side but arms catch me before I fall.

"Seriously, Nate?" I shriek as he closes the door behind us. This must be some sort of private event room. As I glance over his shoulder it's just a huge open space with tables and chairs lined up neatly along the side and a tiny bar against the far wall. "Why do you-"

"Shut up," he barks as he backs me into the wall. And not gently. He crushes me with his body and his mouth is on mine, his tongue instantly searching.

Desire flares within me.

"I need to be inside you right now, Elsi." His tone is urgent, desperate.

My heart stutters and I give into him, wrapping my arms around his neck. His hands are all over me, gripping my breasts, sliding along my stomach, and palming my ass to pull me closer to him.

"I want you to scream my fucking name so every goddamn person in this building knows exactly who makes you feel good. Whose cum you'll be dripping for the rest of the night." As his mouth moves down my neck, his teeth graze my skin making me shudder. His hands find the button of my jeans and undoes them before pulling his mouth off of me and yanking them off.

Next are his own pants and his urgency is thrilling until I glance down at my nakedness and remember we're in a public place where we can very easily be barged in on. I can hear the murmur from the restaurant through the closed door.

"Someone might come in," I protest, a feeling like fear or panic settling in. I glance around the ceiling looking for cameras.

"I'll fucking kill them," he says and I honestly can't tell if it's a joke.

"Nate-"

He cuts me off with a kiss and wraps his hand around my leg, lifting it. I lean back on the wall and he pushes against me, holding me up. My hesitation melts away and gives in to him. Trusting him. He doesn't waste any more time before he is thrusting hard into me.

"*Fuck*," I cry at the sudden stretch as my pussy tries to accommodate his hard length.

He pushes in again, bottoming out and then finding a steady, punishing rhythm. "You're so perfect, Elsi. Such a good fucking girl."

"I love it when you call me that," I confess as his thrusts hit so deep inside of me that I can see stars. I grip the back of his neck, holding him against me, our foreheads pressed together.

"I know. Are you a good girl for anyone else, baby?" His lips brush against mine.

"No," I shake my head.

He groans, "That's right. You're all mine."

"*Yes*," I breathe out in agreement. I'm his. I'm totally his.

His fingers slide into my hair and he tilts my head so my neck is exposed. His mouth glides across my skin, kissing and nipping. The feeling sends shivers through me as he continues to drive into me harder and harder, hitting the perfect spot inside of me, and his pelvis nudging my clit with every movement. His lips find mine, kissing me gently and it's a complete contrast to his harsh thrusts. I edge closer and closer to an orgasm as he fills me perfectly again and again.

"Oh God, Nate. Keep going."

My head falls back against the wall as I feel the tension inside me about to snap and I whimper out a cry of pleasure as the dam breaks and I come apart around him. His motion speeds up and as the orgasm is still spasming through me, he thrusts hard and then stills with a sharp inhale.

"*Fuck. Yes.*" He grunts as he spills inside of me.

As he catches his breath, he lets my leg go so I can stand back up but he doesn't move off of me. Instead, he grips my jaw and brings his lips down on mine in a slow, deep kiss.

When he finally pulls out of me, he helps me get my underwear and jeans back on. I can feel his cum immediately soaking the material.

Again he grips my chin and lifts so that I'm looking at him. "I hope everyone out there can smell my cum on you. All those fuckers who touch you."

My mind flashes to Frank resting his arm on my shoulder. To me, a completely platonic gesture. I hide my embarrassment by swatting at his arm, "Awfully possessive of you."

He shrugs and buttons his own pants, "Maybe." He eyes me up and down and seemingly decides I'm decent, steps to the door, and pulls it open.

I figure the booty call is done and feel awkward as I walk by him to leave the room.

"Elsi," he says, grabbing my arm but when I turn around he doesn't say anything. Instead he steps into me and cups my face before gently planting a kiss to my lips. I'm shocked by the sweetness of the moment and don't move. When he steps back, I look up at him, wondering if he can tell how confused I am by him. But when he doesn't say anything, I just give him a small smile and walk out of the room.

Chapter Fourteen

Nate:

I step off the bus and start up the driveway. Dad's car is already here. Waiting for me. Shit. I close my eyes and take a deep breath, bracing myself before going inside. I walk through the front door and as my foot hits the bottom stair, leading up to my bedroom, he calls me. I should have known. I should have gone somewhere else. And then I want to laugh at myself because there is nowhere else to go. I steel my nerves, take my foot from the step and turn toward his study.

He's sitting in his big leather chair behind his desk, leaning back, a glass in his hand. The brown liquid is nearly gone. I don't look much like my father. His hair is a deep brown that he keeps neatly combed back from his forehead. His face is still young in appearance, which helps him lay on the charm at work, but when he's home, his face is blank. It's as if his emotions get completely wiped when he walks through our front door. His tie is loosened around his neck and his jacket is hanging on the hook behind him. I look him in the eye. They're not green like mine, but so dark they could be considered black. And they have no life in them either. "Hi, dad."

"Want to explain to me what happened today?" he asks, though he already knows what happened. I turned down the internship he set up for me because I had already accepted a position at a local law firm. I didn't hear from the man, Mr. Roberti, who interviewed me for the position that my father set up, for over a week so I took that to mean I didn't get it. I was freaking out about how mad he'd be that I didn't land the job so when McLean's Law Firm called yesterday to offer me the position there, I took it. An internship I thought he'd be happy that I had landed.

"*I took the internship at McLean's, sir. I hadn't heard from Mr. Roberti so I assumed I didn't get that position.*"

"*Even though I had set it up?*" *he says, implying I should have known it was a done deal because he has connections with all of these people. I keep my shoulders from drooping in defeat. I should have realized that but I won't show him weakness.*

"*I hadn't heard from Mr. Roberti, sir. When McLean called, I figured I should take it. It's a great opportunity there,*" *I say this hoping it will soften his anger but knowing it'll do nothing.*

"*You don't make it easy to be your father, Nathan. Somehow you continuously fuck EVERYTHING UP!*" *He spits the last sentence with venom and I can't help the way my body jerks.*

"*Mr. Roberti was very understanding, dad. I explained to him that McLean had already called.*"

"*How anyone will ever put up with your bullshit, I have no clue. You can't even follow simple instructions. I lay this shit out before you and you still fuck it up and embarass me.*"

My eyes drop to the desk, "*Sorry, sir.*"

"*You will write an email to Roberti expressing your gratitude for the interview, your deepest apologies for turning it down, and your hopes to work for him in the future. Do you understand me?*"

"*Yes,*" *I nod.*

"*You will blind copy me on it too so I know you didn't fuck this up as well.*"

"*Yes, sir.*"

"*I will not be so understanding the next time you fuck me over, Nathan. Get out.*"

Without another word, I turn and hustle out of his room, running up the stairs two at a time, and closing myself into my room. I sit on my bed and drop my head into my hands. I'm such an idiot. I shouldn't have taken that spot at the law firm. I should have known the internship at the bank was a done deal but I wanted to make sure I landed one of the two. I couldn't turn down one and not be offered the other. I thought I was doing the right thing. Fuck.

Chapter Fifteen

Elsi:

"Elsi?" I hear Joann call as she pokes her head into my office. She's one of the directors of EmpowerNest and therefore, my boss. She's a great boss and the one that I work the most with. We've become close over the past two years.

"Yeah?" I look up from the document I was working on.

"Is now an okay time to bother you?"

"Yeah, of course!" I push my laptop away and give her my full attention, gesturing for her to take a seat.

She's a tall woman, probably almost six feet and full figured. She was a rugby player for most of her life and still holds onto that power, confidence, and strength. Today her auburn hair is twisted up in a clip and she wears black cut off trousers with a pale pink button down blouse tucked into it. She sits in the chair on the opposite side of my desk and leans back.

"Everything okay?" I ask her, knowing it must be for her to be so relaxed right now.

"Tomorrow we have a meeting scheduled for 10am," she smiles mischievously.

"Okay..."

"With a gala sponsor," she says with a clap of her hands.

"You're kidding!" I jump out of my seat.

"Nope," she beams.

"Joann, you're freaking kidding me!" I say again, not willing to believe the good news.

"I'm truly not kidding."

"How? Who?" I nearly shriek. I've been trying for months and months to find a sponsor for this event. How is this happening out of the blue?

"Capulus Enterprises called today asking if we could set up a meeting for tomorrow. They want to partner with a charity this year, for some good looks I'm sure, and our name was suggested. I suppose they heard we'd been looking for a sponsor for a while now. Seems like it was just good luck."

This is unbelievable. Have I heard of this company? "Capulus Enterprises?"

She shrugs, "They're a tech company, you've probably seen ads or something. They're nationwide but I guess they have a firm based here."

I've definitely heard of them somewhere, but it doesn't matter now. I'm beyond thrilled. "I can't believe it!"

"I know. So we need to throw together some proposals ASAP to show to them tomorrow morning. Not much time but-"

"I already have some done." I spin my chair around and grab the folder off the shelf where I've been holding all my ideas for this gala.

"*Girl*," she says in disbelief. "This is why I freaking love you."

"I'll make sure everything is in order so we have something for them to agree to."

She stands, "Let me know if I can help at all. Let's get this freaking deal tomorrow."

I give her another big smile, "Absolutely!"

When Joann leaves, I get into full work mode. I brew a new cup of coffee and take a big sip before I plop back down in my office chair and get to work. I flip through every page in the folder and go over every single aspect of this gala that I've already gone through one hundred times. The nerves and excitement of a possible big event makes my blood sing and I get lost in a whirlwind of auction items, numbers, and possibilities.

At 9:42am, my leg is jiggling under my desk and Joann takes a deep breath and stands up. We've been talking through my proposals for over an hour. I need a caffeine boost because between the dopamine hit and crash last night, I stayed here way past my bedtime making sure every single thing about the proposal was ready and foolproof for the meeting this morning. I'm fucking beat, but as Joann straightens her power suit, I turn to face the mirror on my wall and make sure my makeup is set and my eyes don't look too miserably tired.

"I'm going to go make sure everything is together in the conference room. I'll have Lisa call you when they get here."

I let out a sigh of desperate nerves, trying to calm the jitters out of my body.

Joann stops in my doorway, one hand on the frame and turns back to look at me. "Listen, El, this is going to go great. You have absolutely everything covered from budget to plans to freaking tablecloth colors. You've nailed these proposals before and I have no doubt in you now. And if they pass, well then it's their loss."

I give her a forced smile and nod, knowing she's just trying to put me at ease. If they pass on this proposal, it isn't their loss. It's *ours*. And she knows it as much as I do, probably more so. But I appreciate her confidence in me and her attempt at easing my nerves.

For 12 more minutes, I stare at the wall, thinking through every possible angle to this deal that I might have overlooked but my brain is honestly on empty and I just need to focus on answering any questions these fancy business bigwigs may have.

I jump when my telephone rings, it's Lisa, and my heart jolts as I pick it up. "They here?"

"Yes, Miss Abbot. They're here and being led to the conference room by Mrs. Milligan."

"Thanks, Lis."

"Go get 'em, Elsi!" she says in a whispery cheer.

After taking a few more deep breaths, allowing them a moment to get to the conference room, I stand and run a hand down my blouse and pencil skirt. I dolled myself up a little extra today for this meeting. First impressions and all. I grab the proposal packets and head out of my office and down the hall to the conference room. I plaster a smile on my face as I push the door open. Taking in Joann on one side with an empty seat for me next to her, I turn my gaze to take in each of the two men now standing upon my arrival. The first is an older man, maybe in his late 50s, with a stylish graying hairstyle, a navy blue suit, and a handsome face. I turn to the other man and-

Oh *shit*.

Oh fucking fucker shitballs.

Nate Croman stands across the table from me with a casual, polite smile on his face.

My own smile falters but only for one nanosecond and I breeze into the conference room with what I'm hoping is an air of confidence. I force myself to rip my gaze from Nate's and focus back on the other man, who I'm guessing is his boss.

"Gentlemen, this is my event coordinator, Elsi Abbot," Joann introduces, gesturing to me as I step up to the chair she has left for me.

"So nice to meet you, Miss Abbot," the older man reaches across the table and I grasp his hand. "I'm Arthur Capulus Jr."

I smile at his introduction, noticing his last name, and nod my head, "So very nice to meet you, Mr. Capulus."

I glance towards Nate, not sure how to proceed but he saves me from having to make a decision by reaching across the table like Capulus did. "Miss Abbot. It's nice to see you." His eyes seem to be laughing at me, though his face is fairly neutral.

I follow his lead, "Mr. Croman. Always a pleasure."

"Ah, yes," Mr. Capulus says with a short chuckle. "Nate here says he knows you from college."

Nate smiles, a very businesslike smile that isn't real at all, and adds, "Yes, we share some friends as well."

I see Joann look at me out of my peripheral vision but just continue to act unaffected, "I didn't realize you worked for Capulus Enterprises, Mr. Croman."

Nate shrugs like it's a non-issue. But it is very much an issue that the man I've been fucking got his boss to seemingly agree to bankroll our next fundraising event. He must have known I work here. No, he *definitely* knew I work here. So what's this all about?

All four of us sit before Joann jumps in, turning the conversation to business and I've never been more grateful for the woman in the two years I've worked here. "We were so thrilled to get your call yesterday to set up this meeting."

"Yes, well, Capulus Enterprises needs to start giving back. It's really about time," Mr. Capulus smiles warmly, his eyes drifting between Joann and me. I instantly like the man. He seems genuine.

He continues, "I have been pushing for something like this for years now but haven't had much time to actually implement it. Luckily, my brother is going to start handling more of the business end of things at CE and I can focus on other things, like charity. Nate knew I wanted to start connecting with nonprofits, like yourselves, and suggested we meet. He had heard that EmpowerNest was looking for sponsors for an event so we looked into what you folks do here and were honestly impressed. We figured it'd be the perfect place to start."

Joann is nodding enthusiastically next to me, "We're truly flattered, Mr. Capulus. Miss Abbot and I have a proposal here for a silent auction gala that we'd love to put together for March. And if I'm being truly honest, Elsi is the mastermind, I was just the sounding board for the past 20 hours or so. But I know you'll be pleased with what she's come up with. We'd be happy to go over it."

"I hardly think we need the full rundown," Mr. Capulus says, looking towards Nate for agreement.

"Perhaps you could just give us the gist? No hard numbers. Just what you have in mind," Nate suggests to me with that fake business smile.

I give him a fake smile in return but when my eyes turn toward Mr. Capulus, the plastic smile melts into a genuine one. "I'd be happy to! This is a duplicate of my own file. You two can take this with you to go through it more thoroughly on your own time. I can also send a digital version," I slide the blue file folder in front of me across the table towards Mr. Capulus. I'm barely surprised though when Nate is the one to reach over and grab it, letting it sit closed in front of him.

"We ran all the numbers and figures for a silent auction gala to be held at The Harborview in mid March. There will be drinks, dinner, and a live band. Formal, of course. Before dinner, we would allow for bids to be placed on the items. After dinner, and before dancing, we would announce the winners of the big ticket items. All other winners would be discretely informed of their winning afterwards. In the budget, you'll notice that in addition to the venue, we allotted for photography and valet.

"In terms of a guest list, we have a running list of attendees for our events, which I also included in the file. We would also be inviting those who are contributing items to be auctioned and anyone else you'd like to be added, as well as a few members of the press. We already have about two dozen items at the ready for the auction. Those are also in the file. A few are fairly large ticket items: paintings, sculptures, vacations, private jet usage, but we'd be happy to find more if you'd like or if you know of anything we might have missed."

When I pause, Joann chimes in, "All profits would go directly to EmpowerNest's renovations, housing, college and career fairs, and counseling."

Mr. Capulus blows out a breath, "You two are efficient. What do you think, Croman?"

I meet Nate's gaze when I turn my attention to him and he responds to Mr. Capulus but doesn't look away from me, "I think it sounds well thought out, sir. And honestly, I think the event will be a great time too."

Mr. Capulus laughs and smacks his hand on Nate's shoulder, "I agree with you there. My wife is going to have a blast bidding on items."

"So you're in?" Joann asks tentatively.

"We're most certainly in, Mrs. Milligan."

Relief, happiness, disbelief all wash through me simultaneously.

Joann leans back in her seat, a weight obviously lifting off of her shoulders as well, as she claps her hands together, "Oh, thank you so much, Mr. Capulus. We're so happy to be working with you."

"It is our pleasure. Now," he shifts to stand up, "I'm sure I have to sign on the dotted line somewhere?"

"Yes, you can come with me to my office."

"Wonderful. Miss Abbot," he turns to me, "Mr. Croman is going to be my man for this job since you two already know each other. He'll be the one to look through the files and run anything by me. So if you have any questions at all, don't hesitate to call him. That work for you, Nate?"

"Certainly, sir," Nate assures Mr. Capulus.

He nods to Nate and turns back to me, "We want to help in every possible way. I'll be seeing you soon, Miss Abbot."

My stomach rolls at the thought that Nate and I will be working together on this one but I play it off, "Absolutely, Mr. Capulus. Thank you so much for your support of EmpowerNest. I know you'll love the event."

He chuckles as he follows Joann out of the conference room.

"I'll be right there, sir," Nate calls to him as the door closes behind Joann and Mr. Capulus.

I look at Nate and the silence seems loud around us. "How do I-" I stop, not sure what to even say to him. Am I mad? Am I happy? Am I thankful? I'm not sure what to think. "Why are you-" I shake my head, "I just can't-"

He smirks and leans casually back on the conference table, his arms crossed and head tilted slightly to the side, as I fumble through what I want to say to him.

"Why did you do this?" He must have some sort of reason.

He shrugs, "You expressed a problem and it was within my means to solve that problem. So I did."

"Just like that?" I ask, still in disbelief.

He gives me a little smirk, and it's not a fake one this time, "Just like that. I have no secret motive. I simply wanted to help you. The work you do here is important and it's important to you. That's enough of a reason."

I feel my shoulders relax and he must notice it too because his smile broadens and he reaches a hand out for me. Reflexively I look towards the door to make sure it's fully closed before I let him pull me closer to him. I stop just an inch or so away from him, so our only point of contact is where his hand is on my wrist.

He leans down slightly and lowers his voice as he says, "Let's keep the fact that I've been fucking you between us."

I give him what I hope is a very unimpressed deadpan look.

He shrugs, "For now at least."

"I hardly think anyone needs to know," I bite back.

"For now at least," he repeats, his free hand coming up to run a finger down my cheek and along my jaw.

Despite my annoyance, my gratitude is growing larger and larger by the second and I find myself saying, "Thank you, Nate."

He leans closer to me. His large frame envelops my vision.

"I can't even begin to tell you-"

"You don't have to tell me anything, Elsi." He closes the distance between us, pressing a soft kiss to my lips, so quick I don't have time to respond. When he pulls away, his eyes connect with mine and hold there. His cocky little smirk tugs at his lips. "I better go help, Mr. Capulus."

I breathe out a quick laugh, "Come on." I lead him to Joann's office, where the door is open. He gives me a nod before walking through and I watch his back as he makes his way to Joann's desk. Before turning away, Joann notices me and mid sentence gives me a quick wink. I hold my thumb up and turn to head back to my office. I have a shitton of work to do now, a huge event to plan and finalize in less than two months.

I sit back at my desk and drop my face into my hands. All of that insane prep between today and yesterday and I'm not even sure it mattered. I think Nate had Mr. Capulus on board before they even got here. It's surreal. But now there's work to be done.

About 20 minutes later, I'm creating my checklist of steps to complete when I hear voices in the hallway and a moment later, see Mr. Capulus and Nate peering into my office.

"Thank you again, Miss Abbot. We look forward to working with you," Mr. Capulus gives me a bright smile.

"Thank you, Mr. Capulus. Mr. Croman. Truly. We appreciate it so much."

Mr. Capulus waves me off and heads down the hall towards the exit.

"I'll be seeing you soon, Miss Abbot," Nate says, knocking lightly on my doorframe, and then he follows his boss down the hallway.

Not surprisingly, the moment I hear them exit, Joann pokes her head around my office doorway. I look at her and do a big dramatic sigh. She beams back at me, her hand on each of her cheeks, and a soft screeching noise escaping her lungs.

"I know!" I yell to her and hop out of my chair so we can hug in the middle of my little office.

"We did it! *You* did it! I can't believe it! They signed the papers without even glancing at any of the freaking documents!"

I laugh, "I know! It's going to be amazing. The best fundraiser we've ever done. Ever!"

"How well do you know Nate Croman? I wonder if he talked you up or something beforehand?" Her question is genuine and not at all accusatory, so it's easy to play dumb.

I shake my head, "Only through our friends and it was a surprise to me that he even knew what we do here. But I'll take it!"

"Absolutely! Ah, God, I feel like I can breathe again," she sighs contentedly.

"I know. I know. This is going to be wonderful."

She throws her arms around me again, "Thank you, Elsi. Let me know what tasks you need me to do or you need me to delegate."

"You got it! I can't wait to get started."

"Once our accountants connect with theirs, we'll be good to start paying out. I'll let you know as soon as I get the all clear."

Chapter Sixteen

Elsi:

F ive business days after meeting with Nate and his boss, I was able to start booking the event and working through my checklist. Nate emailed me a few days after that to give me the list of people they wanted to be added to the guest list and additional auction items, with very thorough write ups, to be donated by hotshots within the company. And in the two weeks since that meeting, I got the venue booked and the invites sent out. The auction items, if physical, are being stored in a fancy, climate controlled storage facility that Capulus Enterprises owns and I have a meeting with the venue next week to discuss color choices, centerpieces, food and drink menus, and room set up. Everything is going smoothly. And Nate has basically disappeared.

Last I heard from him was a week ago by way of a work email:

From: natecroman@capulusenterprises.com
To: elsi.abbot@empowernest.org

Subject: Auction Items

Ms. Abbot,

I received your list of the auction items, their monetary value, and where/how they are being stored. Could you please confirm if the tickets to the opera are for 2 or 4? Also, did you receive the donated item from

---

Chetworth Douglas, a business partner of ours, that I was told would have arrived yesterday?

Thank you,
Nate Croman

All very professional. Like he doesn't even know me. And of course, I expect nothing in a work email but that doesn't explain the complete lack of contact. No texts, no showing up when we all go out to get a drink, no stopping into my office. Nothing. Which has led me to the solid conclusion that I was a short lived conquest for him. Five years later, he did in fact get me, and now he is satisfied to move on. The thought makes me...sad. Just so sad. And for some reason, I feel lonelier than I ever have before.

Last night, I was out with Norma and the rest of our friends and Nate was nowhere to be seen. Trying not to let it destroy my mood was fruitless because even though I was asking her tons of questions about her trip to Las Vegas with Will, within about 20 minutes she nudged my arm and asked, "Are you alright?"

I pursed my lips and made a face, "I'm being a mopey bitch, aren't I?"

"Yeah," she chuckled, "Why though?"

"It's kind of pathetic and a little desperate," I admitted.

"You still haven't heard from Nate?" she guessed.

I took a sip of my gin, "Not a peep. It's like he's disappeared. I keep expecting a text or maybe for him to show up one night and accost me in a janitor's closet." Norma, of course, knows about Nate's habit of finding me in dim hallways.

"Will said he hasn't seen him much around the office lately either. Maybe he's just busy. Have you sent him a message?"

"No, I typed out a few but never hit send. I'm too..." I waved my hand, "I don't want him to think I'm, like, a clinger or whatever."

"El," she sighed. "He got his company to support your nonprofit for fuck's sake. I don't think you messaging him would make him think you're clingy. Aren't you at least friends at this point?"

Are we friends? Yeah, I guess we kind of are. Maybe? God, this is ridiculous. It doesn't need to be so complicated.

"I don't even know, Norm."

She raised her eyebrows, "It sounds to me like our little buddy Nate is kind of a douchebag. You don't even know if you're *friends?* Seriously? If he makes you feel like shit, like you're just a piece of ass, then good riddance. Jeez babe, I'm regretting that I ever thought this was a good idea."

She was right. She was totally right. I shouldn't feel this bad and torn up over a guy I've only slept with a few times, and who I barely even know. "You're right. It's not worth this."

I know I didn't expect much from him, but I just thought after the things he's said and how desperate he was for me, that he would have held on just a little longer. Maybe this is for the best, before I get attached to him in any way other than the incredibly mind blowing sex. I know myself, and Nate is absolutely someone that I could see myself falling into unrequited love with. Not to mention the huge issue that he's going back to California in May. It's better that it just ends. A clean break. And when I do see him again, which I'm sure I will with him being Will's friend and the fundraising gala, we can just be friends. God, *are* we even friends?

I'm comfortable with this decision and have been sitting on it since last night. It's definitely for the best. But the disappointment is still making my skin feel weird and I'm holding onto a little bit of resentment towards him. So when he randomly strolls into my office at 11 in the morning, I almost think I'm imagining things. And like a complete weirdo, I just stare at him for a solid 10 seconds, not saying anything. Even though I know he addressed me as "Miss Abbot" all mischievous and sexy when he walked in as if he's been here 100 times.

"Are you alright, Miss Abbot?" he asks with a grin, walking over and sitting in the chair on the opposite side of my desk.

"What are you doing here?" I ask, my tone somewhere between cold and confused.

"I was in the neighborhood. Figured I'd stop in and see if there was anything I could assist you with for the fundraiser," he says it like it's the most perfectly normal thing in the world.

And now I'm angry.

I haven't heard from this man in two weeks. He fucks me three times within like five days, ambushes me at work, and then completely disappears for two weeks.

I glance towards my office door. The very open door and lower my voice before turning my gaze to him, "I don't need assistance, Nate. I know how to do my job."

"Of course you do," he says, not allowing my anger to deter him even the slightest. "I meant anything CE can help you with."

"No. Mr. Capulus will be happy to know that invites to the guests went out this morning and all of our auction items are either located in storage or are on their way to storage. The items that are merely in writing are filed appropriately in my locked cabinet," I gesture behind me.

"Hm," he hums in an approving tone. Which is infuriating because I don't need his approval.

"I meet with the event planner at The Harborview on Wednesday evening to finalize the details with her."

"What time?"

"Four thirty but-" I mentally kick myself for telling him.

Nate doesn't say anything right away, just looks at me.

I haven't seen this man for over two weeks and I don't think he cares. I don't think he cares that I've been spending my evenings wondering what he was doing...or *who*. Wondering if I should text him and see if he had any nights free. Wondering if he was wondering about me at all. What a fucking idiot I am.

I inhale deeply through my nose, keeping my eyes down at the documents I was just organizing, then calmly ask, "Is there anything else I can do for you, Mr. Croman?"

When I look at him again, some sort of emotion flickers across his face, but it's too quick for me to catch before his features settle back into their normal stoic nothingness. "I'll pick you up at four on Wednesday for the meeting."

I feel my eyebrows shoot up, "What?"

"The meeting with the event planner at The Harborview. I'll pick you up before we go. Will you be here or at your apartment?"

"You're not coming with me to that meeting."

He shrugs, "I'm sure Mr. Capulus would love for me to attend. I won't get in your way. Now, Miss Abbot, will you be here at four o'clock on Wednesday for me to pick you up?"

Anger burns through my chest but I contain it. "If you *insist* on coming, I will just meet you at the venue."

"Don't be silly, Miss Abbot, I'd be happy to pick you up. It's on my way, after all."

"Nate, I'm not-"

"It's settled then. Four o'clock, Wednesday. I'll be waiting out front," he gestures towards the front of the building. He gets out of the chair and bends down, both of his palms resting on my desk as he leans over it. "I've been *quite* busy at work these past two weeks, Miss Abbot. Lots of unexpected overtime." His meaning is clear to me, he hasn't had time to see me but he could have texted or *something*. But there I go again thinking this is something more than what it actually is.

I give him a small nod, but look back down to the papers in front of me, not really wanting to hear it.

He continues anyway, "Time got away from me but my schedule should be back to normal, so I would truly be honored to help you on Wednesday at the venue."

I sigh, defeated, "Don't you get tired of these games?" I didn't mean to say it aloud but now it's out there, hanging heavily between us. I mindlessly straighten my stack of sticky notes.

"Elsi, I-"

But I cut him off. Not really wanting to hear it at the moment. I just want him to go. Looking up at him, I concede, "Okay. Four o'clock out front."

"Thank you." I see his hand lift off the desk and reach toward me briefly, but he seems to think better of it and slides it across his hair, making sure it's all still perfectly in place. Then without another word, he turns and walks out of my office.

Chapter Seventeen

Nate:

Elsi is upset with me. The look on her face won't get out of my fucking head. *Hurt.* I did something to hurt her. I know I haven't been available the past couple weeks but it's not like she reached out to me either. So many times I picked up my phone to message her but what would I say? *Hi?* And I didn't have time to see her so it's not like we could have made plans. What would we have talked about? I'm not great with small talk.

I want so desperately to know what was going on in that pretty brain of hers. I'll pick it out of her on Wednesday. Just five more days until I can see her again. Deciding to attend the meeting and pick her up were all impulse choices but I'm going to make them count. And by the time I go to sleep on Wednesday night, I'll have sunk my dick into her sweet pussy again. Exactly where it belongs. I've done far too much jerking off in the past two weeks to thoughts of her sexy little body. I feel like I'm back to being a hormonal teenager who can't get control of his hard ons. Every other thought is about her lately and my cock jerks angrily with every passing fantasy.

Maybe sending her a text here and there will help ease the ache I feel when I'm not near her. I'll give it a shot tomorrow.

Chapter Eighteen

Elsi:

"So he just walked into your office and invited himself to a business meeting?" Norma asks, knowing the answer is yes.

I nod through my gulp of wine.

"That absolute piece of shit."

"He didn't even seem to realize what my issue was. Why I was upset. I mean, regardless of the implication that he doesn't believe I can handle my job, I haven't seen the man in over two weeks. Like, what is actually happening here? He gets his boss to sponsor this event that he knows is important to me and then completely disappears aside from a couple of business emails? I'm too tired for games."

"I'm sorry, honey," Norma says, gripping my forearm.

"I just thought..." I don't really know what I thought but there were a couple weeks there where I thought that he might actually be interested in me. "I don't know. For about one second, I guess I thought I was beginning to matter to him."

"I know."

"And I feel like an idiot that he matters to me," I sigh.

"He's the idiot," she tells me, being the perfectly supportive friend I need. She knows I don't want solutions. I just want an ear and a shoulder.

"He *is* an idiot," I agree with a nod. "This wasn't anything anyway, so whatever." I wave my hand like I'm brushing it off but Norma and I both know that's bullshit. The real problem here, beyond the fact that he started to matter to me, was that he's the only man to ever make me feel alive. Feel like I matter. Feel good and sexy and desired. But if he can just turn that off on a whim, then I guess it's really not what I thought it was.

"If he's just using you I'll kick his ass or slice his tires or tell Will to stop inviting him around."

"No," I let out a little laugh. "I'm okay, seriously."

"So what are you going to do on Wednesday?"

"Go to this meeting with him and hope he isn't an asshole."

"What if he turns on the charm again?"

I lay my head down on her shoulder and think about it for a moment. What will I do if he goes back to flirty, charming, and filthy-mouthed Nate? "I don't know, Norm."

She rests her head atop mine, "That's okay. Just let me know what I can do to help you. I'm here."

Saturday morning I sleep in and wake up in a better mood than I've been in for the past few days. I'm going to do some chores this morning and then spend the rest of the day lounging around reading or watching movies. I need the day in and I need to just recuperate after yesterday's annoying ass whirlwind. I'm so grateful Norma was free last night so I could go to her place immediately to vent about this shit with Nate. What would I do without her and her unending, nonjudgmental support?

I have a super productive morning doing laundry, deep cleaning the kitchen, and vacuuming my area rugs in the living room and my bedroom. After eating a sandwich for lunch, I throw a bunch of ingredients in my crockpot to make a stew to have for dinner tonight. It's brutally cold outside and the only good thing about winter is that it's soup season. I get everything cooking together and then decide to brew a cup of tea before settling into my favorite spot on the couch to rot for the rest of the day.

As the kettle heats, I hear my phone chime from my bed and pad through the living room and into my bedroom to grab it. Then immediately after seeing the screen, I close my eyes at the mix of emotions, because of course it's Nate.

> Nate: Hey

Hey? I cannot keep up with the ever changing winds of Nate Croman, master of stressing me out. I opt to ignore him for a little while. He doesn't need instant gratification. I walk back to the kitchen and stare at the kettle until it whistles, pour the hot water into a mug, ignore the message, rip open a tea bag, and add some sugar before stirring it all together. Then I slowly move to the living room and put the mug down and my phone next to it. My book is still in my bedroom, so I go to grab it, before returning to the living room to sit in my favorite spot. Leaning my head back, I stare at the ceiling as I take a deep breath, but my patience is at its end and I grab the phone and text him back.

> Me: Hi.

The period at the end sends the message that I'm annoyed, right?

> Nate: It was nice seeing you yesterday

My heart stutters but I refuse to allow this to make me immediately forget the fact that he only entertains the thought of me when he feels like it. As I debate how to proceed from here, he sends a follow up message.

> Nate: What are you up to this weekend?

Is this an inquiry? Or just small talk? I truly have no idea. Whatever.

> Me: Some R&R. Just sat down. Going to read or watch a movie.

> Nate: Anything good?

> Me: If I watch a movie, no clue what it'll be... But reading an Agatha Christie. Do you read?

> Nate: I read.

And then he sends a picture of his side table in his living room. A book is there next to a glass of water and the TV remote. I can also see the TV is on in one corner of the photo. He seems to be watching football or something. I zoom in on the book to see it's called *True Believer* by Jack Carr. Huh, never heard of it. I'll look it up later.

> Me: R&R for you too?

> Nate: I went to the gym this morning but otherwise.. yeah. I wasn't kidding about the insane 2 weeks I just had. I've been looking forward to the weekend to do next to nothing

Don't let him off the hook too easily, Elsi. Just because he was busy doesn't make it okay for him to ghost you for two weeks. Though to be fair, I didn't message him either. Am I being a hypocrite? Ugh, I don't know. I decide to stay in safe territory for my response.

> Me: What was going on at work?

> Nate: A lot of movement with the bosses. Arthur Capulus is stepping aside in a big way to let his brother take the reigns but he's still staying on the company's board, so it's been a matter of reorganizing and falling in line within the new pattern

> Me: Did your position get affected?

> Nate: You worried about me?

I let out a laugh despite my best efforts to remain mad at the man.

> Nate: No, it doesn't affect me much unless you count the insane amount of meetings that were held and therefore, affected the time I had to do my actual work. I generally try to limit my overtime but shit happens

Me: At least it's settled down now

Nate: Right. Now I can get back to other things

I will myself to not read more into that comment than is actually there. But I can't help but ask because I'm apparently a glutton for punishment.

Me: Like what? Hobbies?

Nate: Sure. Hobbies. Relaxing.

Right. That's what I figured. And as I'm about to ask him what his hobbies are, another text comes through.

Nate: You

My heart is definitely stuttering now. I shift on the couch and read it again. *You.*

Me: Me?

Nate: Yeah. Not even 3 weeks and I forgot how good you look in your work clothes

I roll my eyes.

Me: It's not like I wasn't exactly where I always am

Nate: I'm aware. I thought of you being exactly where you always are…often

I close my eyes, absorbing the acknowledgement that he thought about me. Or he's just playing this game very freaking well.

Nate: I'm a jackass

And now I can't help the smile that spreads across my face.

Me: Why's that?

Nate: For letting that much time pass without seeing you even though you were so close. A truly stupid jackass

He's right. He is a jackass.

Me: You said it not me

Nate: But you thought it. I'll make it up to you

Me: Oh really?

Nate: Yes.

We pass the rest of the evening texting sporadically. Sometimes I stop answering for 30 minutes or so and then send him a random message and he does the same. Throughout the day, I tell him what I've been up to for the past couple weeks and I do end up asking about his hobbies. Other than reading, he likes to work out. *Obviously*. He trains in mixed martial arts several times a week and he follows the sport. It's an inconsistent conversation but it's nice to know he's thinking of me as he lounges at home. That's all I've wanted. Just to know I was being thought of.

I tell him what movies I'm watching and he passes judgment, both good and bad, depending on the movie. One time, he even turned the same movie on, sending me a picture of his TV with a scene about 15 minutes behind where I was. I can't help but wonder what it'd be like to do these lazy days together. Lounging on my couch, bickering over what movie to watch, and then settling on something we both like and enjoying it together, not even having to speak.

Chapter Nineteen

Nate:

I was wrong. Texting with Elsi is easy and just having her attention, even for only a moment at a time, is enough. Enough to ease this angst of waiting for her. We've messaged back and forth more times than I think I've ever done in my entire life. Thank fuck I get to see her tomorrow. I'm becoming desperate.

Chapter Twenty

Elsi:

Wednesday moves painfully slow. I'm getting a ton of work done but every time I look at the clock thinking it will have been an hour since I last looked, it's only been 20 minutes. I've tried to not be excited about seeing Nate again, but I fail. He seems to be a weakness. A kryptonite. And my heart keeps telling my brain over and over and over again that this weakness is going to bite me in the ass big time. In a big, bad, awful way. But can I resist? No. That's the whole freaking problem.

His consistent texting since Saturday has softened me to him. Again. Which I'm sure was the entire point. Butter me up in the days leading up to seeing each other so that I invite him home and spread my legs for him. I know I shouldn't. I *know* it. But if he asks, I also know I'll cave. He'll give me one single heated look and I will melt into a puddle, willing to do anything he wants.

At 3:55, I sigh heavily and push back from my desk. *Just keep things on business.* That's my mantra today. We're going to The Harborview for a meeting and when the meeting is done, I will say goodbye to him. This is business. Keep it business. Business.

I pull on my coat, grab my bag, and head from my office to the front door. I say goodnight to Lisa and walk out into the freezing winter air. A gust of wind slams into me, throwing my hair behind me and plastering my coat to my front. I run my eyes along the cars parked in front of the building and see Nate as he climbs out of his and comes around to the sidewalk. I hustle over to him and he opens the passenger door for me without a word. As I climb in, I'm immediately grateful for the reprieve from the wind and the heat blasting from the vents. A moment later, he's opening the driver's door and climbing in next to me.

"Hi," I say. *Business*, Elsi.

He looks at me as he buckles his seatbelt. A small smile starts on his handsome face, "Miss Abbot."

"I'd thank you for picking me up, but seeing as how it was against my wishes, I won't."

He chuckles as he puts the car into drive and pulls out onto the street, steering us toward the venue. "Fair enough."

We drive in silence for a moment and I look out my window, watching the buildings, cars, and people as we drive by. He breaks the silence to ask for the event coordinator's name at the venue and I answer him without looking away from my window. I'm being cold towards him, I know it, but it certainly makes it easier to keep this to business if I simply don't look at him.

"How long do you think this will take?" he asks, breaking the silence again.

I finally turn to look at him, taking in his handsome profile. His almost white hair combed neatly to the side, his slightly crooked nose, his strong jaw, his green eyes. God, he's gorgeous. But that doesn't matter right now. I scoff, "You invited yourself to this, you know. You have plans or something?"

He glances at me before turning his eyes back to the road, "Not at all. My night is wide open."

"I would think an hour, maybe, but I'm not sure."

He stops at a red light and looks at me again, "Can I buy you dinner afterwards?"

I sigh, my lips pressing together, "Why?"

"Because I want to. Because I haven't seen you in a while. Because I'm crashing this meeting for no reason other than to be near you and I want to at least buy you dinner as an..." he trails off.

"An apology?" I supply.

He begins driving again and shakes his head, "Doesn't seem like something I'd do."

I breathe out a laugh, half amused and half annoyed, "Right."

"Please, Elsi," he looks quickly at me again.

I turn back toward the window. I have been coaching myself to say no to this kind of thing for days but here I am saying, "Okay." I don't see his reaction but I know that cocky little smirk is on his face right now. Why am I powerless against him?

Nate pulls into the parking garage of the venue and we wander over to the elevator to be taken to the correct floor. Having been given directions this morning, I know the event coordinator is on the third floor and head towards that office. Nate follows me without questioning anything. When we get to her office, the door is wide open and Lenora Jones is sitting behind her desk, typing away on her keyboard. I knock on the doorframe and she looks up.

"Ah, Miss Abbot! So nice to finally meet you in person." She stands up from her chair and walks around her desk to greet us. She's a beautiful woman. Her hair is black and sleek, stopping at the top of her shoulders. Her features are dark and alluring, her makeup accentuating that fact. She wears a simple white blouse that is tight against her breasts and tiny waist and is tucked into a maroon pencil skirt. She stands tall and confident on black pumps. She reaches out to shake my hand, which I take. I feel mildly frumpy compared to her in my loose fitting gray blouse, black dress pants, and plain flats.

"Ms. Jones, nice to meet you as well."

"And this must be Mr. Croman from Capulus Enterprises?" she asks, reaching her hand out to Nate and looking at his unfairly handsome face.

His business smile is perfectly in place as he shakes her hand, "Nice to meet you, Ms. Jones."

She waves her free hand, "Oh, we can all stop with the formalities. Please call me Lenora."

My eyebrows raise slightly but I brush it off. Is she being polite or is she being flirty with my business partner? But then I chastise myself for being suspicious and jealous for no reason.

Lenora gestures for us to follow her into her office and we take off our jackets and sit across the desk from her. Nate pulls my seat out for me and I thank him as I sit. One of his hands brushes along the back of my neck and across my shoulder. Lenora catches the gesture and quickly averts her eyes back to her computer monitor. Then he sits next to me, pulling his chair marginally closer to mine. I play it off like nothing is amiss and keep my attention on her as she clicks through a few things before turning her gaze back to me.

"I got your response this morning with all of the questions I had posed. I appreciate your decisiveness. It certainly makes things easier. So we are all set with color choices, tablecloths, and napkins. I want to finalize centerpieces first. Then we can go through the menus."

"That sounds perfect."

Nate leans towards me, "What colors did you choose?" I know he's just asking out of curiosity and not because he intends to change a single thing.

"Navy blue and champagne."

He nods, "Nice."

Lenora glances between the two of us and seemingly decides she can continue. "Now, for centerpieces, were you thinking floral?"

"Yes."

"Perfect, so to go with the color scheme, I had put together a few options." She turns the monitor towards me and scrolls through the options. "We have some with hydrangea, orchid, thistle, peony, baby's breath. The options are pretty extensive but I think these two would be my favorite." She points to one arrangement with hydrangea and eucalyptus and then the second arrangement with peony and baby's breath. I look at each and try to envision it with the navy blue table cloths.

"I think I like the peony and baby's breath. I like the height of that too, being a little shorter, so no one has to look around it." I turn to Nate, "What do you think?"

He gives me a sly little smile, probably to indicate that he was hardly listening and says, "I think your choice is perfect."

"Great!" Lenora claps her hands, "That was fairly easy."

I shrug and give her a wide smile, "I think we have the same taste in flower arrangements."

"*Good* taste," she agrees with a chuckle. "Now for the not as simple bit. The menu."

Nate seems to perk up at that, shuffling a little closer to the computer screen and subsequently, closer to me. His knee brushes my thigh.

"Generally we offer a fish, meat, pasta, and vegetarian option."

After indicating that I would like to keep it that way, she continues.

"Wonderful, so let's start with the main course and then we can work our way backwards. Starting with the fish, the options would be here." She pulls up the correct tab and indicates the fish options, "We have blackened salmon, mahi-mahi, or stuffed flounder."

"Hm," I look at each and try to think which would be the most widely enjoyed. I glance to Nate, "Mahi-mahi?"

"Yeah, sure, something people won't be able to get just anywhere."

"Exactly," I agree.

Lenora works us through the side options for the fish and we move onto the pasta and then vegetarian. I ask Nate's opinion here and there and he seems to appreciate that. When we get to the meat option though, he chimes in before being asked, "The ribeye."

"Really? Not the filet mignon?" I ask skeptically.

"The ribeye," he repeats enthusiastically.

I can't help but laugh and not really wanting to argue, say, "Okay. The ribeye, then."

He smiles back at me, showing some of those perfectly straight teeth and I catch myself lingering on his mouth and quickly pull my attention from him.

"You might as well pick the sides too since I'm guessing this will be your meal," I tell him.

"The mashed potatoes, please, and the broccoli rabe."

"Perfect!" Lenora replies cheerfully and then we move on to appetizers, salad, and finally the dessert course. It takes almost 30 minutes just to choose the dinner menu. But then we shift to alcohol and decide on one signature cocktail. Nate insists on top shelf options for the open bar and I don't bother trying to negotiate. It's his company after all that's footing the bill and I'm sure he knows what he's doing.

"Wonderful. So that should be the menu and drinks settled. I will send finalized documentation to your email Miss Abbot on everything you chose tonight," she assures me.

"Elsi," I correct, wanting to be less formal. "Thank you."

"Elsi," she says with a bright smile. "All that's left is just to decide on the room arrangement. Do you two mind taking a walk with me downstairs?"

We follow Lenora out of her office and toward the elevator. When the doors open, Nate ushers me in with a hand on my lower back. We're not being overly professional at this meeting with all of his hidden touches and my ogling his lips but what does it matter if Lenora knows there is something between Nate and I? It *doesn't* matter. So I don't sweat it.

We walk into the ballroom where the event will take place and it looks weirdly empty with no people in it and the chairs and tables all to the side. It's a beautiful room. The walls are a dark gray and there are pretty light fixtures hanging from the ceiling throughout the room and sconces along the walls. There are two bars, one on each side of the large room, and they're made from a deep colored wood, really making the room look elegant. She walks us through the room making recommendations and answering our questions. We decide where everything will be, the auction items, the live band, the high tables for people to mingle around, the dinner tables, how many people to seat at each, and every other little nitpicky detail that you could imagine. Nate gets bored within about five minutes of the walkthrough but keeps a polite smile on his face and nods every so often. When we've finished in the ballroom, we follow Lenora back to her office to grab our things.

"Thank you so much, Elsi. If there is anything else you need, feel free to reach out."

I give her a warm smile as I shake her hand again. I like her. She's efficient and competent and easy to bounce ideas off of. I'm glad she's who I am working with for what is easily becoming the biggest event of my career.

"Thank you, Lenora."

"And Nate. It was nice to meet you."

"Yes, thank you," Nate politely shakes her hand and then turns, gesturing for me to walk out of the office first.

I head down the hallway back to the elevator to head up to the parking garage.

"That was successful," I say as we wait for the elevator.

"Hm," Nate hums. "Who fucking knew there were so many decisions for an event?"

"Me," I laugh.

"Yeah, I suppose you would, but *Jesus*. So many options for damn salads. It's all the same shit!"

I smile at his teasing as we step onto the elevator and the doors close in front of us. Nate stands close to me and the second the doors close, he reaches his hand around my waist and pulls me toward him, turning me in the process so that I'm pressed chest to chest against him. I tilt my head back so I can look up at him, my heart fluttering as our eyes meet. His hand around my waist tightens and the other reaches up to land on my face and neck, his thumb runs along my cheek softly. Then he's leaning down and his lips press firmly against mine. God, I missed this. His mouth on me. The elevator doors begin to open and he presses his lips to mine one more time before stepping back, grabbing my hand, and leading me towards his car.

"After all that menu talk, I need a steak," he groans as he unlocks the doors.

I smirk at his whining, "We can go wherever you want. I never have trouble finding something I like."

He takes us to a pub and we get a table in the back where the lights are pretty dim and it's far enough away from the noise of the bar that I can hear him when he speaks. He asks me lots of questions about the event and what else I need to get done between now and then. I ask him about work and the new restructuring. When our food is done, his steak and my fish, Nate insists on paying and sends the server with his card before even getting the bill. Now we're waiting while he leans back in his seat sipping his drink. He looks comfortable and relaxed. He ran his hand through his hair a few times through dinner and it's now falling around his forehead rather than being neatly combed to the side and it looks very, very good.

He turns his attention from the people at the bar and leans onto the table, moving closer to me in the process. I watch his movement and take a drink of my wine, my eyes locked on his.

"Let me take you home." It's not a question, though I'm sure if I said no, he'd accept it.

But I don't say no. I say, "Okay."

Cue the cocky smile and the subsequent tightening in my lower stomach.

The ride to my apartment is quiet but it's this strange sort of quiet that's a mix of anticipation and comfortable silence. I give him directions and in the meantime, hope that I haven't left clothes on the floor and that the toilet bowl is clean. He's able to find parking a block over from my place and as we walk to the door, he leaves his hand on the small of my back. I can barely feel it through my coat but I still know it's there.

He follows me up the flight of stairs and then down the hall to my door. Having already been at his very expensive place, I'm suddenly a little self conscious of my very tiny one bedroom apartment. I unlock the door and lead the way, flipping on the light. When I start to pull off my coat, he helps me out of it.

"Thanks," I smile, suddenly nervous. I take my coat from him and hang it on one of the hooks by the door before heading toward the kitchen. "You know, I think I have some bourbon."

He smirks, "Is it any good?"

I scrunch my nose, "No clue. It was a Christmas gift. Let me look." I walk over toward the cabinet where I usually keep all my alcohol. I glance back at Nate and he's taking in my apartment, the living area with the couch, ottoman, small TV, and bookcase. His attention migrates along the walls with some photos and art that I've collected over the years.

I reach into the cabinet and pull out a bottle of wine and the bottle of bourbon. "Want to check this out?" I ask, holding it up.

He comes over and grabs the bottle with one hand and my outstretched arm with the other. He pulls me closer to him. I hesitate slightly and I think he can tell because instead of kissing me, he just leans down and presses his forehead to mine. He breathes a long, slow breath out of his nose. "I'm not trying to play games with you."

He apparently couldn't help answering my question from the other day. I so desperately want to believe him. I let out a shaky laugh, "Nate-"

"I just want you," he confesses.

I completely understand. His fingers land along my neck and jaw, gently tilting my head back so he can look into my eyes before he plants a soft kiss to my lips. I'm immediately filled with warmth. My body is always more willing to overlook his bullshit than my brain is. But if I'm doing this, then I'm really going to do it but I'm not going to let him have sex with me and leave. We can talk like actual adults first. Though his tongue in my mouth is trying to convince me to just skip to the sex. But I won't!

Before I even attempt to end the kiss, he pulls back, "This bourbon is shit, by the way."

I can't help the laugh that rips out of me, my head dropping back even further. The smile he gives me in return is blinding. It lights up his entire face, showing his perfect teeth and causing creases in the corners of his eyes. I don't think I've ever seen him smile like that. It makes him more human, more real.

"Figures," I say through the final waves of laughter.

"I'll take one for the team though and start working on it," he puts the bottle down and I find each of us a glass. He pours his own drink as I uncork my bottle of wine.

He leads us over to the couch and I sit next to him. "Tell me something about yourself. Something none of our friends know." I take a sip of my wine as I wait.

He makes a humming sound like he's thinking, "I was raised by my father."

I narrow my eyes at him, "No one else knows that?"

He tilts his head to the side in a half shrug, "Never really came up."

"And you grew up in New England right?" I remember that vaguely from college.

"Yeah," he seems surprised that I know that. "In Connecticut."

"Your mom?" I ask tentatively, not really sure how to word the question.

"In Florida. She and my dad separated when I was six and she moved there shortly after," he turns a little to angle towards me and his arm drapes across my shoulders.

"Do you see her often?"

He shrugs, "Once or twice a year. She remarried when I was 10 or so. She's a busy woman but she calls fairly often."

I don't push for more on that subject, not wanting him to shut me out. So I switch back to his father, "What's your dad do for a living?"

"We're doing a lot of talking about me. This feels like an interrogation."

"You can ask some in a minute," I brush him off with a wave.

He raises an eyebrow at me but answers anyway. "He's a businessman. CEO of his company for at least the past 15 years," he sips the bourbon and purposely makes a funny face to emphasize that the bourbon is, in fact, shit.

I smile at his antics. But I'm not letting him distract me. I want to know more about him, "Is that why you went into business?"

"Yeah. I guess it was all I really knew. And to my father, the only way to be a successful man is to run a business, work insane hours, and make a ton of money. To have power." He twirls some of my hair around his fingers.

"He works a lot?" I ask as chills run down my spine.

He just nods, very obviously wanting to stop talking. "But what about you? Where did you grow up?"

"Tennessee."

"You don't have an accent," his tone is somewhere between a question and a statement.

"Norma says you can hear it with certain words but otherwise it's pretty mild," I shrug. My parents' accents are mild too and I think mine has gotten less pronounced every year that I've been away.

"What do your parents do?"

"My dad's a preacher and my mom's an elementary school teacher."

He glances down at my necklace, a small silver cross, and then his eyes narrow, "You're fucking with me."

I can't help but laugh at his disbelief, "Nope. My father is a preacher at the church in town and my mama teaches first grade. Everyone in town knows them and they know just about everyone else. My older brother, Elijah, is a preacher too actually. A couple towns over from them."

"This makes so much sense. I *always* suspected you were an innocent little Christian girl."

"I don't know about that," I scoff.

"Do you see them often?"

"Not really. It's expensive to fly and they don't make much extra money. And I'm not in much of a different situation with my pay, so we mostly just call and send photos when we can. We try for at least once a year, but it's usually me going to them. But it's tough because most holidays when I'm off is when my dad is busiest."

"You didn't want to move back there after college?"

I shake my head dramatically, "Absolutely not. There's not much available for work in my interests and I knew from the moment I met Norma that I wanted to be wherever she was."

"Yeah, you guys seem pretty tight."

"She's my soulmate," I say in the corniest voice but with absolute honesty.

"Will's not her soulmate?" he asks incredulously.

"Of course not. He's just her husband."

He laughs at my joke and I beam back at his smiling face.

"Are you close with your brother?"

I shake my head, "Not really. He's eight years older than me. We have incredibly different interests and he was always involved in the church and volunteer work. He never had much time for me."

"Mm," Nate nods. "I have a step brother. Jaxon. He's younger, like five years, but we don't have anything in common either. To be honest, I can probably count on two hands how many times we've ever really spoken."

"It's weird," I say, "being tied to someone like a sibling or stepsibling or parent, even, and just having no...connection with them."

"Yeah, it is. You'd think a connection would be automatic but it's not. Sometimes you have to work at it and sometimes you just kind of don't."

"Who *do* you have a connection with?" I ask leaning in toward him.

He shrugs and avoids my eye as he sips his drink again, "Will's a good friend and a couple guys from work." Then looks back at me with a grin, "And I like to think we have a connection."

I laugh and tease, "Well I'd say so since I'm somehow the only one who knows you were raised by a single father. It's so basic."

His eyebrows shoot up and he nearly laughs, "I'm telling you, it just never came up!"

"Right," I say skeptically but now I'm ready for a change. "So," I point, "the bathroom is through that door. I'm going to go use it."

I hustle into the bathroom, glancing around to make sure it's fairly clean. I pull the hand towel down and throw it in the hamper before replacing it. I quickly scrub the toilet bowl and then lift the seat to make sure it's clean under there since I never really check. All is well. So I pee, wash my hands, and then give myself a quick determined nod before heading back out.

Nate isn't on the couch anymore. He's standing next to the TV, looking at some of the photos I have hanging up. He's taken his suit jacket off and laid it over the back of the couch. His dress shirt sleeves are unbuttoned and he rolls them up while he looks at the photos. A tattoo of a beautiful weeping willow on his forearm catches my attention and I look up at my wall to the new painting Norma got me for Christmas. Two weeping willows. What are the chances?

"Your parents?" He asks, pointing to a photo of me with the two of them right after I graduated college. It was a day or two after the ceremony and we had gone hiking. Norma took the photo for us.

"Yeah, right after graduation." I point to another one taken at my dad's church, "And that's Elijah." He looks at my brother for a long moment. Taking in his short, stocky frame, his light brown hair combed perfectly to the side, his polo shirt and chinos, and his beaming smile. Elijah's arm is draped over my mother's shoulders. My dad's arm is across mine in an almost exact mirror image.

He nods but doesn't comment and continues to look from photo to photo. Most of them are of Norma and I or of the few places I've visited. He asks me about a few of them, seeming to be genuinely interested in where I've been, what I've experienced.

"I had fun today," he says.

I chuckle, "I actually did too. I'm not mad at you anymore for inviting yourself."

"You were mad at me?" He knows fully well that I was.

"Yes, I thought you were going to steam roll me."

He steps closer, "Nah, you're the expert. I just wanted an excuse to see you."

"So you've mentioned," I reply, remembering his comment from earlier.

His hands are on my hips now, pulling me into him. God, I forgot how small he makes me feel.

"Can I have you now?" he almost whispers the question as his lips briefly connect with mine again.

"Yes," I tell him, looking into his intoxicating green eyes. My stomach rolling with anticipation.

"Yes, what?" he asks with a wicked smirk.

"You can have me now."

The words are barely out before his mouth is there, his tongue desperately searching for mine. I press up onto my tippy toes, my arms wrapping around his neck to pull him closer. A wave of need ripples through me from head to toe and as he pulls my body to fit against his, I whimper into his mouth at the desire that's flaring inside me.

"Bedroom?"

"Come on." Grabbing his hand, I pull him to my room where he makes quick work of laying me down gently on the bed. His fingers undo my dress pants so he can work my blouse out and lift it over my head. He barely breaks our lips apart as he rids me of my bra, pants, and undies. He lays over my naked body, one of my legs between his knees. He's still completely dressed, his hands roaming across my stomach and over my breasts, and I can feel his cock hardening against my thigh. My fingers are threaded through his hair, holding him to me as our tongues taste each other with equal desperation.

When we split apart, his mouth trails down my neck and along my collarbone, planting kisses here and there, some soft and some open-mouthed and wet, tasting my skin. His attention makes me squirm, the desire already pooling between my legs, needing him there. But he takes his time. He runs his tongue along each nipple, until their stiff peaks, and then kisses below each breast, his breath giving me goosebumps as he goes. When he gets to my hips, his fingers dig in as his teeth graze the skin there, making my back arch and a gasp escape my throat.

He hums in approval, the vibrations feeling nice, "I want to taste every inch of you, Elsi."

"Yes," I agree, the lust speaking for me.

"You're a work of art. Perfect," he says against the top of my thigh. "It drives me fucking crazy."

"*Nate-*" I whine from need. His teasing and his praise. It's too much.

"Not yet, baby," he says as he plants a kiss to my little daisy tattoo. "So goddamn sexy."

He continues to kiss along my thighs and calves until he eventually settles between my knees. He reaches under my legs and wraps around, his palms landing on top of my thighs, his fingers digging in. He pulls me closer to him. The anticipation may seriously kill me. And just when I'm about to tell him that, his tongue reaches out and flattens against my clit.

I inhale sharply. Finally. He groans at my taste, his fingers pushing harder into my skin. I look down at him and his eyes lock with mine, they're burning with lust and desire. His tongue works hungrily against me. His hair is a complete mess. It's the most sinfully sexy thing I've ever seen. When he wraps his lips around my clit and sucks, my head falls back as I breathe out a cry. Feeling the pressure of release beginning to build, my hips jerk against his face.

Nate releases one thigh to rest his hand on my stomach, his fingers spreading out across my sternum and touching the bottom of my breasts. Such big hands. He holds me down as I start to squirm around him.

"You taste heavenly," he tells me between his ministrations.

Needing to touch him, I reach down to thread my hand into his hair, the soft strands slide between my fingers.

"Pull it," Nate commands and when I do, he moans against me, the vibrations heightening the pleasure.

I continue to tease his hair as he works me into oblivion. The orgasm is seconds away and my legs fall wider apart as the pressure of his tongue increases.

I whimper. My grip on his hair tightens and with another perfect swirl of his tongue, I plunge over and explode. My whole body feels like it's floating as I throb and jerk against him. He slows his motions but doesn't pull away until my body stills.

My breathing is heavy as he crawls over top of me. "My perfect girl," he whispers before pressing his wet lips to mine. As his tongue dives into my mouth, I can taste myself on him.

He keeps his mouth pressed to mine as he rolls over to his back, pulling me with him so that I end up straddling him and I can't help noticing that he is still fully dressed.

When I push to sit up on his lap, he resists briefly but then lets me go with one final swoop of his tongue against mine. Looking down at him, he seems satisfied, maybe even happy. There's a lazy smile on his face as he looks at my naked body. His hair is a complete mess, standing up in all directions from my pulling on it. A feeling of rightness washes over me.

I sit back, my center pressed firmly against his trousers where I can feel his erection straining. His hands land on my hips and he rocks slightly so his cock rubs against my entrance. I ignore the sensation as I find the top button of his black shirt. As I undo each button, purposely slowly, he continues to grind his erection against me. I must be making a mess of his pants. I can barely keep my eyes open from how good it feels but I resist, wanting his shirt off of him. When I get the last button undone, I push his shirt open and look down at his annoyingly perfect chest and abs, muscled and strong. The tattoos across his chest and down his ribs are a mixture of black and color, some words, some larger pieces, all melding together to create this story of Nate. One I want so badly to know.

My gaze locks on his collarbone, on two lines of poetry I somehow recognize in my lust induced haze, "*I am the master of my fate, I am the captain of my soul.*" I smile at the lines from Henley's "Invictus", one of the best poems I read in college. My fingers follow the lines and I wonder if that's where he first read it too.

"My unconquerable soul," I quote, remembering my favorite part of the poem.

I look back at him but he isn't returning my smile, instead he's just watching me with a look that I can't quite decipher. It's wonder or desire or confusion. Either way, I lean forward and kiss him, just needing to. It's slow and heady, our mouths moving perfectly together, our tongues sliding lazily against each other. His fingers grip my face and jaw, slide into my hair. Again, that feeling of rightness spreads through me, along my arms, down into my toes, making my heart jump.

Blinding need ripples through me and as if he's on the same page, his hips rock again. I respond with a moan, which he captures with his mouth and his kiss becomes urgent.

He makes quick work of reaching between us and unbuttoning his pants, I lift off him to allow him to push them down. His cock springs out and he grabs it, pumping once, before lining the tip up with my entrance. Without a word, I sink down onto him. He slides in smoothly from how completely soaked he's made me. When my ass rests on his thighs and he's deeper than I can possibly believe, he breathes out a guttural moan that goes straight to my core.

"*Nothing* in this world," he says slowly, his voice strained, "feels better than being inside you, Elsi."

My heart squeezes and I put my hands on his chest for leverage as I lift up slightly before sinking down onto him again. His hands find my hips, his fingers digging in as I start to repeat the motion. It's intoxicating how he watches me, his gaze dancing along my face and down my body, landing on where he is sliding in and out of me. He doesn't adjust my rhythm or speed, just lets me move how I want to with encouraging groans and grunts as I go. Have I ever felt this powerful before? This needed and desired? It's almost too much.

"Such a good girl making those pretty sounds. Be nice and loud for me."

Wanting to do as he asks, I sink down on him and breathe out a whimpering sigh at the feeling of being so full. Then, needing more friction on my clit, I try rolling my hips forward a little as I move against him. I get that touch of pressure I need and my eyes fall shut as Nate lets out a strangled noise.

"*Yes.* Fuck-"

I do the motion again, returning my eyes to him but his head is back, his eyes closed. His fingers dig into my hip bones.

"Just like that, baby."

I continue the motion as the orgasm builds, coiling tighter and tighter with each rock of my hips and my clit hitting his pelvis. I move faster, my fingertips digging into his stomach, my breathing ragged with the need to cum. Nate must be getting close too because as I slide down along his length, he jerks up to meet my thrusts.

"*I can't-*" his tone is desperate. "I need you to cum, Elsi."

My eyes close at his pleasure, my head falling back as the pressure builds and with one final motion, I come undone, crying out as my pussy clamps down on his cock.

"Elsi," he moans as he jerks harder into me, his grip on my hips holding me down so he's as deep as he can be when he pauses, his cock spilling, a ragged grunt leaving his throat as he cums.

I collapse forward on top of him, my face nuzzling against his neck, my cheek on his shoulder. He's breathing fast and wraps his arms around me, holding me to him as we come down from the high.

I slide off of him and lay pressed against his side, my arm still draped across his chest. He keeps his arm under me and wraps it around my back before giving me a small smile and a quick kiss. I close my eyes and just enjoy the closeness. Have I ever felt so content before?

After several moments of very comfortable silence, he speaks through the quiet, "Elsi?"

"Huh?"

"Do you consider yourself successful?"

This is so out of the blue that I can't help but eye him suspiciously.

"Really. No games here," he says and I look at him for another second before giving in.

"I think..."

His eyes dance across my face, waiting for my answer.

"Sometimes I think so. But most of the time I think success is something you can only evaluate at the end of your life. Like you're 80 and you're looking back on your years and the regrets you have, the choices you made, the stuff you overcame, and you can say, 'Yeah, I did it.'"

He seems to muddle this over as he stares off into space, his fingers twirling circles along my side.

"What do you think you need to do in your life to be 80 and be satisfied?"

I commit to the vulnerability, "A family, I think. A husband. Some kids, maybe three or four. Quiet Sunday mornings eating pancakes together. To travel. To try new things. To continue helping other people better their lives."

He nods as if accepting this answer.

"What about you? Are you successful?"

I'm not sure if he'll answer me honestly, but he surprises me, "I think people look at me and *see* success."

I wait, feeling like there is more.

"Every time I'm working on a promotion, I think to myself, 'This is it. I'll level up and I'll have made it.' But then I get the promotion and I feel the same. Nothing changes. I don't know...maybe you're right. Maybe it can't be evaluated yet."

"Is success only measured through work for you?"

He shrugs, "It's all I've got."

"Right now it is, but will it always be? You don't plan to settle down? Have a family?"

"I don't think love is in the cards for me."

I ignore the disappointment that nags at my brain. "Why? Are you anti-love?" I roll my eyes. "Or do you think you're unlovable or something?" I let out a quick laugh and then catch myself because maybe this isn't a joke. Maybe that's what he thinks.

"I think it's not in the cards for me," he repeats with little emotion, staring up at my bedroom ceiling.

I go to say something but a weird echoey noise comes out of my open mouth. He thinks no one will ever love him? Does he really think that? And before I can stop it, a thought flashes through my brain: *I can love you, Nate. I can love you if you let me.*

"I'm sure that's not true," I say just above a whisper, willing him to believe me.

He sighs and slides his hand along my hip. "It's late. I should probably go."

"No," slips out before I even have time to think it through. "You can stay?" It comes out as more of a question but it's out there now and because I'm a coward, I add, "If you want."

He looks at me again, hesitation so obvious on his face. But I won't push it. Whatever he decides is fine and I will not let it affect me in any way.

"Okay."

I can't help the broad smile that stretches across my face.

"Let me just..." he gestures to himself, completely disheveled, with his shirt open and his pants down around his thighs, "fix myself."

I breathe out a laugh, "Yeah, sure." I sit up and start to scoot to the end of the bed.

"You stay right there," he points at me and I know instantly that he wants me to sleep with his cum inside me again.

I lay back down on the bed and watch him strip off his shirt, pants, and boxer briefs before turning out my bedroom lights. He lays down how he had before and holds his arm out for me to drape myself over him again.

"Goodnight, Elsi."

And I fall asleep with the feeling that *this is right.*

When I wake up to my alarm blaring, I'm no longer draped across Nate, but our legs are entwined. He shifts around, having been woken up too, and I reach to my nightstand to silence the damn thing.

I flop back down and groan.

"I'll drop you off." Nate's voice in the morning is this gravelly, deep sound that makes my insides melt.

I smile at the ceiling, "Thank you. I need a quick shower and a vat of coffee." I push the covers off myself and with a slight twinge of embarrassment, crawl out of bed completely naked and stalk to my closet to grab clothes for the day. I see his clothes piled up on the floor. "I should have thrown your stuff in the laundry."

"No need. I'll stop home before going to the office."

I don't respond. What I want to say is that my cum is definitely all over his dress pants but if he doesn't care then oh well. Plus, his clothes probably get dry cleaned.

Leaving him still in bed, I pad out to the kitchen, clothes in hand, to put on a pot of coffee before heading into the bathroom.

The hot water is soothing along my muscles and I stand under the spray for a few moments just absorbing it. Then I start to make quick work of cleaning myself so Nate doesn't have to wait too long.

A knock on the door makes me jump. "Els? Sorry. I just really have to take a leak."

I chuckle at his desperate tone, "Totally okay! Come in!"

I hear the toilet flush as I finish rinsing my hair, then turn off the water. Wrapping myself in a towel, I push the shower curtain back and see Nate leaning against the sink with that sexy little grin of his. He's dressed in his clothes from yesterday and I can't help but glance at his pants. I'm grateful when I can't see any traces of myself there.

Before I have time to feel self-conscious, he grabs the front of my towel and gently pulls me to him, so my chest is on his.

"I think you like it when I'm naked and you're fully dressed."

"Of course I fucking like it," he says with a laugh.

The sight of him smiling is becoming familiar to me, and I won't deny how much I love it, so I push up onto my toes and kiss him. His hands grip my soaking hair and he tilts my face so he can kiss me deeper. It's a soft kiss, gentle and swoon inducing.

Once I'm ready for work and we both have coffees in our hands, Nate drives me to my office since I left my car there yesterday. He pulls up in front of the building and pushes his door open so he can usher me to the building's entrance. How chivalrous.

When we stop by the door, I turn to him, "So when can I expect you to randomly show up in my life again?"

He shrugs and gives me a cocky smirk, "Guess you'll have to wait and see."

I sigh, a cool breeze stinging my cheeks, "Are you going to dinner with everyone on Saturday?"

"Yeah, Will invited me."

"Norma must not have told him about..." I'm not sure what to call what we're doing so I settle on, "this."

"And why would that matter?"

"Norma thinks you're just using me. I don't think she's a fan at the moment."

His face shows some emotion I can't decipher. "I'm not using you," he says.

"Aren't you? It's not like you actually care about me," my heart pounds at the admission. I shouldn't have said that. It gives away that I care. That I want him to care.

His face remains stoic except for that muscle in his jaw as he steps over to stand in front of me. He reaches out and grips my face, his fingers digging into my cheeks as he leans down so we're eye to eye. I can feel his breath ghosting across my lips. "Don't pretend like you know a *thing* about the way I feel for you." His lips press against mine gently before he lets me go and walks back to his car. The brutal wind slams into my face now that he isn't in front of me to block it. I turn toward the door and walk inside feeling confused and hurt and oddly hopeful.

Chapter Twenty-One

Nate:

Elsi takes up all of my thoughts. I try to distract myself but she's still there. The feel of her, the sound of her voice, and the conversation we had about success.

So much of my life has revolved around needing to prove that I'm successful, craving the feeling of it but I can't seem to achieve it. I've followed all of the steps I have laid before myself. I'm good at my job. I keep climbing in rank. People respect me. But still, there's that feeling of something missing. Maybe Elsi is right and I won't feel successful until I'm older.

She wants a husband and kids, to help people in her work, but she's not consumed by a need to prove herself. But as I think about it, that makes sense. She doesn't need to prove herself to anyone. She's *loved*. How she doesn't already have a doting husband is beyond me. She's perfect. She's kind and loving and loyal. She's beautiful and funny and smart. She's everything. Someday the right man will come along and realize that and he'll put her on a pedestal. Then she'll give him children. Perfect little blonde babies with big smiles and wild laughter. The thought of it makes my insides churn. She deserves that more than anyone I know but the thought of another man touching her, making her giggle, making her moan. It makes me murderous. It shouldn't. I have no claim on her. No fucking right to be taking up the time she's already been giving me. But I've never wanted anyone like this and I'll keep taking up her time until she realizes the mistake she's made letting me have her. And then she'll end things and go find the right man, a man who can give her what she needs, and the world will make sense again.

I'll at least be left with the memories of her. The crease between her eyebrows when I've pissed her off. The face she makes when she's feeling overwhelming pleasure. The sight of her straddling my lap, naked, touching my skin, and reciting my favorite poem. Those moments all belong to me.

My father laughs. It's a cold and chilling sound, meant to be threatening and cruel and it is, "You think your mother will take you for the summer?" He swallows the last of his drink, which he's had many of. His voice is louder than usual, his eyes half closed, and there's the tiniest slur to his words. He's hammered.

"No," I quickly respond, my stomach tight. "No, I just thought I could visit for a little while. Maybe a week."

He laughs again, "You think she'll want you for that long even?"

"Well-" I start, remembering my conversation with her about coming down in July and her telling me that 'we'll see'. "She seemed to be..." I hesitate, I hate talking to him about this shit, about anything, especially when he's drunk, "willing to talk about a visit. I haven't been down there in a few years." I've only been to visit my mother twice since she left eight years ago. She comes here a couple times a year to see me and her other family members.

"Sure, sure," he waves his hand. "If she's willing to take you for a week, be my guest and go. Though when's the last time she took you? When's the last time you saw her for more than a few hours at a time?"

"I-" I want to protest but I have nothing to say. He's right, but all this time I always blamed him for that. She's obviously afraid of him, afraid to defy him even though she's my parent too.

"I'm the only one who can put up with you, boy. Your mother doesn't want you. Why do you think she left when you were a kid?" He chuckles again and refills his glass.

I don't believe that she doesn't want me. She just doesn't know that I want to come. I finally mentioned a visit last week to her and I think it was the first time I ever asked to come see her. In all honesty, I'm hoping to spend a week with her and ask if I can move there. Permanently. I can't take being here anymore. I can't take the constant worry. His constant watching. His criticism. The sting of the back of his hand. The obvious dislike, maybe even hatred, he has towards me.

"So I can go if she says so?" I ask, ignoring his cruelty.

"Certainly." He lifts his drink in a cheers motion before taking another swig.

"Hi, honey," my mom's soothing voice carries over the phone.

"Hi, mom. I talked to dad. He said I could visit this summer. You know..." I stall, suddenly nervous to ask, "if that's okay."

Silence. One, two, three, four. A breath. "Oh."

My father's voice rings in my ear, "She doesn't want you."

"Well, when were you thinking?"

Hope bubbles inside of my chest. "Maybe early July? First week? Or the end of August? I have an internship from the second week of July through the second week of August, so it'd have to be around that."

She hums, "I'll have to check my schedule, okay? Summer's busy down here but that sounds nice. A few days would be great."

A few days. My stomach dips at the difference I definitely notice between a week and a few days. Doubt crawls up into my throat. But it's okay, she just needs to check her schedule. "Okay, mom. Let me know when." I'll have to fly down alone but I've done that before so that's okay. She just may have to talk me through buying the airline tickets. Excitement rattles around inside me, I feel like I'm vibrating.

"Sure. I have to go though, sweetie. Talk soon," she says abruptly.

"Oh okay, b-"

The click of the call ending stops me from finishing my goodbye. But that's okay, my excitement to be gone from here, even if only for a few days, is too good to ruin my mood.

"So, I'm actually going to be too busy during those times, honey, but I already have a trip planned to come up mid-September. So I'll still be seeing you soon."

I'm numb. I hear this weird ringing in my ears. It's irritating. My eyes are burning as a stupid, traitorous tear streaks down my cheek. I angrily swipe it away. "But mom, I can just hang out at your house or something. It's okay."

She gives me a forced giggle, "Don't be silly, Nathan, you won't have any fun sitting in my living room for a week. You'd rather be home with your friends, enjoying your time off from school."

"I don't really get to see my friends too much, mom. Dad doesn't really approve of them and if I do anything without his permission, he gets mad."

"I'm sure you can go out and see your friends, honey," she says dismissively. She's not freaking listening.

"No, mom, I can't really. He won't let me go do what I want." I'm desperate now, "Please, mom. I thought if I came down and liked it that maybe I could go back and stay with-" I cut myself off at the confession. I wasn't going to tell her my plan.

She's quiet for a second, "You have a good life up there, Nathan." Her voice is stern, serious, "You go to a great school. You have a lot of opportunities that you won't have down here. Internships and scholarships and connections. Just do what he asks, sweetie, and you'll be glad you stayed there. You're just going through a hard time."

I'm grateful she can't see the embarrassing stream of tears on my face. "It is always a hard time here with him. It is always hard, mom. He's angry all the time and he..." I don't finish the sentence. If she doesn't care, then I'm not laying it out before her. Forget it. "I actually have to go."

"Nathan-' she starts to say but I end the call. Really, what can she possibly say that will fix this? She doesn't want me. She doesn't care that my father probably hates me. Hits me. She doesn't want to stand up for me. Dad was right. She doesn't want me. He doesn't want me. No one wants me.

Chapter Twenty-Two

Elsi:

"Hey ma," I say into the phone on Thursday evening.

"Hi sweetpea, how's your week going?" Her voice is soft and loving, one that has calmed me time and again.

"Great, actually. I've been insanely busy at work with the gala but I have everything in place and am checking things off. I met with the venue's event planner yesterday to make all the decor and menu decisions. So at least that bit is done. I'm feeling good about it all now."

"Oh, good for you, Elsi. This is probably a no-brainer for a pro like you."

I laugh, "Thanks, mom."

"What colors did you decide on?"

Last week, I went on a rant to her about not being able to decide on color choices. "I went with the dark blue and champagne. I think it's the most elegant and regal for all the rich donors that are coming."

"Ooo, yes, I agree. And the menu?"

I sigh, "That was a hassle. We have to have a lot of variety even though it's a fixed menu, but we settled on everything even though it took forever. I had some help from a friend with that which was nice."

"Which friend?"

"Oh," I say, not expecting the question even though I was the one to bring him up. "My friend, Nate. He works for Capulus Enterprises, the company who is sponsoring the event."

"Well that was nice of him to offer to help you. Or did his boss make him?"

"He volunteered. I knew him back in college."

"Is he single?"

I roll my eyes even though she can't see me. She can hear the sigh I let out though, loud and clear. "Yes, he's single, and before you ask, yes, he's already taken me out on a date." Was it a date? It was certainly more than a date, but my mother needn't know any of that.

"What? You haven't mentioned him before!"

"It's not serious, mom. Just casual."

She groans, "Aren't you all growing out of the casual thing?"

I breathe a laugh through my nose, "Maybe someday, mama."

"I'm holding you to it, sweetpea! Your brother has a new *casual* girlfriend too that he won't let me meet." Before I have time to respond she changes the subject, "Oh! Did I tell you that Sally McNeil took over planning the annual town carnival? Bertha Allen came into the town meeting last month and announced to all of us that she wouldn't be doing it anymore. So we were in a panic but Sally stepped up and has been doing a great job. She has a lot of fun new ideas and has been taking care of everything. I told her she was just like you planning these big events!"

A pang of annoyance at Sally's accomplishments being compared to mine zips through me. But I immediately feel guilty about it since this probably is a big deal for Sally. So I control my voice and say, "That's really great. I'm glad the carnival will still go on for another year."

"Right? I couldn't imagine not having it. Bertha has since volunteered to run a booth, so we all forgave her for dropping it at the last moment. Carl Foxhall is going to do his hayrides again this year and Cindy South is going to host the pie baking competition. All should be as it usually is except for the new things Sally has come up with. Did I tell you that she..."

I zone out and hum in agreement and understanding every few seconds. This carnival is the same every year but it's what has my mom's attention, just like the people of our town. They all have her attention. I've shared that attention all my life and of course it has only gotten worse since I moved away for college almost a decade ago. I try so hard not to hold it against her. She needs hobbies and I want her to be happy and stay busy, but sometimes I don't want to hear about the town's people. Sometimes I just want to talk about her and dad and what's going on with me. Even Elijah I can stomach. Had she asked me more about Nate, I'd have told her but she stopped after hearing it's just casual and moved onto something she found more interesting.

But I realize that I'm being bitter and selfish and I don't want to be, so I refocus on what she's saying and ask all the right questions and hear her pleasure at my taking interest in what's happening back home. I don't get a chance to ask about dad before we're saying our goodbyes so I just tell her to give him a kiss for me.

Thursday night or Friday, I don't see Nate but he texts me here and there which I appreciate and also constantly wonder if it's something he does because he wants to. Or something he does because he knows I don't want to be ghosted in between our nights together. I could ask him, of course, but I'm too chicken to learn that it's just for my benefit.

Things have been busy at work with throwing together this event but everything is falling into place. Joann checks in regularly to see how progress is going and to see if I need any additional help, which I usually don't. I love being busy and being efficient, putting my organization and planning skills to work. It's fulfilling. But also exhausting, so Saturday morning, I'm thrilled to sleep in and have most of the day to myself, lounging around. The only plans I have this weekend are dinner tonight with everyone. We're celebrating Sarah's first full week of teaching.

While I had planned on lounging, I end up scrubbing my kitchen stove, sweeping, mopping, changing my sheets, doing some laundry, and bleaching the entire bathroom. Once I got started, I just couldn't stop and my place really needed a deep cleaning. Not to mention, I constantly have a little voice in the back of my mind reminding me that Nate could come by any of these nights and I don't want to have to worry about if there's dust in the corners or crumbs on the carpet. So with a sigh of relief and feeling content, I plop my ass on my couch to chill for about two hours before I have to get ready and leave for dinner. I grab my phone off of my coffee table and see a message from Nate from over an hour ago.

> Nate: I'll be there at 5.

> Me: Be where?

> Nate: Your place…I'm picking you up for dinner

> Me: Since when?

> Nate: Since now, Elsi. Don't be difficult

I laugh at his annoyance.

> Nate: Be ready at 5

> Me: Yes, sir

A moment passes before he answers.

> Nate: Call me sir again later

Tingles run along my arms and heat flares low in my belly at the thought of him being turned on by that. And feeling turned on myself, I respond.

> Me: Make me.

> Nate: Deal

And I swoon at his acceptance and that he most definitely isn't joking. God, this man really knows how to work me up.

At quarter to 5, a knock sounds on my front door and I can't help the smile that spreads across my face.

"One sec!" I look at myself in the full length mirror in my bedroom. Tonight is a casual dinner, so I'm in my favorite jeans and a fluffy knit sweater. My hair is in two thick braids that hang down to mid chest. I grab a knit hat from my dresser and head to the front door.

When it swings open, I give Nate a beaming smile, not bothering to act unaffected by him picking me up tonight. I like that he wants to drive me. I just like being near him. "Hi!" I say cheerfully and step back to let him come in.

"Hey." He looks at me from head to toe and steps into my apartment. He's in jeans, a black zip up sweatshirt, and some canvas sneakers. His hair is covered by a black baseball cap that is really, really working for him. It's always a bit shocking when I see him out of his black on black suit for work. He looks casual, comfortable, and sexy as shit.

I close the door and turn to him, pulling my beanie on, it's like 8 degrees outside or some ridiculous crap like that. "I just need shoes," I tell him, turning back toward my bedroom. I grab my shoes from the closet and head back out to the living room to sit on the couch. "Thank you for coming to get me," I say as I pull my first ankle boot on.

"Don't thank me. It's purely selfish."

I raise an eyebrow as I slide on the second boot, "Selfish?"

"I'm taking you home with me tonight. Easier to have one car."

I stand up and head toward the door to grab my coat off the hook, "What if I have other plans?"

"Plans can be cancelled," he shrugs, knowing fully well, I'm sure, that I don't have any plans.

I pull my jacket on, not feeling the need to respond since he already decided for the both of us apparently. Once my jacket is zipped, he steps closer to me and grabs one of my braids, letting it slide across his palm and then dropping it.

"You look incredible."

I feel my cheeks burn, "You've seen me much more dressed up than this."

"I like you dressed up," he nods, "but your ass in jeans just might kill me."

I can't help but laugh as I swat at his arm. He catches my wrist, jerking me forward so that I stumble into him. His arms wrap around me and my big winter coat and I look up to see his green eyes dancing across my face before he leans down to kiss me. It's innocent, sweet, and far too short.

We talk easily as we drive to the restaurant, conversation at some point became natural between us. The entire way though, I wonder if this counts as a date, if he'll touch me in front of everyone, if this means something.

Nate parks on the street in front of the restaurant and opens the door for me, his hand landing on the back of my coat as I walk through the door. Sarah, Alina, and Frank are already here and flag us down from a round, corner table.

"Hey, guys!" I greet them all cheerfully, having not seen any of them in a couple weeks.

Nate greets them in his usual disinterested tone, giving them a nod. As they all echo hellos black to us, I climb into the booth seat and slide over, stopping once I'm next to Alina. Nate follows me in, sliding until his thigh is pressed to mine under the table.

"Congratulations on your first week!" I say to Sarah, reaching over Alina to grip Sarah's arm and give it a squeeze. "How'd it go?"

Sarah lets out a long breath, "I don't even know. I'm exhausted. There is so much to figure out at the same time as teaching and creating lesson plans but I was assigned a mentor, this incredible woman who's been a teacher for 17 years. She's firm but sweet to her students and is basically insane, which I think you need a little of to survive in this profession."

We all laugh, Nate even grins.

"The kids assholes?" Frank asks.

She gives him a small chuckle and shakes her head, "They're okay. Some are wonderful and some are definitely testing their limits with the new teacher. But I like it so far!"

The waitress comes over and takes my and Nate's drink orders while we wait for the Blackburns and Charlie to arrive. I order some cucumber, vodka drink from their specialty cocktails and Nate orders a seltzer. I raise my eyebrow at him when she walks away and he shrugs, reminding me he's our driver and that he's saving his one drink for when we order our meal.

"Did you ride here together?" Alina asks, a hint of disbelief in her tone. Her and Sarah know basically nothing about me and Nate.

I glance around for the waitress because I have no idea how to answer, when Nate does it for me, "Yeah."

"Oh," Sarah says, her voice higher pitched than usual.

I turn my head to hide my face from Nate and shoot her and Alina a look that I hope says to shut up and that I'll explain later.

Norma, Will, and Charlie arrive at that moment and I'm beyond grateful for it. We all greet them and as they sit in the remaining seats between Frank and Nate, Alina leans over and whispers in my ear, "You've got some 'splaining to do."

I turn to her and stick out my tongue.

We get our drinks, the rest of them order theirs, and then we finally check out the menu. As our food comes out, and Nate finally gets his bourbon, we all cheers to Sarah having a successful first week in a terrifying new career, and then we dig in. Conversation shifts and flows between all of us. Sometimes there is one big conversation, sometimes there's two or three smaller ones. At all times, there is laughter and a comfortable ease between us all. I hadn't realized how well Nate seems to know Frank and Charlie already. They must have all hung out separately from the rest of us, because the four guys chat amongst themselves easily. Nate's leg stays firmly pressed to mine, but that's the only contact we've had since sitting down.

"What's up with your work friends? They used to hang with us all the time."

He shrugs, "Nothing. Just haven't invited them around."

"Why not?"

He shakes his head, "No reason. The group's big enough as it is."

"Hm. Okay," I say even though that seems like a flimsy excuse. I wonder if Will doesn't like Nate's other friends or maybe Frank or Charlie.

Alina begins telling me, Norma, and Sarah more of the ridiculous soap opera drama from her job and we roll our eyes and protest at the absurdity of it all.

When she fills us in on the impromptu mandatory sexual harassment training they had to have this week, I can't help but roar with laughter, my head tilting back and my body shaking. Our raucous laughter catches the guys' attention and Will asks what's so funny. As Norma and Alina fill him in, Nate shifts back, stretching one arm behind me on the booth's backing. His arm doesn't touch me but his fingers lightly toy with the braid on that side. I pretend like nothing is out of the ordinary.

He leans towards me so he can whisper in my ear. His voice is so low, I'm positive no one else can hear him as he says, "I want to fuck your mouth tonight. Will you let me do that?"

Immediately heat flares low in my center as I look around at our unsuspecting friends. I've never been overly enthusiastic about giving blowjobs, but the idea of having his cock in my mouth, making him moan above me, makes me shiver. My undies are getting wet just imagining it. So without turning to look at him, I just give a subtle nod.

His breath tickles my neck, "Good girl."

My eyes shut at his comment and I shift in my seat to try to ease some of the tension I'm suddenly feeling.

I take a sip of my drink to try to cool myself off and as I put it back on the table, I meet Norma's gaze and her eyes narrow suspiciously. I give her the tiniest shrug and her lips shift into the smallest, barely there smile. Norma knows how Nate's been since ghosting me. But she hasn't given me much of her opinion, has just been listening and not judging. She turns her attention back to her husband and I rejoin the conversation

We have another round of drinks after we finish eating and then we all chip in to cover the bill, not allowing Sarah to contribute. Once we slide out of the booth seating, we say our goodbyes. When I hug Alina and Sarah, they both say they'll text me tomorrow and Norma tells me to call her. I refrain from rolling my eyes and just squeeze all my friends tight and follow Nate to the restaurant's front door.

Nate leads me through his apartment door, flipping on lights, and kicking his shoes off. I follow suit, leaving my shoes next to his, and then hang my coat up by the door, shoving my beanie into the sleeve. He walks towards the kitchen and grabs two glasses.

"Drink?"

"Sure."

"I'll bring it over," he says, nodding to the living room, which I assume means he wants me to sit down.

I pad over to his couch and sit, pulling my legs up and getting comfortable and begin to undo each of my braids. "Have you hung out with Frank and Charlie a bunch? You guys seemed to know each other pretty well."

"Yeah," he says as he pours us some brown liquid, which I'm assuming is bourbon. "We get together with Will every once in a while, usually to watch sports."

"I figured." I run my fingers through my hair.

He brings the drinks over and hands me one before sitting down next to me on the couch. "I see Charlie at work sometimes too when I go over to their office."

"Oh, right. I forget you work with them. Man, you really get around," I tease.

"Don't worry, Elsi. You're my favorite co-worker."

I take a sip of the bourbon and it burns a little going down. I tap my finger to my chin a few times like I'm thinking, "I wonder why that could be?"

"It's truly not fair. You have an advantage having the sweetest pussy imaginable."

I roll my eyes, "Jeez, Nate." But I'm not really annoyed. I'm on fire.

He gives me a broad grin, the kind that I love, that shows his teeth and makes his eyes bright, "Do you have plans tomorrow?"

"No," I tell him after another sip of my drink, which is growing on me.

"Good, we can sleep in then."

"Sure," I confirm.

He holds my gaze for a few seconds and then brings his glass to his lips, tipping his head back slightly, and finishing the drink. He leans forward, setting the glass on the coffee table, and standing up. "Come with me," he says, holding his hand down for me.

I finish my drink, following suit, and let him pull me to his room. He doesn't turn on the overhead lights, instead clicks on the lamp on one of the nightstands which gives off a dim glow. Not bright, but just enough to illuminate the room.

As he steps up against me, one hand cups my cheek gently but the other wraps into my hair, fisting near my skull and yanking. It doesn't necessarily hurt but it's forceful and sexy and I nearly groan from it.

"Call me sir again," he demands.

Embarrassment flares through me, remembering our conversation earlier. But the bourbon is making me brave and my desire to please him causes me to push it even further. "I'll do whatever you want," I say, looking up at him, and then add, "*sir*."

He makes a growling sound from deep in his throat as his mouth slams down on mine. His tongue explores urgently. I grip the front of his sweatshirt as I press myself against him. He finds the hem of my sweater. We separate so he can pull it off and before he can kiss me again, I do the same with his. We're moving frantically, desperate to have more of each other. When we're both naked from the waist up, he pulls me against him again, the kiss hot and thorough. I'm definitely soaking through my undies and want to make him feel good too. So I pull my lips from his and with my hands on his hips, drop down to my knees in front of him.

I glance up at him briefly, seeing obvious desire there, and I start to undo his jeans. His fingers gently land on my cheek and glide along my skin. I get his pants undone and then pull his jeans and his boxer briefs down to his thighs, letting his hard cock free. I take in his length, wondering how I want to taste him first but before I do anything, he hooks two fingers underneath my chin and lifts, forcing me to look up at him.

"Never in my entire shitty life did I think I'd see something as perfect as you on your knees for me, Elsi Abbot. You look so fucking beautiful."

I'd be embarrassed if I wasn't so turned on and I give him a small smile before turning my gaze back to his cock and leaning forward. With one hand on his thigh for balance, I use the other to grip him, sliding along his length a few times before running my tongue along the bottom of his cock from base to tip, nice and slow.

He gives me a satisfied exhale and I meet his gaze again as I take him into my mouth, my tongue flat along the bottom of his cock. I let him slide into my mouth as deep as I can take him and then pull back off, swirling my tongue along his tip, tasting his precum. I begin a rhythm and use my hand to cover what I can't get into my mouth and before long, he's groaning above me, watching me the entire time.

His fingers travel into my hair and grip tightly again, but he doesn't make any effort to move me or change my pace, he's just holding on. As he watches me and groans, I feel myself getting more and more turned on. I'm positive I've soaked through my underwear already and can't help the heady moan that escapes as my lips are stretched around him.

His breath stutters at the sound, "Are you wet?"

Not wanting to stop my motion, I hum an agreement.

"Touch yourself for me."

My eyes shoot up to meet his. I've never touched myself in front of someone else before.

"Do it," and I'm sure he's trying to sound demanding but his tone is weak from the pleasure I'm giving him.

Feeling brazen from how much he's enjoying this, I keep his cock in my mouth as I unbutton my jeans, spread my knees apart, and I slide a hand inside my panties. I regrip his cock with my free hand. Then as I take him to the back of my throat again, I find my clit with my fingers and give a muffled cry at the feel of it.

"*Holy fuck.*" His voice is strained and I look to see him watching me and then glancing further down to where my hand disappears within my pants. My hips are rocking as I work my clit and I'm definitely going to cum quickly. I've never enjoyed giving a blowjob so much before, but he's so fucking pleased.

"Such a dirty little thing you are. You're doing perfectly. Fucking perfect."

I release him from my mouth so that I can kiss his tip and then run my tongue along the bottom of his cock, before taking him inside my mouth again. This time I suck hard, hallowing out my cheeks.

He lets out a strangled groan, "*Again.*" I look up at him and his eyes are blazing, "Jesus, yes. Do that again, baby."

I do the entire thing again, licking his length and then sucking him hard. His hips jerk forward this time, pushing deeper, making me gag a little but I don't stop. I keep my cheeks hollowed, taking him too deep. Gagging. I brush my fingers along my clit, sure that I'm going to cum any second.

"Fuck. Stop," he pulls out of my mouth abruptly. "I'll cum down your throat next time. I need to fuck you."

I pull my fingers from my jeans as he lifts me and then grabs my hand, the one that was working my clit, and guides it to his mouth. My entire core clenches when his tongue runs along my fingers and he sucks them clean. I need him inside me now.

He pushes my jeans to my knees and then tells me to sit on the edge of the bed, where he kneels in front of me and pulls them off the rest of the way.

He guides my legs open, looking at the mess already there. "Such a pretty pussy for me to play with. It's all mine, isn't it?"

"Yes," I say and it sounds strange, low and throaty.

He hums in approval, leaning forward. "You're such a good girl for me, I bet you'd let me do whatever I wanted to you."

"*Nate-*" I jerk as his tongue just barely touches my clit.

"You already let me fill you up whenever I want and, fuck, do I love thinking about my cum dripping out of you." He leans forward and kisses the inside of my thigh before standing up and pushing his own jeans off and stepping out of them. "Get on your hands and knees."

With only a second of hesitation, I do what he asks, kneeling on the bed and then bending at the waist to be on all fours. From where he's standing, he has a very clear view of me spread open for him and I've never felt so on display before. So vulnerable.

I can feel the bed dip as he climbs up behind me and I look over my shoulder as he kneels between my calves, lining himself up with my already slick entrance. He looks up to find me watching him and holds my gaze as he pitches forward, thrusting into me until his pelvis rests on my ass. As he pulls out and slams back in, I gasp, my eyes closing and my head dropping between my shoulders. *Holy shit. Holy shit, he's so deep inside me.*

He slows his thrusts as he leans forward, so his chest is pressed along my back and winds his arm along my waist and then up, wrapping his fingers loosely around my neck. His forehead rests on my shoulder as he continues to push in deep and slow. "You were made for me to fuck. You know that?"

"I know," I agree because I think I was. I think we were made to be together like this, to make each other feel like this.

He's hitting a magical spot inside me that makes me see stars and he pulls himself off my back so he can grip my hips and increase his pace into punishing thrusts that rock my whole body. I push back into him, needing more.

"Play with your clit."

I shift to balance on one arm and reach between my thighs. My fingers graze against his dick pounding into me before they land on my clit. I swirl them exactly how I need and let out a gasp, feeling suddenly overwhelmed.

"That's it, baby. Such pretty sounds you make." He drives into me harder. I'm not sure how much more I can take. He releases my hip with one hand, his palm running slowly up my spine. It's a gentle caress, almost loving, before it settles on the back of my neck and he pushes me down. I let him, collapsing forward, my forearm flat on the bed next to my face, my other hand still working myself into a whimpering mess.

His hand shifts, his fingers in my hair and his thumb digging into my cheek as he holds me down, my face pressed into the mattress, and he fucks me hard and *properly* like he once told me he would. This is exactly what he meant and I fucking love it. I cry out at the punishing thrusts, feeling like I might lose consciousness from pleasure. There's too much. He's everywhere. I am completely at his mercy and he is making me feel so good.

My orgasm is a breath away. *"Nate-"* It sounds like a sob and then I am crumbling apart beneath him, my hand curls into the blanket on his bed, my whole body spasms as he continues with his pace.

"Oh fuck, Elsi. *Fuck-*" He's sputtering random words and his rhythm falters. He presses hard against me, cumming as deep as possible inside of me, and then he falls forward on top of me. His breathing is ragged. He shifts and pulls me with him as he lays on his side, keeping himself inside of me. He kisses my hair and asks, "Are you okay?"

I feel warm. I nod and let out a little giggle, "That was..." but I'm not even sure what to call that. It was perfect. It was intimate and desperate and right. I've never had an orgasm like that in my life. I grip his arms, pulling them more firmly around me.

He lets out a contented breath.

When I wake up the next morning, we've shifted around a bit. I'm flat on my back and Nate is curled around me. His forehead is pressed to my temple, his arm across my stomach, and one of his legs is hooked around mine. I don't move. I don't want to disturb him so I just lay there, looking at his ceiling and any other part of his room that I can see by just moving my eyes. But there isn't much. So instead, I daydream about our time over the past couple months. How well we fit together, how compatible we are, and then sadness washes over me that he seems to expect this to be temporary. How can I tell him this doesn't feel temporary to me? How does he expect me to wake up like this with him and not feel something?

I'm not sure how long I lay awake but when he starts to shift around, I turn so I can curl around him, wanting to touch him while he's still half asleep. He moves his arm to be underneath my head as I press my face into his chest. His top arm winds around my waist and lands on my lower back, pulling me closer.

His nose burrows into my hair and he takes a deep breath before settling himself again, relaxing into me. He doesn't speak but I know he's awake.

"Nate?"

"Hm?" he hums against my forehead.

"What were you like as a teenager?"

He breathes out a laugh, "Always so many questions from you."

I don't respond. I can't help how badly I want to know him.

"I was good in school. I had a few friends that I spent time with. I did whatever it was my dad expected me to do."

"Like what?" I tilt my head so I can look at his face.

"Clubs, National Honor Society, internships during the summer. The only thing I had for myself was baseball and I'm pretty sure he only allowed it because I was good. He liked seeing his name in the paper. I played for my school and when I was old enough to drive myself, I played travel. I was shocked when he didn't protest about me playing in college."

The memory of him in that baseball uniform is one I hope to never forget. He played center field and was definitely a good outfielder but hitting was where he shined. "You were good. Pretty good on base percentage if I remember correctly? And high RBI stats."

"You watched our games?" he asks, curiosity causing his eyebrows to come together.

"Whenever I could make it to home games, I watched both baseball and softball."

"I didn't know that," he has a sort of entranced look on his face.

I shrug, "I played through high school. I loved little else more than softball. When I went to Cort, the softball coach asked me to try out but I didn't have the time. I needed to work to cover my textbooks and food and going out with Norma."

"Oh."

I wonder what's running through his head. He probably didn't realize I had to pay for most of my own things. I could have asked my parents for more money but I had no intention of straining their already slim budget. But I move past his possible discomfort. "I was a catcher. Where did you think these thighs came from?" I joke, slapping my hand down on my leg.

He laughs, "I haven't ever thought about where they came from, just thanked God for them a few times."

I giggle at his compliment and blatant flirting.

His fingers trace along my cheek, tucking loose hairs behind my ear, "I'd have remembered you being there if I'd noticed. But I never really looked into the stands."

Meaning no one was ever there to cheer for him. Not his dad or mother. But he wouldn't have cared seeing me anyway. "You wouldn't have noticed me even if you had seen me."

"Yeah, I would have. I don't think you realize how much I did notice you, Elsi."

"Mm," I hum, not really believing him and not sure what to say. I give him a small smile, trying to hide my disbelief. It doesn't matter if he noticed me. Nothing came from it and if it had, I'd have been a stepping stone for him. I'm not even sure I'm more than a stepping stone now. "You didn't seem to lack in the company of ladies."

"Yeah, well, I've always been better *company* than long-term material." It's a self-deprecating comment, one I wasn't expecting, and I don't know why he'd think that. Has he ever even tried to be relationship material? I don't ask though because at that moment he tilts my head back and presses his lips to mine softly. When he pulls away, he smiles down at me again, "Let me make you some coffee and eggs."

"*Finally*! What is going on with you and Nate?" Norma asks the second she picks up the phone. On the first ring might I add. This morning I messaged her to tell her I'd call her when I got home and she has apparently been impatiently waiting.

"I don't know, Norm. We're just..." What do I call this? "We're just hooking up, I guess."

"But he drove you to dinner?"

"Yeah, so he could bring me home with him," I explain.

"I don't know, babe. I feel like I keep misjudging this. The way he looked at you. It was like you were his gravity. The entire night, he was consistently always leaning just a little bit toward you."

My heart flutters at the thought. My brain running a mile a minute. But no. I won't let this give me hope. This isn't more than hooking up. "He has made it fairly clear that this isn't more than that. This morning he told me he isn't relationship material."

She groans, "What a cop out. I didn't realize Croman was such a fucking coward."

I shrug, though she can't see it, "I'm really struggling to keep a line drawn, Norm. I just- We talk so much and it *feels* like a relationship but then he goes and says stuff like that. I don't know what to do."

"Babe, if it's too much, then you need to tell him. Or just tell him you're done with the arrangement."

"I don't want to be done with the arrangement," I say obstinately, like a stubborn toddler.

She sighs, "I'm worried about you getting hurt. If he's not looking for what you are, then you need to get out of this before it'll hurt you when it ends. Has he even mentioned moving back home in May?"

It's already going to hurt me when it ends. I don't even want to think about it. About how much I'm denying to myself that I'm already in love with him. How I want to always be with him or at least talking to him. How he makes me feel more than anyone else ever has. How he seems to know me without trying. It's natural and organic and it feels so right. But I keep freaking forgetting the most important part. He's here temporarily. So of course, *I'm also temporary.*

"No, he hasn't. But I know you're right. I know," I say with a defeated tone.

"I'll support you with whatever you decide, babe. And if he breaks your heart, I'll kick his ass, but I'll be there for you. You know that."

"I do. Thanks, Norm." She's always there for me. I couldn't ask for more.

"So the sex is good?" she asks shamelessly.

It rips a laugh out of me, completely changing the tone of the conversation. "Norma Belle, the sex is better than anything I've ever even fantasized about. It's like..." I try to figure out a way to explain it. "It's like he can read my fucking mind. It's - mind numbing, toes curling, makes me want to weep - incredible."

"*Shit*," she says, impressed. "No wonder you're all messed up about him."

I chuckle, "It's a real problem."

"Explain to me again your plans this weekend?" Nate asks the following Friday night as he's wrapped around me, his chest against my back. We're both sated and I can hear the exhaustion in his voice. I've spent almost every night with him this past week. Sometimes he messages me early in the day to ask if I have plans and sometimes he just shows up at my door after work. We haven't been having endless sex either. Sometimes we just talk. I've never talked to anyone but Norma like this. It's like he doesn't mind hearing the random shit I have to say and he's gotten over his annoyance at my endless questions. Sometimes he comes over and we just make out in my bed for a while until I'm too tired to open my eyes. But regardless of how the night goes, I like sleeping next to him. He's warm and seems to want some sort of contact with me throughout the night.

"I'm meeting the girls in the morning and we're driving to the casino. We're going to eat and drink and gamble and get massages. I'll be home Sunday afternoon."

"But I just don't see why you have to be gone basically the entire weekend," his voice is whiney and teasing. It's not even two full days, the big baby.

"They're my besties, Nate. It's an annual tradition," I chuckle at his childish tantrum. I also can't help but love it. I love that he doesn't want to be away from me for the weekend. It makes me feel important.

"Yeah, but we're friends too," his teeth graze my ear.

"Friends? Is that what we are?" I ask, with the gnawing hope that he'll say we're something else. Something more than that.

"Of course we are. Friends who fuck," he adds with a nod I can feel against my shoulder.

My hope drops out from under me but I force out a short laugh. "Well I'm sure you can survive without fucking me for a day and a half."

He gives a sleepy chuckle, "I suppose you're right. Goodnight, Els."

I close my eyes, letting his voice, gravelly from sleep, wash over me, "Night, Nate."

Chapter Twenty-Three

Nate:

W ill takes the drink I hand him. Since the girls are out of town, we decided on a sports bar so we could watch tonight's MMA fights. I don't watch weekly but my favorite fighter, TJ James, is fighting for the championship belt, so I'm pretty locked in. The main card doesn't start for another hour though.

"What's going on with you and Elsi?" Will asks after taking a long pull from his beer.

I sit across from him, "We going to talk about girls, man?"

He shrugs, "We're going to talk about Elsi. Listen, I don't particularly care what the answer is. I'm just asking because Elsi is important to me. I love her like a sister. She's always there for Norma. *Always.* She's family."

His vulnerable honesty takes me off guard, we haven't ever really talked about shit like this, but I smile at him, "Is this the part where you tell me if I hurt her, you'll kill me?"

Laughing, he says, "No. Just..." he pauses, running a hand through his hair, "Just be honest with her or whatever. Don't toss her to the side when you find something better. Though, I dare you to try to find someone better than her."

I take a long sip of my own beer, "I'm not planning to toss her aside. I'm sticking around until she finds the right man or just tells me we're done."

"Hm," he grunts. "And what if that never happens? What happens if you're still doing this when it's time to go back to Cali?"

I stare down at the foam on top of my beer because I've been avoiding this shit within my own brain. So I hardly want to talk about it with someone else.

Will continues, "Elsi's not the type to be looking around for the right man when she's looking at *you.*"

He's right. He's totally right. I wish I was the right fucking man. And if I'm being honest with myself, I haven't even thought about looking at another woman since seeing Elsi again in November. "Yeah, you're right."

"Just something to think about. And Nate?"

I pull my gaze from my glass to catch his eye, "Yeah?"

He leans forward and changes his tone, "You hurt her and I'll fucking kill you." A small smirk spreads across his face.

I give him a similar grin, "Understood."

He lifts his glass to clink it against mine and then thankfully, changes the topic.

Chapter Twenty-Four

Elsi:

My trip with Norma, Alina, and Sarah was wonderful. We drank, danced, gambled a little, ate delicious food, and spent a few hours at the spa. It was exactly what I needed, a day to relax and recoup and be caught up in my friends' drama rather than my own. Norma has zero drama but Alina always has good stories to fill us in on and Sarah has a new guy she spent much of the trip talking about. She was adorable with her shy smiles and blushing cheeks when he would message her. Of course, Alina and Sarah asked me at least 50 questions about Nate, that I answered, but then they didn't bring him up again, which I was relieved by. Norma, who knows more the extent of my feelings for him, definitely had more questions she wanted answered, but she didn't bring any of it up in front of the other girls. She knows me well enough to know that I don't want to commiserate with anyone but her.

Nate messaged me here and there, saying he didn't want to bother me too much but still asking about my time and what our plans were. He went out with Will last night to watch mixed martial arts and I know he had a great time because his favorite fighter won some championship. As I walk into my apartment, I'm happy to be home and feeling great, actually relaxed. I unpack my stuff, throw in a load of laundry, and take a long, long shower. Since I'm not planning to go anywhere else today, I pull on some jammies and march to my kitchen to try to figure out what I'm going to scrape together for dinner. I find some lettuce and tomatoes and pull bacon from my freezer, deciding BLTs are easy and delicious.

Once I get a romcom on the TV, I begin frying bacon. I've only cooked a few pieces when there's a knock on my door. My stomach, the hopeful bitch, clenches with anticipation just knowing that it must be Nate.

Sure enough, I pull the door open and see his teasing smirk.

"How did you know I was home?"

"I didn't," he says, stepping through my door and scooping me into his arms. "I was just hoping."

My heart spasms in my chest as his mouth moves to rest on mine, the kiss soft and familiar. He pulls away before I even have time to wrap my arms around him and melt into it.

"How was your trip?" he asks, kicking his shoes off.

"It was great. You have fun last night with Will?"

He nods, "Yeah."

"I'm having a BLT for dinner. Want one?"

"Please, but I'll do it," he says, walking into the kitchen. Familiar with my apartment from being here more regularly than I want to acknowledge.

I laugh, "You don't have to make it, Nate."

He grabs the tongs and flips the bacon in the pan, "You're supposed to be relaxing this weekend. Let me cook. You tell me about your trip."

I narrow my eyes at him, suspicious of him being so nice.

"I just showed up unannounced," he points toward the front door with the tongs. "The least I can do is cook your bacon and put your sandwich together."

"Alright," I say skeptically. "Want a drink?"

"Are you having one?" he asks over his shoulder.

"No. I had plenty last night. It's water for me."

"Then water is good."

I fill him in on the trip and watch him chop the tomatoes and lettuce. He's liberal with his mayonnaise and bacon. Finishing each sandwich with salt and pepper, he hands me a plate.

"Thank you," I say before turning to the couch to watch the end of the movie I had put on before.

"What's something you like to do that I don't know about?" He asks as he plops down next to me.

I'm surprised by the randomness of it and that he'd even care to know. But I suppose it's payback for all the questions I'm always asking him. "Hm," I finish my bite, which is delicious, "In the summer, I do a lot of hiking and I play in an adult softball league."

"Really?" he says, his interest obvious. "Co-ed?"

"Yeah," I laugh at his enthusiasm. "Have you played since college?"

He shakes his head, "Not at all. Didn't even think of an adult league. That'd be awesome though." His smile is radiant. He must truly love and miss playing.

He stays the night. Before we fall asleep, he runs his fingers along what seems like every single inch of my skin, until I'm writhing beneath him and he takes mercy on me. It's slow and overwhelming. His constant praise, adulation, and admiration make my head spin and my blood heat and I come apart beneath him as he spills inside me, moaning my name. Afterwards, he wraps me in his arms and sinks his nose into my hair before whispering goodnight.

How am I supposed to experience this with him again and again and not feel something?

Every single day, Nate finds some sort of reason or excuse to see me and every single night we spend together whether it's at his place or mine. I'm accustomed to him being near me whether it's at work, at home, or at his apartment. And my whole life, I've coveted alone time, have craved and cherished it, but I can't deny anymore that I like Nate's presence even more. We know each other's nightly and morning routines. He knows that I go to yoga every Monday night and how I take my coffee and where I keep the chapstick in my nightstand. He knows all of my favorite books. I know his favorite athletes and the names of the guys he trains with on Saturday mornings. I know now that he started getting tattoos when he got to college because it was something he solely had control over but then he loved them so much that he hasn't stopped getting them. I know what all of them are and what they all represent or mean to him. I even have my own favorites now: the Henley poem, of course, but also the willow tree on his left forearm and the raven on his thigh.

I know I should set boundaries, I know I shouldn't let him infiltrate so much of my time but I want him around. I like being with him. He stops in my office two or three times a week to 'check on things' for the gala but he knows fully well that I have everything under control and I take no offense, knowing he's only there as an excuse to see me during the day. The only thing he doesn't crash is my time with Norma and Will and I'm not really sure why that is. Why that's the line he isn't willing to cross. Especially since he's friends with Will. I eat dinner with them regularly and he moans and groans about it, obviously jealous that I'm so close with them, but won't come when I ask him. Then always shows up at my place when I tell him I'm heading home.

All that this is achieving is making me more and more attached to a man who frequently reminds me that we're not in a relationship, that he isn't interested in one, and that he moves back to California really freaking soon.

This morning he stopped into my office, asking me what my plans were for the night, and I told him that I was going out with Will and Norma for dinner.

"We could double date you know, they'd be happy to," I said, not even really thinking about the wording I used, half distracted by the document I was checking over.

"No," he replied sharply, making me look away from the computer and over to where he was lounging in one of my chairs.

A feeling like being in an ice cold shower washed over me, "I didn't mean-"

He made a face like he was totally unbothered, "Of course not. I know you didn't mean it that way."

But the way he said it was like I'm the one who would never consider what we're doing dating, but that wasn't why I was correcting myself. I was just worried that it'd bother him.

"I just mean you can come. I'd...I'd like you to," I pulled my gaze from him as I said it, not willing to face his rejection.

Which of course followed, "No, you go out with your friends. I'll see you later."

A jolt of sadness shot from my chest straight to the back of my eyes and I blinked a few times ensuring I didn't cry.

I walk with Norma and Will into their favorite spot and sit at the table with them as their usual third wheel, except lately it's been really bothering me that there's someone who could be sitting beside me but who just isn't willing to. It puts me in a mood that Norma almost immediately notices.

"No, I'm okay, Nor. Just feeling kind of 'eh' today," I tell her, taking a sip of my wine.

"You're sure?" she double checks. Will looks at me inquisitively. These people know me too well. But there isn't anything to share.

I give her a little chuckle, "You know I'd tell you if anything was wrong."

She nods and accepts that as truth when the waitress comes over to take our dinner order. Afterward, we talk about the gala and how things have been going with that and I'm grateful for the safe topic. I don't think I have it in me to discuss Nate tonight.

As the waitress comes to take our plates, Will looks over my shoulder and it's clear from his expression that he spots someone. My traitorous guts jolt, assuming it's Nate, but when I turn around, I see Scott heading our way with a big smile.

"Hey, man," Will says first, standing briefly to shake his hand.

Scott looks wonderful, as he always does, in a quarter-zip green jacket and gray chinos. He shakes Will's hand and then turns his attention to Norma and me, "Hi, ladies. How's everyone been?"

"We're great!" Norma says with her radiant red-lipped smile.

"How's everything going with you?" I ask, "Good start to the new year?" I feel comfortable asking him, grateful that I feel no lingering awkwardness from not having seen each other since the break up a few months ago. I'm genuinely happy to see him.

His hand lands on the back of my chair and he leans casually, putting his weight on it. He definitely seems okay. "Yeah, excellent. My mom came up from the city for a little during the holidays which was awesome. Just been keeping busy, you know?"

"How is Elena doing?" I ask, knowing he's super close to his mother who raised him on her own in New York City. She's a wonderfully kind woman, I met her twice while we were together.

"Oh, she's awesome. She retires in June, so she's getting herself ready for that. She's actually going to move up this way to a small suburb. She wants to be a little closer to me."

"Wow! Retirement. Good for her. What's she going to do with all her free time?" Will asks.

"Her plan is to get a part time job somewhere she likes to shop so she can get a discount," he shrugs.

Norma and I laugh. "That's perfect for her," I say, "she loves talking with people."

"Yes, she's quite the social one."

"So how's work been for you guys? El, I heard you have a gala planned for next month. Kudos."

"Yes! Thank you. It's been a whirlwind for the past month but it's coming together."

"You always were good under pressure. Thrived, if I remember correctly," he teases. His head turns then, someone catching his attention and I don't think anything of it until Will smiles and gives a mini salute.

Before I can turn to see who it is, Norma says, "Hey, Nate. We didn't know you were coming."

My insides clench as Nate gives a general greeting and I turn to see him step up to the table and hold out his hand to Scott, "Nate."

Scott clasps his hand and introduces himself. When they let go, Nate's hand lands on my shoulder, with his thumb on the back of my neck, his fingers spread out along my collarbone, and his index finger stopping at the base of my throat. It is a *very* possessive hold and in any other situation it would completely turn me on. But in this moment, he's definitely doing it to lay a claim in front of Scott and it just pisses me off. He doesn't even know him. He's just making an assumption.

"I wasn't intending to come but I just got done with work and Elsi said you guys would be here for dinner." His index finger slides just slightly higher on my throat. It gives me the chills. I can't believe he's acting this way after initially refusing to even come out tonight. After reminding me again that we're just friends.

Wanting to avoid any more discomfort, I turn my attention back to Scott but Norma breaks the ice before I can think of something to say. "Who are you meeting tonight, Scott?"

He glances at his watch, "A date. She should be here in about five minutes. I better go get us a table."

"It was nice to see you!" I say honestly.

"You too, Els," he says with a quick glance up at Nate, who of course is much taller. "Bye, guys," he says to the other three, giving a quick wave, and walking back toward the front of the restaurant.

I look at Norma, annoyance bubbling along my skin, and I can tell by her eyes that she knows how I'm feeling.

"You going to sit?" I ask Nate, my tone not as casual as I was aiming for.

He doesn't say anything as he pulls the chair out next to me and sits down. His hand shifts, letting my neck go, but his arm stays draped across the back of my chair.

"We ate, man, but do you want to order something?" Will asks, seeming to be completely oblivious to the dick swinging contest Nate just attempted to put on.

"Nah, I had a late lunch today. I'm good." He jerks his head in the direction Scott just walked, "Who was that?" He's looking at me for an explanation.

"We'll grab the next round," Norma says with a forced smile, nudging Will with her elbow.

They head up to the bar, leaving me with Nate.

"What the fuck was that?" I ask him.

Realization that I'm pissed hits him quickly and he leans toward me, "I didn't mean-"

"You don't own me, Nate. We're just *friends*, right? So you don't get to storm into a conversation and put your hand on me like that just because you're feeling jealous."

He shakes his head, "I wasn't-"

"You were! I don't belong to you. You only acknowledge me in public when you want to and you can fuck right off if you think I'm going to allow shit like that. You can't lay a claim on me only when it's convenient for you."

He looks in the direction Scott walked. "Who is he to you?"

I wait until he looks back at me, feeling my pulse thudding. "Really? That's how you're going to respond? Fuck. You. Nate."

To anyone else, Nate might look like he always does, stoic and unbothered. But I know him well enough now that I can see he's concerned. It's in the turn of his lips and the corner of his eyes. And I suddenly hate that I know him well enough to decipher that. I hate that I'm so upset with him because I *want* him to be possessive of me.

"I'm sorry," he says quietly. "It won't happen again. Please, just-" he cuts off and leans closer to me. "The way he was look-" he cuts off again, shaking his head. "I'm sorry."

I nod at him, seeing the truth there and hearing the things he's not saying. He was jealous. He didn't like the way Scott looked at me. But why can't he just admit that he wants me? Does he truly not want a relationship that badly?

I let out a reluctant breath. "Thank you. Scott's my ex-boyfriend."

"Okay," he says, his voice still quiet.

Norma and Will come back over and give us our drinks. Norma gives me a questioning look, knowing full well that I probably just ripped into Nate. I just roll my eyes at her and give her a quick smile so she knows everything is okay. We spend the next hour or so chatting and having a good time. I put the Scott fiasco out of my mind as much as I can. Nate is being overly sweet to me, trying to make up for his shit behavior, I'm sure. It almost makes me sad at how much fun the four of us are having together. It could always be like this. If only he wanted that.

When we leave, Nate walks me to my car and my irritation returns, pricking up my spine. I walk quickly through the bitter cold, holding my coat tight around me. When I reach for my door handle, Nate grabs my arm gently, "Will you come home with me?"

I don't answer him. Instead, I turn toward him, crossing my arms over my chest and looking down at the pavement between us. "I broke up with Scott back in November."

"Oh."

"After I saw you again," I nod. I shouldn't be confessing this but here I am again being utterly vulnerable for a man who doesn't want me. "I didn't expect anything at all to happen between us. I actually didn't think I'd even see you again after that, I figured it was a fluke. But I remembered the way I felt that night in college. So...*overwhelmed* by you. And I guess I realized that he had never made me feel that way. We'd been together for almost a year."

He doesn't get closer but he reaches out to run his fingers along my cheek. They're warm. "I feel overwhelmed by you too," he says and it makes my heart jump. "I'm sorry."

I finally look back up at him, his eyes still tell me he's concerned. My initial thought is that I need to reassure him, tell him it's okay, but I need to be honest now and I need to be honest with myself. "In a different circumstance, I'd have liked your hand on me like that but we're not..." I swallow against the lump rising in my throat. "We're just friends."

I so desperately want him to deny that. To tell me we're so much more than that. I've never needed to hear anything more than that at this moment. But he drops his hand from my face and nods solemnly. It cuts like a rejection and immediately my eyes burn.

"Goodnight, Nate," I say and my voice cracks. I quickly turn away from him, hoping he didn't notice it, and get into my car, glancing back at him before driving off. He doesn't move, just watches my car. I somehow manage to keep the tears from falling.

Chapter Twenty-Five

Elsi:

The next morning, after an awful night of sleep, I wake up to an apology text from Nate.

> Nate: I messed up. I'm sorry, Elsi.

I don't respond, figuring I can let him stew for a few hours. I get ready for work, feeling like I'm in a dark fog. I wonder if this is the end of us. I don't want that. That's the last thing I want. But maybe it's the right thing. Maybe cutting ties now while I still might retain some of my heart in the process is for the best. I know it will crush me but I'm getting so fucking attached to him. *And he's leaving soon.* The thought of not seeing him every day makes my lungs feel weird, like they can't get quite enough oxygen, and a pressure builds at the base of my throat. I realize as I organize my desk and figure out what's on my to-do list today that it's fear. I'm scared of this being the end of us. I put down the documents I'm shuffling and drop my head onto my desk.

I don't know what to do.

"Elsi?"

I jump, my heart hammering in my chest at the unexpected voice. One I know so well. I pick my head up, looking to the door and see Nate there, his face blank. "I didn't mean to scare you."

I press my hand to my chest, "It's okay."

He steps into my office with a to-go cup in his hand.

"What are you doing here?" I don't hear the bite in my words that I gave him last night. Already I'm softened to him.

He raises the cup slightly, "Bringing you a coffee." He walks forward and sets it down on my desk. "An apology coffee."

"You're doing a lot of that for someone who doesn't typically give apologies," I point out, picking up the cup and taking a sip of hazelnut coffee. My favorite. "Thank you."

"Sometimes I do. When it's actually necessary." Again, I see through his empty facial expression to the concern beneath that I don't think many others, if any, could decipher. I *know* this man.

"How flattering that I'd make that cut," I give him a smile and he returns it tenfold, relief obviously washing over him, making my already speeding heart clench.

"I don't want last night to..." his sentence falls off.

I don't want last night to happen again? I don't want last night to make you hate me? I don't want last night to end this thing between us? He says none of those.

"Will I see you later?" Maybe he *is* worried this is over. I take inventory of him. A man I know so intimately now. He's wearing an all black business suit that hugs him perfectly. His impossible height looms over me in my little office. His hands are in the pockets of his pants now, his white blonde hair combed perfectly to the side, his just barely crooked nose, his green eyes searching for an answer.

I should say no. I should end this now. Save myself even more heartache.

"I'd like to see you later," he adds.

But I'm a masochistic idiot and have no power against him. And I also don't want to waste a single second that I potentially have left with him. "I was thinking of making enchiladas tonight."

He gives me another relieved smile. "Perfect. I'll bring tequila."

"Okay. I'll be home by 5."

"See you then," he steps backwards, giving me one last grin, and turns to walk out of my office.

I'm placing a rolled enchilada into the baking dish when there's a knock on my door. "It's open!" I call, knowing it's Nate.

He pushes the door open and comes through with a brown paper bag in his hands. "Hey."

"Hi! Whatcha got?" I ask as I begin rolling another tortilla.

"Drinks," he sets the bag on the counter and takes his coat off, hanging it up. It leaves him in a black long sleeve shirt and gray sweatpants. I fucking love casual Nate. "I got chips and guacamole too. I wasn't sure if you had any but I know you love the stuff from that market by me."

I instantly smile at him remembering my love for that specific guacamole. Such a small detail to latch onto. "That's perfect. I was craving a snack and these need to bake for a bit after I roll them up."

As I fill the next tortilla with all the ingredients, he pulls the chips and dip out of the bag, opens them up, and then scoops a chip through the guacamole before holding it up for me. I smile at him and open my mouth. His fingers brush my lips as he feeds it to me.

It's as delicious as I remember with chunks of tomatoes and plenty of garlic. He helps himself to one as well. "Super good. Thank you!"

His response is to lean forward and kiss me. I close my eyes as my heart does the swoop in my chest and my fingers halt what they're doing. His lips part and his tongue slides into my mouth. I hear myself inhale sharply as I kiss him back. His hands cup my jaw and hold me to him. We lose ourselves in the kiss for a few moments, taking our time with it, and I wish that my hands were clean so I could touch him back. When I can feel his breath getting heavier, he pulls back slightly and rests his forehead on mine. And I remember what he said last night about me overwhelming him too. I just wish I knew what that meant for this. For us.

He mixes us drinks while I finish making the enchiladas and put them into the oven. I wash my hands and grab my drink, taking a sip and then gesturing to the living room couch.

"Work okay?"

He sighs, "Yeah, but I found out today that I have to go to Dallas for two weeks."

"When?" I ask, trying to hide my disappointment.

"It was supposed to be next week but I asked them to postpone it until after the gala."

"Oh good. That'd have been a bummer to miss after all the hype about the ribeye."

"Yes, all the hard work *I've* put into it, it'd have been a shame to miss it," he laughs. "I'll have to leave the day after though. They booked a morning flight for me on that Sunday."

"I'm glad you'll be there." Though I'm not glad at the realization that we'll lose two weeks of our already dwindling time together.

"Mm," he agrees. "What are you planning to wear?"

"To the gala? A dress."

"Did you get it yet?"

I give him a skeptical look, "Yeah, it's in my closet. Why?"

He shakes his head, "Just curious. What color is it?"

"Light gray. *Why?*"

He laughs, "I'm just curious. Really."

"You're being suspicious," I tell him, still giving him an inquisitive look.

"Maybe I'd have offered to buy you a dress if you didn't have one."

"Really?"

He shrugs, "Yeah, maybe."

Why does that make me happy? It's just a dress. But that he even thought about it is...sweet.

When the food is done, we scoop it out and eat together on the couch watching a new action movie that he's super into. He recognizes a bunch of the actors and makes predictions of what's going to happen. The small bits of comedy are my favorite though because he laughs along with it, so carefree and relaxed. After the movie, we put on some sitcom and spend a lot of time talking about our favorite shows and movies and books. Through it all, I fall more into a pit of deep freaking feelings that I'm worried I'll never climb out of.

"Any plans this weekend?" he asks, his fingers sliding along my arm as I lean back on his chest.

"Chores and I have to run a few errands tomorrow. But nothing Sunday."

"I have training for a couple hours in the morning." I know now that he means his mixed martial arts. He goes every Saturday morning. "But that's about it. Maybe we can crash on the couch most of Sunday?"

We.

"Sounds great." It sounds perfect.

His fingers find my cross necklace. "You don't go to church much," he says it as an observation, not with any sort of judgment either way but it's still wildly out of the blue.

"Oh." A weird creeping sensation goes up my spine. One I often get when people ask about my faith and I worry that they won't really understand. But I know Nate is just curious so I blink those doubts away. "I go sometimes. Always on holidays."

"Mm," he hums in understanding.

"It's a bit of a sore subject with my parents but I'm more of a believer that God is everywhere and I don't have to be within a church in order to feel close to Him or talk to Him."

"That makes sense to me," he replies genuinely, still fiddling with my necklace.

"Are you religious?" I tilt my head back so I can look up at him.

"I believe in God but I don't practice anything. I just like to think there's a Heaven, a paradise to make the shit days worth it, you know? And I try to be decent so they'll let me in when the time comes." He laughs at himself but I know he actually means it.

"Yeah, I try to do the right thing too. And not even always just because it's what God expects me to do or anything like that. I like to do the right thing *because* it's the right thing. It just feels good. But an eternity of paradise will be pretty wonderful, don't you think?"

"It's the fucking dream."

I give him what I'm hoping is a warm smile, "I think you're doing pretty great so far."

"Thanks," he gives me an embarrassed sort of look and my heart sinks further into the pit. "I know you'll be fine. You're all that is good in this world. At least in mine anyway."

The unexpected compliment creates a burning in my eyes and I blink a few times to work it away. To cover it up further, I shift back and press a slow kiss to his lips.

Chapter Twenty-Six

Nate:

"**N**athan!"

My father's voice rises through the quiet, empty house to the solace of my bedroom and I groan aloud. It's already 11pm but I wasn't expecting him for another hour at least.

"Coming!" I yell, hopping off my bed and heading out into the hallway. Once on the stairs, I hear him closing a cabinet and the familiar sound of ice being dropped into a rocks glass. A knowing dread starts to wind its way through my guts.

"Hi, dad," I say as I enter his study.

He leans on the edge of his desk and takes a slow sip of his drink.

I don't dare sit in the empty armchair right next to me without him telling me to. That's a mistake I've made before. As I stand in front of him, I can feel the tension building in the muscles of my neck.

After what feels like an unnecessarily long time, he opens his mouth. "Explain to me why you were not in attendance at Tony Walker's retirement party tonight."

Fuck. Here we go. I shift in my seat, "I had a baseball game, dad. An important one."

"I do not ask you for much, Nathan, but I asked you specifically to attend this party and then I find out in front of my colleagues from my secretary, my fucking secretary," he spits as he says it, "that you responded 'no' to the event."

I almost roll my eyes at the idea that he doesn't ask me for much. Everything I do is dictated by him. Everything except baseball, of course. "Dad, this was the most important game of my senior year. It was sectionals. The Cort University coach came to see me play."

We won too. I hit in the winning run in the bottom of the 9th inning with two outs. My blood is still pumping hard from the memory. The swing, the knowledge the very second the ball hit the bat that it was going between the center and right fielders, the screaming at the top of my lungs for Smitty to 'RUN, RUN, RUN!' Watching him score and then my team sprinting out to the field to pile on top of me. It was the best moment of my entire life.

Does he ask me any of that, though? No.

He points at me with the hand holding the glass, "When I allowed you to continue playing that silly game, I was under the impression that it would not get in the way of the things that matter for your future."

I try to understand how a retirement party for a man I barely know is important for my future, but it's never really mattered what I think.

"I have done everything *in my power to get you in the good graces of the people who can leverage you into positions of importance and you do everything in your power to defy me! And I have to hear about it from my FUCKING SECRETARY!"*

"I'm sorry, sir, but I couldn't miss that game."

His hand swings before I even have time to react, the back of his knuckles connecting with my cheekbone. I stagger back a step on impact. He hasn't hit me in a long time, not since my growth spurt in 10th grade, but I react as I always have, by fixing my posture and looking down at his feet. Too ashamed to meet his eye. I don't grip my burning cheek, not wanting him to know it hurts.

"You embarrass me, you ungrateful little shit. You will go fucking nowhere with your self importance and inability to listen."

I don't say anything. I notice a scuff mark on the toe of his left shoe.

"If you *ever* embarrass me again, you will be cut off. Do you understand me? No college tuition. No car. No allowance. No bank account. Nothing."

I nod my head.

"Do. You. Understand. Me?" *he repeats, his voice venomous.*

"Yes, sir."

"Get the fuck out," *he flicks his hand toward the door.*

I turn and walk out of his office, the adrenaline I felt earlier from joy now replaced by anger and resentment. I fucking hate him. I wish I didn't need his money. I wish I could walk out that front door and never return. Only four more months until I leave for college and then I plan to figure out a way to never have to come back.

I close my bedroom door quietly and climb onto my bed. Now that I'm alone, I allow myself to reach up and touch my cheek. The skin is tender and feels warm on my fingertips. I don't know why I got it in my head that he'd never hit me again. It's been so long and I let my guard down. Not that there was anything to do to stop it, but at least expecting it makes it less shocking.

I wish desperately that I had somewhere else to go. But there isn't anywhere to go. Not to my mom's. Not to a friend's. Nowhere. My mother's voice telling me to 'just do what he asks' ricochets through my brain.

My eyes prickle at the memory and at the shame of being hit again when I'm old enough and big enough to defend myself. But I just take it. Why do I take it? Why do I do nothing but apologize to him and do exactly what he tells me to? And then I try to talk myself into standing up to him but I very quickly remember all of the things he can deny me and I realize there is nothing to do.

Just four more months. Then I'll be free. I don't fucking need anyone else.

I take another sip of my drink as the memory fades away. I stuck to my goal of finding a way of never returning, though it took me longer than I'd hoped. I had to return between freshman and sophomore years of college but I spent nearly every free moment working and saving money of my own. The summer after that, I was able to get an apartment with a few of the other guys on the baseball team. I spent that summer working an internship that my college advisor helped me set up. It was the first job I chose for myself. Something I actually enjoyed. I got paid very little but I *liked* what I was doing and didn't have my father's shadow looming over me.

Surprisingly, or maybe not, my father didn't object to me never calling or coming home. Maybe it was an arrangement he preferred. I know he checked in on my grades, which were excellent, and he kept tabs on my employment, but I must have been doing the right thing since I never heard any complaints. When

I got my job with Capulus, he called to congratulate me and ask me when I was moving to California. How he even knew any of that, I still don't know. But after about two minutes of talking on the phone we hung up. In the five years since, I've gotten a call from him on Christmas and a card on my birthday, which I'm sure his secretary sends, and that is the extent of our relationship now.

I hear from my mom weekly and see her once or twice a year but it's always very formal and stilted. My relationship with her is okay but I wouldn't call it comfortable. I wouldn't call it motherly. She tells me she's proud of me and knows the names of my close friends, but she doesn't ask if I enjoy my job or if I have any hobbies or if I'm happy.

I was right to think, back when I was 17, that I don't need anyone else because I don't. I made it here on my own. I can be 80 and look back on my life and see this as a success. But then, of course, that thought brings about the feeling of strawberry blonde hair pressed against my cheek and a fleeting, hopeless idea passes through my mind that maybe when I'm 80 I won't want to be alone. Maybe when I'm 80, I'll want to roll over in bed and look into caramel colored eyes.

Chapter Twenty-Seven

Elsi:

"**A**re you okay?" I ask Nate, who's been really distracted since I got here tonight. He's moving the salad around on his plate, not actually eating much of it. The TV in his living room is playing an action movie he likes but he's not paying much attention to that either.

"Yeah, just caught up in some shit," he waves his hand around the side of his head.

"Work stuff?"

"No, just..." he fades off.

I want to ask what it is but I don't want to push either. I watch him thinking it through, I can see the thought process of him deciding what to tell me, if anything.

"Just my dad," he shrugs. "I don't even know why he's stuck in my head today."

"Did he call or something? Is he okay?"

He gives a soft chuckle, "He didn't call. We only talk on Christmas."

I can feel my eyebrows shoot up on my forehead and quickly school my features back to neutral. Only on Christmas? Not even on Nate's birthday or anything? "You only speak once a year?"

"Mm," he hums in agreement. "My preference, really."

He's never said much about his father other than him being controlling and what he does for a living. I don't know anything about their relationship. I don't know much about his relationship with his mother either, now that I think about it. He doesn't talk about either of them.

"So what's been on your mind then?"

He shakes his head, "Just memories."

"Are you missing him?"

"Oh God, no. They're not good memories, Elsi."

"Do you-" I stop and try to figure out how best to approach this. "You can tell me about it. If you want to."

He looks up from his plate and locks eyes with me. The smile he gives me is small and sad. Breathing in through his nose, he looks away on his exhale. "He's a very controlling man. I dealt with it for as long as I had to."

I know his dad dictated most of his life, making sure he was included in all the right activities, setting him up with jobs at his company or his friend's companies. I also know he didn't go to his baseball games which was the one thing Nate chose for himself and loved.

"When was the last time you saw him?"

"Seven years ago."

"Oh." It comes out sounding surprised before I can catch myself. He hasn't seen his father, who only lives one state over from him right now, in seven years?

"It's my preference," he says again. "I couldn't wait to go to college and then I couldn't wait to get my own place so I didn't have to go home over the summer. He wanted to control every single portion of my life to make sure I didn't embarrass him. He got very..." he pauses to think of the word he's looking for, "*upset* when I did the wrong thing. It was so important to him that I be successful. It was all he ever cared about."

"But you're not sure that you're successful," I suggest, remembering our conversation weeks and weeks ago. I wonder what his father being 'upset' looked like. I have an idea but I don't ask. Not today.

"I'm not sure if I'm successful but I am sure that I don't care what he thinks anymore. I haven't for so long now." He looks at me again. "You know, I took that job in California after college just because it was the job farthest away from him," he ends the line with a laugh.

"I didn't realize..."

"I just needed to be *away*."

"But you came back when they asked?"

"Yeah," he shrugs. "I knew he wouldn't try to see me now so I figured I could make the six months work. I didn't want him controlling my decisions anymore. I wanted to make my own choices."

"You deserve to make your own choices, Nate. You should do the things that make you happy."

"Yeah," he says as if he knows that, but I don't think he really does. "Yeah, I guess so."

"What's your mom like?"

He barks out a laugh like I just told a joke. "Busy. Wrapped up in her life in Florida. She's married to her insanely rich husband and spends most of her time at their fancy country club."

"But you see her sometimes?"

"She tries to visit me at least once a year."

"Well, that's good. Do you ever go down there?"

"Nah. She doesn't really like me in her space. I haven't been down there since I was probably 10."

"Oh," I say, unsure how a mother wouldn't want her son to visit her at home.

This is a lot. His father was definitely verbally abusive and maybe even physically. And now he lets slip that his mother kept him at a distance and only saw him on her terms. Who the hell are these people? And there's no way his friends know, right? No one even knows he was only raised by his dad except me. Nate's been carrying this on his own. His whole life.

"What are your parents like?"

I'm somewhat surprised he asks, but I'm sure it's with the hope that we can get the conversation off of him, "They're nice. We talk all the time. They're pretty busy people. They're kind of like parents to my whole town."

"Makes sense, I guess, him being the preacher."

"Yeah, exactly. It was hard sometimes though. I've always had to fight for their attention with not only Elijah, but the entire population of our town. Their focus wasn't usually on me for long periods of time. Someone else was always whisking them away. It took a toll sometimes, especially when I was younger, wanting their approval so freaking bad. But I understand it now and I know that it's a privileged complaint."

"You don't have to minimize your feelings just because you love them and other people might have it worse. They can be good parents but still let you down sometimes."

"Yeah, you're right," I agree. "I'm sorry your parents let you down so much."

He breathes out a laugh through his nose, "Thanks, El, but they weren't ever really parents to begin with."

"I'm piecing that together. I know I've never met your father but I can tell you that you're nothing like him."

He looks at me quizzically, "Don't try to make me out to be some sort of martyr, Elsi."

"I'm not. I'm just saying that you're not him. You care about people. You're kind. You do things because it's what's right, not because it will leverage you to a better position. You're a good friend to Will and you got that sponsorship for me. I think that's something to be proud of. That you're the way you are in spite of him."

He looks down at his plate, "I think you just see what you want to see."

"I just see you, Nate," I respond defiantly, annoyed that he is brushing me off. He needs to know that despite everything, he's kind and good and deserving of people who care for him.

He sighs in response and cups my cheek before leaning over and brushing his lips against mine.

Chapter Twenty-Eight

Elsi:

The following week is completely bonkers with last minute gala issues, resolutions, questions, and concerns. Everything somehow gets worked out and on the day of the gala, I'm thankful that we chose The Harborview for the event because Lenora Jones is extremely good at her job. She foresees problems and has solutions ready. She's happy to help me delegate where the auction pieces will be placed, how the timeline will run, and figuring out best ways to improve our chances of making a shitton of money. All in all, she's thorough as hell and with time to spare, we have everything set up and the venue looks absolutely perfect. Before I get dressed, I sit in on her staff meeting. She tells her team exactly where they should be stationed, what their roles are, and general expectations. My favorite bit is when she tells a handful of them to be sure to always have their trays filled with champagne so that the attendees get boozed up immediately and bet big on the items.

With 45 minutes until the beginning of the event, I finally feel like I'm in a good spot to go change into my dress when Joann arrives all dolled up with her husband and tells me to take a breather and get myself ready.

"Everything looks incredible, Elsi. This is going to be our best event by far. I cannot thank you enough."

I brush her off, "It's my job, Joann. It was my pleasure."

"You go beyond the call of duty though and you know it. So thank you. Go have a glass of champagne and get yourself ready. It's going to be a long night."

"Yes, ma'am," I say with an excited smile.

I head toward the suite designated for these events. I'm sure it's often used as a bridal suite for wedding parties. Now though, it's basically just for me to use to shower and get ready. I head into the room and sure enough, there is a bottle of champagne on the center table and a tray of meats, cheeses, jams, and fruits. I know Lenora had it sent here for me so I make a mental note to thank her later.

I pour a glass of champagne and plop down at the table, running through my inner to-do list, making sure I checked all the correct boxes. Feeling pretty confident that everything is going to go well, I grab my duffel bag and garment bag and bring them into the bathroom. I shower quickly and blowdry my hair while wrapped in the very fluffy towel. I twist my hair up into a low bun that's functional but still looks fancy. I swipe some eyeliner and mascara on, then some lipstick, and figure I'm plenty dolled up for the event. I leave my silver cross necklace on and change out my pearl stud earrings for a pair of silver slightly dangly ones. The last bit is just to slide on my dress and heels. Afterward, I put all of my stuff back into my duffel bag and head back out to the suite to get a final look in one of the floor length mirrors.

I look pretty elegant, I'd say, and a small thrill runs through me at Nate seeing me dressed like this. I hope he'll like it. The dress is spaghetti strapped and shows off a respectable amount of cleavage and a decent section of my back. It is fitted through my hips and then flows out around me. A slit goes up one side to mid thigh. I can see my black strappy heels as I step away from the mirror.

At the table, I throw a few more pieces of cheese in my mouth, swig some champagne to wash it down, and steel my nerves, ready to get to work.

Once back in the event space, I find Lenora and double check she doesn't need anything from me as the first guests begin to arrive. She assures me she's okay and I let her know that I'll be circulating through the auction area during the cocktail hour in case anyone has questions about the items.

As people begin to arrive, my nervous jitters calm down as soon as I spring into action. Joann is with me as we mingle throughout the auction space, welcoming the attendees, speaking for a moment or two with the people we know, thanking the donors. I greet Mr. Capulus enthusiastically as he comes into the room and is immediately handed a glass of champagne.

"Miss Abbot! The event looks marvelous. Thank you for all of your hard work."

"It was my pleasure, sir. Thank you again for the donation. This will be a huge night for EmpowerNest."

He introduces me to his wife and then they wander into the auction space, looking at all of the items on display.

A few moments later Norma and Will come in, looking gorgeous. I always give them invites to my events, perks of being the event coordinator. Will's dark hair is getting long but he has it neatly arranged around his face. His suit is black with a white shirt and a mauve colored tie that matches Norma's dress. She's stunning as always, and traded out her signature red lipstick for a light pink that matches her gown. Her dress stops at the shin and shows off her pretty silver chunky heels. They come over and each give me a kiss on the cheek before I steer them toward the auction items and tell them to talk up everything. They walk away chuckling together, each holding a glass.

Nate sneaks in somehow. I continue looking toward the entrance, waiting for him, but he ambushes me from the side about 30 minutes into the event. "Miss Abbot," he says and I spin around to see him. He looks incredible as always but instead of his usual all black attire, he's wearing a light gray dress shirt under his black jacket and tie. And it just so happens to perfectly match my dress.

He matches me.

I give him a wide smile, "Mr. Croman, thank you for coming."

"Getting to see you in that dress would be worth just about anything," he says in a low voice so no one else can hear him.

"You like it?" I ask, looking down and sliding a hand along the material at my thigh, suddenly nervous and wanting his approval.

"Very, very much," he praises, looking down the front of me and not being subtle about it.

"Thank you," I can feel my cheeks heating and I turn to look at all of the people wandering through the auction items. "Everything is going well so far."

"I had no doubts. I bet you'll exceed your goals."

I sigh, "Hopefully."

Nate catches Mr. Capulus' eye and tells me he'll check in later before wandering off, his business smile firmly in place as he walks towards his boss.

The silent auction part of the evening is almost over. People are doing some serious bidding here. Some of the larger pieces are hugely popular. We have a few art pieces with the artists stationed near them to talk with the attendees. A few free vacations, financial advising, a private chef, concert tickets, gift baskets, private wine tastings, country club memberships, and so much more. All of the items are bid on. Thoroughly.

Norma and Will find me a few times to check in.

"Will told me to bid on a few things! I doubt we'll win anything but it's still thrilling!" she squeals with excitement, looking around at all the options. "When will we find out who won?"

Will laughs at her elation, wrapping his arm around her waist.

"The bigger items," I point toward the one side of the auction space which holds the top dollar items, "will be announced after dinner. The winners of the other stuff will be notified privately."

"This is so exciting," she says, sipping her champagne.

"That's the idea, babe," I smile at her and catch sight of Lenora heading out of the room. "I have to go do my job, I'll see you guys after dinner."

I wander to the back of the venue and into the back room where Lenora, her staff, and some of the EmpowerNest interns are working.

"Can we do the 10 minute warning announcement?" I ask Lenora, looking at the clock on the wall above her head.

"Yes," she nods and looks around. "Shane? Can you take care of that, please?"

One of her staff wanders out to the event and we hear him a moment later making the announcement and encouraging everyone to find their seats in the dining room.

"Everyone ready for the real work?" I ask, clapping my hands together.

The interns of EmpowerNest, the company's accountant, Joann, the other higher ups, and I are quickly put to work identifying the winner of each item, calculating the winning price, noting everything down, and then checking and double checking our work. Once every item is sorted, identified, and properly labeled, we allow the venue's staff to move everything into the storage room and lock it up. We'll get the contact information for each winner today and items will be sent or provided to them over the next week or so. Lenora makes copies of our list and gives them out with clipboards. I delegate who will notify who and Joann is given the list of big item winners that she is going to announce in a few minutes when dessert is served.

Throughout this entire ordeal, Lenora had food delivered to us and we've taken bites here and there when time allowed. I'm honestly too excited to be hungry though because like Nate had predicted, we went way beyond our expectations and made EmpowerNest a ton of freaking money. I'm excited, in disbelief, and for the first time tonight, relieved. It was so much work and it was so worth it. Joann hugs me with tears in her eyes and endless words of thanks and thanks and thanks.

"This is incredible, Elsi. Incredible."

"I know, Joann. It's amazing. We have to make sure we thank Mr. Capulus thoroughly. Make a huge deal about it out there, okay?"

"Yes," she wipes her eyes. "Yes, absolutely."

Joann composes herself before making her way out to the dining room. I follow her, standing along the side of the room with the rest of the EmpowerNest employees who all whisper happily to each other, feeling ecstatic about the outcome of the evening. As I stand along the wall, I scan the faces looking for Nate, Norma, or Will. My eyes snag on Mr. Capulus, and I look at the other faces at his table until they land on Nate, who is already looking at me. My stomach dips and I give him a broad smile, bouncing in my heels in excitement. He understands my reaction and he smiles back, giving me a wink.

Joann stands behind the microphone, her clipboard in her hand. She looks lovely in a black gown with pastel colored flowers scattered along it. She beams at the attendees and begins, "Ladies and gentleman, in just a moment I will announce a few of our big winners. Before that though, I would like to thank all of you for attending tonight and bidding on all of these wonderful items."

There is a round of applause and she pauses before continuing, "Next, I would like to thank the numerous donors who are here tonight. Not only did you donate wonderful items to this event but many of you also took the time to bid on the other items. We are so grateful to each and every one of you. EmpowerNest cannot survive without the supportive people like you and I'm happy to announce that we almost *doubled* tonight's fundraising goal."

More cheering and applause, "This event could not have happened without some very key people that I'd like to thank now." Joann gestures to where Mr. Capulus is seated, "First, Mr. Arthur Capulus Jr. and Capulus Enterprises for sponsoring this incredible event and raising the money that will allow EmpowerNest to continue to provide the support and services to some very deserving and unbelievably grateful individuals."

Mr. Capulus raises his hand as a gesture of thanks to Joann.

"Second, the most beautiful Elsi Abbot," she holds her hand out towards me and I immediately feel myself turning pink. "EmpowerNest's event coordinator and overall mastermind who without, we'd be stuck very far in the past. You are a blessing to us and you care more about other people than I can comprehend sometimes. Thank you, Elsi." I give her a tight, slightly embarrassed smile, and blink against the rising tears as everyone claps for me.

"I'd also like to thank Lenora Jones, the event coordinator here at The Harborview who is an absolute genius. Nate Croman, who has been a bridge between Capulus Enterprises and EmpowerNest." I turn to smile at him and he keeps his eyes locked on mine. "The other generous and loving employees at EmpowerNest who worked hard to organize all of tonight's items. All of the staff members working tonight who have helped make this event run so smoothly. Thank you to all," she raises her glass and everyone mimics her, yelling their cheers.

"Now, for the part you've all been waiting for..." and with some laughter, she begins naming the winners of tonight's top items.

After the announcements and dessert, comes the dancing. At this point, all remaining work has been delegated and I can spend the rest of the evening socializing and enjoying myself. I sit with Norma and Will, watching the other attendees on the dancefloor and mingling around the room.

Joann's husband, Theo, finds me fairly late in the night and asks for a dance. I'm happy to oblige and follow the man out onto the dancefloor. He's a tall, very handsome Black man who has been with Joann since they were in college. He's very sweet and he carries our small talk throughout the song we dance to.

"Joann is feeling much better now that everything is done and over with," he gestures to where she sits with some of her friends, laughing and having a great time. "She's very thankful for everything you've done for the company."

"Oh, I know, Theo, but I'm happy to do it. She's a wonderful boss."

As the song comes to an end, I spot Nate approaching us and give him a confused look.

"Can I cut in, Mr. Milligan?" Nate asks Theo and my confused look turns to surprise.

Theo smiles at Nate, "Of course." He shakes my hand before stepping back and wandering over toward his wife.

"Can you dance?" I ask as Nate steps up to me, one hand sliding around my waist and the other taking my hand.

He chuckles, "Nope. Can you?"

"No."

"Good, it'll be more fun then," he smiles and we start dancing to the band's version of a Leon Bridges song.

"Thank you again, Nate." I look around the room, "This was incredible."

"I didn't do anything but provide a name to Arthur. *You* did this."

To anyone watching, we probably look like two people who are work friends, but I can feel the familiar way his fingers dig into my lower back and the way his eyes seem to alternate between looking at my eyes and lips. I can also hear the things he begins to say, which are far from platonic.

"You are the most beautiful woman in this room."

I roll my eyes to try to negate some of my embarrassment from the unexpected compliment.

He holds me marginally closer and says in my ear, "Really, Elsi. I remember the first time I ever saw you. I've still never seen anything more beautiful than you."

"Nate-"

But he just gives me a soft smile, his green eyes seeming to shine in the light, and continues, "You're most beautiful in the morning though, when your eyes are sleepy and your hair is kind of messy. You always give me these pretty little smiles first thing in the morning."

I beam up at him even though my insides are heating with embarrassment and something like pure fucking joy. Again, tonight my eyes feel like they're burning.

"I'm going to spin you now," he says and before I can react, he raises our clasped hands and pushes me away from him. I somehow don't stumble as I let him twirl me out so our arms are outstretched. I can't help but laugh, throwing my head back. He pulls me back in close to him and laughs with me, his face falling closer to mine. His eyes narrowing and his teeth showing. My free hand lands on his chest and I can feel the vibrations there. It's perfect. Have I ever been happier than this?

"I cannot believe you guys won those concert tickets," I say again to Norma. Will wandered off to the bar with Nate a minute ago.

She flips her hair dramatically, "VIP box seats, girl!"

"That'll be so great. And thank you guys for coming, this was genuinely fun."

"Thank you for the invite, babe! We love coming to these things. I'll never say no to free drinks and fancy ass food. More importantly though, Nate is smitten with you."

"What?" I say incredulously. "No, he isn't. We're just..." I trail off not sure how to end the sentence.

"When you two were dancing, I've never seen him smile like that, least of all the laughing."

"He smiles all the time," I tell her, wondering what the hell she's talking about.

"No," she shakes her head, "he doesn't. Maybe with you he's fun and laughs, but the rest of us don't see that. We see Nate, who is serious and usually bored. We don't see Nate with Elsi."

It doesn't matter. "He doesn't want a relationship. He moves back to California in a couple months."

"I stand by my previous comment of him being a coward."

I breathe out a sigh, "Norma-"

"That man is 100% yours, Elsi, he just doesn't want to admit it for some idiotic and probably ridiculous reason."

I don't respond because I can't let my hopes get up but I don't have time to anyway because the two guys come back over.

"You about ready, baby?" Will asks Norma.

"Yeah. Are you all done for the night?" Norma asks me.

"Yeah, I think Joann already left so I'm good but I have to go get all my stuff together, so you guys go. Thank you again for coming!" I hug each of them and Nate shakes Will's hand.

"You leaving too?" I ask Nate when they wander off toward the coat check.

"I got a cab here. Did you drive?"

"Yeah," I turn toward the suite where all of my stuff is stashed.

"Good. I'll drive you home."

"Don't you have a flight tomorrow morning?" I ask over my shoulder as I push into the suite.

"Not until noon."

"So you're coming home with me?" I raise an eyebrow at him.

He lifts one shoulder, "Only if you'll let me, of course."

I respond by giving him a smile.

Before I can grab my bags, Nate grips my forearm and pulls me toward him, wrapping his arms around my waist and kissing me deep and slow, taking his time to get me thoroughly worked up before stepping back and grabbing my bags for me.

"Anything else?" he asks, holding my duffel and garment bags.

"That's all," and I lead him out of the suite.

I find Lenora to give her a big hug and another few thank yous. She eyes Nate knowingly as she wraps her arms around me. Nate and I take the elevator up to my car and he drives me home, knowing the way.

Once back at my apartment, we shower together and he rubs his soapy hands all over me, making me squirm and giggle with his unintentional tickles. He smiles at me through it all and Norma's words from earlier echo through my brain.

After what feels like a never ending day, we end up in my bed, naked and facing each other. Nate props himself up on one arm and uses the other hand to lift my chin so he can press his lips to mine. It's another gentle kiss that's slow and thorough and makes my blood heat and thump through my body. Eventually he shifts, settling himself between my legs and kissing along my jaw and down my neck. His tongue glides along my collarbone and I shiver. When he lines his cock up with my entrance, he kisses and gently sucks his way back up my neck, stopping just below my ear. With a gentle push, he slides slowly in, stretching me as he goes. His hips meet mine and my back arches slightly, trying to take him even deeper.

His lips are still below my ear and I feel his breath on my skin as he says, "Sometimes I think you're not even real. That you're some divine being sent from Heaven just for me. To fucking ruin me."

He sits back on his heels and pulls me against him, his knees underneath me. He runs his hand along one of my thighs and lifts my leg, kissing the inside of my calf before he shifts it up to rest on his shoulder. Then he rocks against me in these long, slow thrusts that go blindingly deep. He watches where he slides in and out, seeming to be mesmerized. "You look so sexy wrapped around me."

When he looks back up to meet my eye, he gives me a lusty smile that shoots from my core through every inch of my body. His fingers begin a motion on my clit but he's in no hurry, keeping a slow rhythm that matches his thrusts. Every time he's fully seated inside me, he pauses, and I feel like I could cry. I hover just before an orgasm, the sensations feeling better than anything I've ever experienced. He's on full display in front of me, his ab muscles working as he thrusts, his hair falling loose around his face, his eyes constantly watching me.

As the pressure grows, I can hear the jumble of whimpers, cries, and groans escaping my mouth and I have no control over it.

"You're fucking perfect," he breathes.

He reaches out with his free hand, gripping my throat firmly as he leans down, stretching my leg and allowing his cock to go even deeper. His thumb pushes into my chin as our lips connect and he glides his tongue along mine. My body is on fire and I don't know how much more I can take. I close my eyes and grip the wrist of the hand he has wrapped around my neck and he squeezes a little tighter. *Holy shit.* It's too much. He's everywhere and it's too much. Too good.

"*Nate-*"

His tongue is firm against mine and he rocks his hips back and slams into me harder. His mouth slides from mine and I can feel his lips on my ear as he whispers, "I want you to look at me when you cum, Elsi. Can you do that?"

I open my eyes and meet his.

"Yeah, that's my good girl."

As he shifts back above me, his hair falls down around his eyes. His palm is firm on my throat and his fingers on my clit are relentless. He pushes in, hitting some magical spot inside me and I come apart around him, gasping out his name or a prayer or maybe both. And he watches me through it all, his eyes blazing. His thrusts quicken as I throb and cry around him, clutching his wrist and digging my fingers into his thigh. Our eyes are still locked together and it's the most intimate moment of my life. Especially as his breath comes harder and he leans closer to me, his mouth coming down onto mine and connecting as he lets out a guttural moan. He stutters as he spills into me and his tongue frantically runs along mine as his thrusts slow. My leg slides from his shoulder, and his fingers leave my center, as his body presses completely into mine. He kisses me deeper. Seeming not to be able to get enough, his newly freed hand slides into my hair, his thumb on my cheek as our lips and tongues work together.

Something is happening here. Something is passing between us. And I can't help it when my mind repeats again and again for only me to hear: *I love you. I love you. I love you.*

I lose track of how long we lay like this but my heart continues to hammer and the things I feel for him continue to get deeper. He pulls back and gives me one more soft peck. He looks down at me and I can see that he wants to say something. But instead, he gently pulls out of me and lays on his side, wrapping me in his arms like he's done so many times before. His face presses into my hair.

Finally through the silence, he says, "It's never been like this with anyone else."

I kind of hate it because it makes that fluttering feeling quicken in my heart. It makes me think he cares about me like I do for him. As much as I want to play this cool and ignore the comment, my brain is overrun and I'm shaking my head, "Never." I hold his arms tightly against me and not too long afterward, I fall asleep to the sound of his steady breathing.

Chapter Twenty-Nine

Nate:

"What can I get you tonight, sir?"

I look up at the woman. The first three nights here the bartender was a very boisterous and friendly man in his early twenties. At first he was a bit overwhelming but he grew on me, so as I look up at her, I feel a little bummed that it's not the same guy that I'd gotten used to.

"Bourbon would be great. Neat." I give her a polite smile.

She nods before wandering off to the liquor shelves. This new bartender is probably in her late 50s, dressed in all black with her graying hair twisted up into a clip.

"Here you are, honey," she says with a thick accent, sliding the drink across the bar to me. "By yourself tonight or expectin' company?" She glances at the empty seat next to me.

I take a long sip of my drink, "Mm. By myself tonight."

"No lucky lady?" she asks in a motherly sort of way.

"I'm here on business."

She reaches beneath her and pulls something out of a mini fridge. Lemons. She arranges a small cutting board and grabs a paring knife.

"How long they got you for?" she asks without looking up.

"I'm four nights into a two week stint."

"Two weeks in a hotel?" she makes a funny face as she slices through the lemons.

I shrug, "Not so bad. Also not the first time I've had to."

"Sheesh, I hope they pay you well." She looks at my business suit and shrugs, "Seems like you're doing okay."

I laugh at her mild teasing. My thoughts then unwillingly turn to Elsi as they have over and over and over again since leaving her Sunday morning. I take another sip of my bourbon. "My girl's back home in Boston."

"And what does she do while you're gone for two weeks at a clip?"

I should correct her that this isn't something she *does* because Elsi's not really mine but I don't. I can pretend in this moment that she really is back at home waiting for me. "Works mostly. She's a bigshot at a nonprofit."

Her eyebrows go up, "Wow. She get paid for work like that?"

I chuckle, "Yeah, but probably not nearly as much as if she used her talents at a major company." I have no idea what Elsi makes but I'm sure it isn't much. "But she's a good girl and wants to help people. And she's very good at it."

"Sounds like a keeper."

"You have no idea," I agree. I'm desperate to keep her. If only I could fucking keep her.

Lucy, the nice bartender, continues to chat with me for the duration of the time it takes me to have two drinks. She's kind and has a great sense of humor and doesn't mind how much I go on and on about Elsi. She seems to enjoy it, actually, asking me questions about her. I love that I know Elsi well enough to answer them. And that, of course, leads me to question *why* I can't keep her. I know her and she knows me better than anyone in my entire life. But is that enough for her to want to stay with me? I'm not long term material. If I'm being honest with myself for five seconds though, this is already a relationship isn't it? I've called her every night before bed since Sunday. I've been texting her randomly. She sent me pictures of the books she bought Sunday afternoon, one of which I had recommended. I can't not talk to her or think of her. It's only been four days but I can't wait to get back to her.

But then reality, *my* reality, chimes in. No one has ever wanted me around. Not for long. The shit in my past...I'm not sure I can be the man she wants. I don't know that I can truly give her what she needs and I can't bear the thought of her resenting me some day for not having enough to give her. She's far too deserving to settle for a life with me.

I don't know what to do. I wish I knew what to do.

I'm a little early to my class today but I had a team workout this morning and after showering and grabbing something to eat, there wasn't much else to do other than wander to find the classroom. I'm not particularly looking forward to this class. It's an English class that I need as a prerequisite for my business major and English hasn't always been my thing. I like to read, love it actually, but they rarely assign anything that's within my interests. Though this class mostly focuses on poetry I think, so that'll be new for me.

Van is in this class with me too which is good, he's a freshman like me and one of the second basemen on the team. He's a solid guy. He ran back to his dorm before class though, and will probably be late, so I'm sitting alone as other classmates trickle in. This is my first time in the Humanities building and it's definitely got a different vibe from the science and math buildings. I think it's an older building. In the science building, the rooms are all steel and white and gray. There's nothing on the walls other than posters of the safety rules, a smart board, and a whiteboard, which half the time the professors don't even have markers for. This classroom though is dimly lit and filled with posters, photographs, and print outs of literary figures, poems, landscapes, idioms. The corners of most of them are all curled in like they've been on the walls since before I was born. It's kind of chaotic.

I'm turning every which way to take it all in before too many people get here, there's only a handful of students so far and no professor. I'm reading an Edgar Allan Poe info poster when I hear a feminine laugh. It's a pretty sound. Sweet and innocent. Without thinking of it, my eyes search for the source. A girl sitting two tables to the left of mine is looking down at her phone, her thumbs typing away. Her hair, tied up in a ponytail on top of her head, is blonde but has a slightly red tint to it. Little strands of hair fall around her face, blocking me from getting a good look at her. She's wearing a fluffy purple sweater, black leggings, and duck boots. She laughs again, her hand over her mouth to muffle the sound, and a little spike of dopamine shoots through me, making me smile unexpectedly.

"Hey, man, not as late as I thought," I hear from beside me. I turn to see Van yank the chair next to me back from the table and flop his spastic ass down in it.

"Mm," I agree, "Professor's not even here yet."

"Excellent. What's this class again? Poetry or some shit?"

"Yeah, or some shit." Van doesn't give a crap about his education, he's very clear about only being in college to play baseball and hook up with women. He's not a brainless idiot either, he just doesn't care. I have no idea what his major even is.

The room is filling up now. The girl in purple isn't alone anymore, another girl is sitting with her. The new girl's back is to me, turned to face the giggler, blocking my view of her. Van is going on about this morning's workout with the team. We're all pretty jazzed up because it's the final stretch before the season starts. We've been doing daily workouts and indoor practices to prepare for the warmer weather when we can get outside.

Over Van's shoulder, I see an obviously frazzled girl come into the room with her arms completely full of books and her shoulder bag, which seems to be holding even more books, swinging dangerously by her hip. She's looking around in a panic for somewhere to sit but every table has at least one person seated at it so far. She must not know anyone here. Her colossal bag swings off her hip as she turns to squeeze between two tables and it hits an unsuspecting person's water bottle, knocking it over with a loud clatter. The stressed out girl turns abruptly and apologizes incessantly to the victim's reassurances that it's no big deal.

Another girl, wearing a purple sweater and leggings, goes quickly past me.

"Let me help you!" she says as she approaches the panicked girl. As purple sweater takes the books from the girl's hands, I take in the shape of her legs. She's not very tall but her legs are thick, toned, and curvy as hell. They're insanely sexy. Like she's a runner or something.

"Oh gosh, thank you so much. I went to the bookstore this morning and I thought I'd have time to run back to my dorm but the store was so busy! I wasn't sure I'd even make it here on time," her anxiety is palpable as she speeds through her explanation.

Purple sweater laughs and it zips through me. Again. What is up with me?

"I totally understand. I work at the bookstore actually and it's been a nightmare for like a week. Why don't you come sit with me and my friend?" she jerks her thumb over her shoulder. "We have an empty seat by us."

"Really?" the panicked girl looks near tears from her relief.

"Of course, come on." Purple sweater turns around to lead the girl to her seat.

I finally see her face.

She's beautiful. Like, masterpiece *beautiful.*

The blonde hair that's escaped the elastic falls haphazardly around her face. Her skin is slightly tan despite it being mid winter and looks like it'd be perfectly smooth to the touch. The light brown of her eyes is like caramel and they're framed by long lashes, making her eyes look wide and alert. Her nose is small and round. And her lips are full and shiny, from lipgloss or chapstick probably. As she talks to the other girl she just seems...kind. She looks back at the girl she's helping and when the girl thanks her again for her help, purple sweater gives her a smile like nothing I've ever seen. It's like she's fucking glowing. It changes her whole face, lights her up. Her eyes come alive and her teeth show. I've never seen anything like her. And I can't look away.

I watch as she walks the panicked girl to her table with her friend, who looks vaguely familiar, she's taller with black hair braided down her back and a pretty face. They all chat amongst each other but I can't hear what they're saying. Purple sweater smiles again, this time at her friend, and I clench my teeth together. She looks past the two girls she's sitting with, surveying the room, and eventually catches my eye. God, I probably seem like a creep but I can't look away. She keeps her eyes locked on mine for a moment and then gives me a shy smile before turning her attention back to her friend.

I reluctantly look away from her and lean over to Van, "You know those girls over there?" I nod my head in their direction. Since Van isn't overly concerned with his academics, he knows far more people than I do. Especially the women.

He leans forward to look past me. "Uh, I don't know the clumsy one that just came in but I know Norma."

"Which one is Norma?"

"*Black hair. Looks like a Greek fucking goddess. She's on the basketball team. She was at that freshman athlete's mixer thing in the fall.*"

Oh, yeah, that's how I recognized her. "*What about her friend? In the sweater.*"

"*That's her roommate. They do fucking everything together. I think her name is Elsi.*"

Elsi. *What are the chances I can get to know her? We're here for four years. So I'm sure it'll happen, right? Jesus, she's just so beautiful.*

The whole class laughs at the joke Professor Tucci made. It was corny as hell but I can't help the small chuckle I let out as the room howls at her. This is probably my favorite class of my entire degree. It's a marketing class which I didn't think I'd enjoy so much but everyone in it is in their final semester of business school and at this point I've had at least one class with everybody, so there's some familiarity between all of us, even if we're not necessarily friends. It's made the class more casual and far less stressful despite the rigorous assignments.

Will leans over and nudges my arm. "That was the stupidest joke I've ever heard," he says on the tail end of his laugh, his smile wide across his face.

I nod in agreement.

"Okay! Now, we've finished a little early today but before I let you all go, I want to hear everyone's plans for post graduation. This is the first time I've ever had an entire class of graduating students. Who wants to start?"

As people share, it's obvious that just about everyone has some sort of plan mapped out for after graduation, whether it be continuing their education, starting a job, or even some who have plans that have absolutely nothing to do with their business degree.

"Mr. Croman? Mr. Blackburn?"

"I have a marketing job lined up in Boston starting in July," Will shares.

"Yes! I hoped someone would say marketing!" Professor Tucci cheers.

"Well, I owe it all to you that I even considered it. I wasn't interested in marketing originally," Will says in a sickly sweet voice.

Professor Tucci flaps her hand, *"Oh, you're just saying that!"*

Will continues to kiss ass for a few seconds before she turns her attention on me.

"Moving to California. I got a position with Capulus Enterprises."

"Ooo," she coos, *"big tech company."*

"Exactly," I confirm.

"Miss Grant?"

Norma Grant smiles wide before sharing, *"I have a job lined up with a bank in Boston, working in admin."*

"Excellent! That's two for Boston!" Professor Tucci points back at Will.

Norma turns and glances in Will's direction. They smile shyly at each other and I have to keep myself from rolling my eyes. Will's been into her this entire year and has done absolutely nothing about it.

What a fucking hypocrite I am.

"Miss Abbot?"

I focus my eyes on Elsi. I seem to always focus my eyes on Elsi whenever she's near. For years I've been drawn to her, hanging onto the very few words she shares in classes, watching her smile easily at our peers. I wish I'd had a reason to talk to her over these past few years but somehow we never got grouped together on anything and she keeps pretty much to herself. Not to mention, she is very rarely without Norma. Plus, what would a guy like me say to someone like her? I couldn't ever, in four years, bring myself to approach her. I just know I'd be attached to her from the very first second of attention she gave me. For fuck's sake, I'm already attached to her and have barely said 20 words to her in all this time. I'm just not sure I could provide her with what she probably needs: commitment, communication, love. I have no experience with any of those things. We're from different worlds. She's a quiet, kindhearted saint and I'm a borderline depressed dickhead. She flushes slightly at the class's attention and gives Tucci a big smile.

Jesus, she's incredible.

"Three for Boston, Professor. I start at a nonprofit in June."

A few of our classmates lean towards their neighbors and start whispering as if working for a charity is unbelievable information. But knowing Elsi, which I really don't, but the little I do know about her tells me that this makes perfect sense for her. She's got the right vibe to help people.

"A nonprofit? What made you choose that?" Professor Tucci asks earnestly.

Elsi shifts in her chair, obviously unprepared for the follow up question. She runs her hand through her pretty hair, one finger getting caught in the strands.

"Well-" she starts, while still trying to free her finger. It's fucking adorable. "Well, I just wanted to work somewhere that helps the less fortunate and I figured nonprofits are the best kind of thing for that."

"Good for you, Miss Abbot."

Elsi smiles and drops her eyes to the table in front of her, definitely embarrassed. "Thank you, Professor."

"Who's next?" Professor Tucci asks, moving to the next group of students.

Elsi frees her finger and Norma leans over to whisper something in her ear. Elsi turns to her and laughs quietly, pressing her cheek to Norma's shoulder. She whispers something back to her and they giggle again. Then Elsi picks her head, looking at Norma, but her eyes glance behind her friend and land on mine. I'm caught staring and when her smile widens, I realize that I was already grinning at her. Seeing her laugh made me smile. She's fucking radiant and for just a moment I let it absorb into me. But before she can think I'm a creep, I turn my attention back to Professor Tucci.

Chapter Thirty

Elsi:

"**H**onies, I'm home!" I call as I let myself into the Blackburn apartment.

"Hey, El!" Will's voice calls through the bedroom door.

I kick the front door shut behind me and head into the kitchen where I drop the grocery bag on the counter. I head back to the door and hang up my coat and kick off my shoes before returning to the bag to empty its contents: all the makings for chicken parmesan and a bottle of wine. I lay everything out neatly in front of me and then turn to grab the bottle opener. As I pour the wine into the first of the three glasses, Will comes out of his bedroom, pushing up the sleeves of his long sleeve shirt that I'm guessing he just changed into.

"Hey, Norma's running a little late. She called a few minutes ago," he says, coming over and planting a kiss on my cheek.

"No problem. Here," I hand him the glass I just filled with wine.

"You're a saint. What's for dinner?" he asks, looking at the contents spread across the counter.

"Chicken parm. I had a craving."

He groans, "Excellent."

"How was work this week?" I ask him, washing my hands so I can start cooking.

"Eh, it was the usual. Working on a new marketing proposal but it's a long shot."

"I'm sure it'll be great regardless."

He shrugs as I turn back to start working on the chicken. "What's on your agenda now that the auction is over?"

I sigh, "Well now we have to allot where the money is going to go, though most of that was already planned out."

"Croman doesn't need to stop by to help anymore, I suppose?"

I give him a side eye, "He was just checking in. Didn't actually do much helping, other than picking that ribeye dish."

"Which was fucking delicious."

I laugh at how easy it is to please him. Such a man. He just needs his wife and a good steak and he's happy.

"He treating you alright?"

I'm not surprised by the question, he knows everything and he's a good listener. He's like the brother I always needed - caring, level-headed, and overly protective.

"Yeah," I nod earnestly. "He is. I just wish I knew what this was that we're doing."

"You haven't talked about it?"

I finish preparing the chicken and wash my hands, the cutting board, and knife in the sink. "Nope. He's mentioned a few times that he's not interested in a relationship but this feels like more than a fling." *And I've been too scared to ask.*

"Do you want it to be more than a fling?" He slides onto one of the counter stools across from where I'm working.

"Yes."

"You like him?"

I stop what I'm doing and place my hands down on the counter, the surface is cool against my skin. I look at Will and sigh, "I think I love him." There. I said it. I voiced it out loud. Fuck. Fuck. I shouldn't have said it. It makes it real. But I can't take it back now. I can just take a deep breath and listen to my friend.

"El," he says on an exhale, his eyes sad.

My heart breaks a little. I think a tiny part of me was hoping he'd tell me it was possible that Nate might love me too. I give him a knowing smile, "I know, Will." I know that Nate doesn't love me. I know that this is getting out of hand. I know I need to stop all of it.

"You deserve someone who wants a relationship, Elsi."

"So he really doesn't then?" Will would know. Nate's his friend.

"I don't know. I don't think *he* knows what he wants and that's maybe worse."

I nod and pick up the carton of eggs.

"I just don't want to see you hurt. And I know he doesn't want to hurt you but that doesn't mean he won't."

The backs of my eyes burn, "I don't know what to do."

"You really love him?"

I close my eyes against the tears that are blurring my vision and let out a breathy laugh, "Yeah. How pathetic is that? The first man I've ever loved only wants me at night."

"I don't buy that. I think he cares about you. I *know* he does actually. I just don't know if he's capable of committing to you. Which we both know is what you want and it's what you should have."

My heart tears a little and I look back up at him, "When you started dating Norma, how soon into it did you know she was it?"

He answers immediately. "Our second date. We already knew each other pretty well obviously and I took her to that coffee shop she loved back by Cort," the smile on his face tells me he can see the memory as he shares it with me. "She helped an older man read the menu because he forgot his glasses, which was adorable and totally something Norma does, but then when we finished drinking our coffee and got up to leave, she turned back to say something to me and walked right into the closed door." He starts laughing. "She was so embarrassed and when I laughed, she flipped me off with the biggest smile on her face. That was the moment I knew I loved her and that I'd marry her some day."

Tears fall as I laugh at his story. Both happy and sad. I swipe them away with the back of my hand, "She told me that story that night. She was so freaking embarrassed."

"The look on her face was so cute. I knew I was doomed in that moment."

"I'm so happy you found each other."

"Even though I stupidly waited until that last freaking moment in college to make my move."

I shake my head, "But you made it and you have her now."

"I do."

A comfortable silence falls around us as I continue making dinner. The sauce is bubbling on the stove and the crusted chicken pieces are frying on the cast iron.

"You'll find what you're looking for Elsi. If anyone deserves it, it's you."

I feel my shoulders drop, tension leaving them, "Thanks, Will."

"Please don't settle for less than what you deserve."

"I won't," I promise him. I owe it to myself to figure out once and for all what this thing is with Nate and if it's nothing, then it needs to firmly be nothing.

Chapter Thirty-One

Elsi:

S hifting the grocery bag to my left hand and attempting to balance it, I reach into my purse for my keys. I get the door unlocked with some difficulty, kick it open, and walk inside. I get the few groceries I brought in put away and turn on some mindless reality TV to have some background noise. It's been a good day. Things at work were smooth and steady, nothing crazy or demanding. It was a great way to end the week. Will and Norma have to go to some fancy dinner with her bosses, so I'm on my own tonight and am honestly not upset about it. I bought some wine and a frozen thin crust pizza. I plan to heat up the pizza and eat on the couch while I watch this new romantic comedy that came out last week.

After a quick shower, I throw on some underwear and a big tshirt, one of Nate's, and toss the pizza in the oven. A few minutes later, I plant my ass on the couch with two slices of pizza and a huge glass of wine. I'm half way through the movie when I hear a knock on my front door. I tap my phone and see it's 7:00 so Norma is definitely still at dinner. Have I ordered something recently? Realizing I have no pants on to open the front door, I go to sneak a peek at who it could be before I go to hunt some sweatpants down. But looking through the peephole, I see it's Nate. I rip the door open.

"What are you doing here?"

With a big smile, he steps forward and wraps his arms around me, squeezing me tight enough to lift me off the floor. He steps into my apartment and kicks the door closed behind him. "I missed you," he finally says.

He missed me.

"I thought you'd be home tomorrow night?"

He sets me back down but doesn't let me go, "I was supposed to be but I got done early today and didn't feel like hanging around any longer."

"I'm not complaining." I shift so that I can look up at him and then push onto my tippy toes to press a kiss to his perfect mouth.

He gives an appreciative hum and crushes me to him, changing my quick kiss to something deeper, something hungry and wanting. His hands find my hair and twine through it to hold me against him. His mouth opens and his tongue meets mine and my heart flutters. God, I missed him too.

Too soon, he pulls away with a smile, "You taste like wine."

I let out a giggle, "And probably pizza. Are you hungry?"

"Starved," he says with a glance down my body. "This is my shirt."

"Mhm," I confirm and turn toward the kitchen to grab him a slice of pizza and a glass of wine. He takes them from me with a kiss to my cheek and follows me to the couch. I change the movie to something else so I don't have to pay as much attention to it.

"How was Dallas? Hot?"

"Hm, yeah, pretty warm but I didn't really get to enjoy it much. The days were fucking long but we got everything done we needed to."

"With time to spare apparently," I point out.

"Exactly. But I'm glad to be home now."

I smile but am struck with the reminder that this isn't his home. He'll be leaving here in just over a month, back to California. Then what? There will be no more of this.

Knowing I need to know, but so scared to ask, I take a deep breath. I can feel my heart starting to beat faster and a weird tightness in my chest forms as I open my mouth, "Nate? What are we doing here?"

He bites his pizza and looks at me, obviously confused. He chews quickly and swallows before answering me cautiously, "What do you mean?"

Don't chicken out, Elsi. You need to know. "You told me once that I have no idea what you feel for me and you're right. So I'm asking you now."

He leans forward and puts his plate on the coffee table and then shifts on the couch so he's facing me, "I don't..." He trails off, looking at me, I can see his wheels turning, trying to figure out how best to answer. "We're having fun, I thought?"

A pang of disappointment hits me in the chest, "Yeah, we are. But what do you feel for me?"

He turns away from me, looking at the TV.

I wait. And wait. "Nate-"

"Why are you doing this?" he asks softly, still looking at the TV. He looks...sad.

Heartbreak like I never imagined settles into my soul. It's like this ripping feeling, like a part of me is being pulled away. My stomach clenches. I feel my eyes burning and my vision begin to blur. He doesn't want more than this. I let myself hope and now it's going to end. I should have fucking known. I did this to myself.

He looks at me then, "I don't have anything else to offer you, Elsi."

It's my turn to look away. I nod, "I understand. You're going back to California soon and this wasn't supposed to be more than what it is. I just-" a depressing little laugh blows past my lips though this is anything but funny, "fucked it up."

"You haven't fucked anything up," he says, confused by my meaning.

I look down at my fingers twisting around the hem of his shirt that I'm wearing. "You matter to me, Nate. This thing between us really matters to me and sometimes I think maybe it matters t-"

He cuts me off, "People get tired of having me around, Elsi, and if we became more and then something happened..." He looks down at his feet. "I just don't think I could survive you regretting me."

So this is fear?

"I could never regret you. Nothing could happen between us that would ever make me regret you. Do you think I'm not scared too? I'm scared all the time, of every day being the last one I have with you." I take a breath and add, my voice cracking, "I'm scared right now."

His eyes shoot to mine, hearing the hurt there but he just shakes his head, "I was trying to keep a line drawn so you wouldn't get hurt."

But I'm hurt now and fucking angry too and I'm determined to make him at least answer the damn question. I need to know, even if it hurts me further. I ask again, "What do you feel for me?"

He runs a hand down his face, "My whole life people have proven to me that I'm hard to love. I just-"

"*I* love you, Nate."

He visibly flinches back. His face utterly bemused. "You what?"

The tears begin to fall despite my best efforts to hold them back. *Keep going, Elsi.* "I've loved you since you told me love wasn't in the cards for you."

He shakes his head, "You'll change your mind."

I sigh in defeat knowing this is a lost cause, knowing it'll only hurt more and more, but going on anyway. "I've tried not to. I tried to only think of you as a friend but I can't help it. When we're together my whole body just relaxes. It just feels *right.* Even when you piss me off, you're the one I want to talk to about it. Loving you is so easy for me. But if this will never be anything more than what it is, then I can't see you anymore. I deserve to be important to someone."

He's looking at me like I'm a crazy person, like he doesn't even understand the words I'm saying. Before I can continue to make a goddamn fool of myself, I get up off the couch and walk into my bedroom. I just need a second. Frantically wiping my tears away is pointless because they keep falling so I try to focus on my breathing as best as I can. This is really it. The end.

His voice comes from behind me.

"You think you aren't important to me?"

"I don't know anything about your feelings," I say truthfully, keeping my back to him.

"Elsi," he sighs, walking around to stand in front of me. He doesn't continue until I look up at him. "You're my best friend. You're-" he cuts off and runs a hand into his hair and tugs. "Since November all I have wanted is to be near you. You know me better than anyone has in my entire life."

He's leaning down towards me slightly and continues, "Every moment of every day I think about you. When I'm at work, in meetings, I find myself daydreaming about the feel of your hair running through my fingers or the sound of your laughter. If I wake up in the morning and you're not there, I feel..." Again his hand grips into his hair. "I don't fucking know! Lost? Like my day won't really matter unless I get to see you. It's like a part of you lives here," he gestures to his head. "Even when I'm not thinking of you, you're still *there*. I don't even know how to explain it. I just feel you."

He reaches his hand out and traces a line down my cheek. That stupid feeling of hope breaks through some of the pain. His thumb swipes my tears away. His eyes dance across my face as he continues his confession, "Six months ago, if you asked me what my happiest memories were, I'd have told you a bunch of big hits, good plays, and wins. For the past five years, I thought my life had already peaked. I had come to the understanding that the rest of my life would probably just be about being comfortable, you know? But then I saw you again..."

He laughs softly and slides his fingers through my hair this time.

"Now if you asked me, I'd tell you that every single one of my best memories are you, Elsi. Every. Fucking. One. Watching movies, making dinner, talking about books, dancing with you at the gala, hearing you recognize my favorite poem. These past few months are the happiest I've *ever* been. I didn't know that I could feel like this."

His hand drops out of my hair, "But then I remember. I *always* remember that people have a hard time staying with me. That I don't know how to be the man you need."

"It's just you that I need, Nate."

His smile is sad again like he doesn't quite believe me. "Please tell me you understand. You're more important to me than anyone or anything has ever been."

I breathe out a sigh and I do understand. I do accept that that's the truth. So this whole thing...The entire reason he's holding back is because he thinks he isn't enough. That he can't make me happy. But he's already providing me with everything I need. Everything.

"I understand. But then you also need to understand that I want this. You. *Us*. I don't need you to be anything other than yourself. It's more than enough. My whole life, all I have ever wanted is *this*. You're all I need, Nate. And I don't find it hard to be around you. I hated you being gone. And you're moving back to California and when I think about it, I feel like I can't breathe. I don't want to go back to how life was before you."

He lets out a shaky laugh, "I could barely handle two weeks away from you. I told the freaking bartender about you. I told her all about my girl. Els," he takes a deep breath as his fingers graze down my cheek, "I requested a permanent transfer here."

"*What?*"

"I knew I'd never be able to go back to the other side of the country. Even assuming that this was temporary, I figured I could at least stay your friend when you decided to end things."

I shake my head violently, "I don't want to-"

"I know," he soothes, stepping closer. He closes his eyes and drops his forehead to mine. He stays like that for a few moments before taking another deep breath. His eyes open and he says, "I'm such an idiot. If I thought for one second that you'd feel for me the way I feel for you, Elsi, I'd have told you so fucking long ago how much you mean to me." He kisses my forehead and smiles down at me, "I want to be the man for you. And I want you to be mine. Really mine. I want everyone to know it. I want to be able to put a possessive hand on your neck and you feel good about it. I want to fall asleep with you every fucking night. I want to marry you and see you pregnant with our babies. I want to be 80 and talk about how successful our lives were. Together. Tell me that's what you want. Tell me you belong to me because Elsi, a part of me has belonged to you since fucking college."

I'm crying again but this time it's good. Better than anything I ever imagined. It's relief and joy and love. "I want that."

"I love you." He lets out a laugh that sounds like a mixture of shock and elation and his hands are back on my cheeks, gently tilting my head up to look at him. "*Jesus*, I never thought you'd love me back. I love you so goddamn much."

I laugh through my tears, "I love you too."

"I'm so sorry it took me so long."

"It doesn't matter,' I shake my head.

He leans down and presses a kiss to my lips, they're wet from my tears but he doesn't seem to care.

Chapter Thirty-Two

Nate:

How could I have been so stupid? I wasted so much time. Not even just these past few months, but years. I could have spoken to her in college. We could have been together since then. I'm such an idiot. I should have known that Elsi was different. That she'd accept me for me. I let the shit from my past almost ruin this with her. I let it keep me from talking to her in the first place. I knew that first day I ever saw her that I wanted her, wanted to be near her, to talk to her.

I might have gone my whole life without this.

Her face is wet from the tears that I caused, both from hurting her and then finally telling her the truth. I won't hurt her again. Not ever.

She steps in closer to me and deepens the kiss, her lips are so soft against mine. When our tongues meet, she lets out a breathy sigh that goes straight to my heart. I will never ever get over the sounds she makes. They're sweet and light, so feminine and pretty. They're an immediate dopamine hit, straight into my fucking blood.

Her hands dance across my chest and stomach before they land on my jeans and begin to work the button loose. My dick is already straining for her. Two weeks without her is far too long. I reach down to the hem of the shirt she's wearing, which is mine and huge on her, and run my hands up the back of her thighs.

She lets out a little giggle as my finger tickle her skin and I smile against her mouth. She pushes my jeans and boxer briefs down marginally and then her fingers are on my cock and I could scream from relief. Her thumb works the slit where precum is already leaking and I can't help the moan that escapes my lips.

I hook my fingers into her panties and begin to pull them down. She has to let my cock go as I bend to help her step out of them. Then I yank my shirt over her head so she's standing beautifully naked in front of me. I take in the sight of her, curvy and soft and perfect. Her breasts taunt me and I know my hands wrap perfectly around them. She reaches for me again and grips my shirt, pulling it over my head with my help and then pressing her sexy little body against mine as her lips return to my mouth.

"I need to be inside you, baby." Pulling her with me toward her bed, I push my jeans down further so my cock is free and then sit on the edge, guiding her to straddle my lap. She follows me willingly, always so fucking willing.

Situating herself on her knees, her pussy warm against my cock, she threads her fingers through my hair as I reconnect our mouths. The kiss becomes desperate and my hands glide along her soft skin, up her back to her neck, down her sides to her thighs. I need to touch her everywhere.

"You're so fucking perfect for me," I tell her. She needs to know.

She shifts slightly and slides her pussy along my shaft slowly and we groan simultaneously.

Yes.

When she pulls away and looks down between us, I get the message immediately and grip my cock to line the tip up with her entrance. She looks back at me, our faces only inches apart, and watches me as she sinks down onto my length. Eyes fluttering, she takes me inside of her, holding my gaze. Her mouth opens just slightly, the prettiest little moan escaping. My body comes alive as I slide into her. Nothing will ever compare to this feeling. When her round, sexy ass lands on my thighs and I'm as deep as I can possibly be inside her tight pussy, she presses a soft kiss to my lips and then circles her hips.

"Oh, *fuck-*" I grunt out. I'm not going to last long if she does that again.

She gives me a naughty little smile, like she knew that would drive me insane, and then pushes up on her knees, letting me slide out of her slightly. She wraps her arms around my shoulders and when she drops back down, huffing out a breath of pure pleasure and my heart thuds in my chest.

She finds a rhythm she likes and I can't take my eyes off of her, her breasts bounce between us, her nipples rubbing against my chest, her head drops back as she rides me. How did I ever deny to myself that I'm in love with this woman?

I do everything I can to show her how much I worship her. I press kisses along her collarbone and up her neck as she fucks me into oblivion. I whisper praise. My hands grip into her perfect body as she moves. They finally land on top of her thighs, pushing her harder down onto my cock. Her moans and whimpers are consistent now with each movement. She's close.

She slides down again and circles her hips like before and I can see stars. She drops her forehead to mine as she continues this little movement, obviously it's hitting the right spot for her because her breathing is completely erratic.

"*Nate,*" she moans and I can barely take any more. She lets out a whimpering cry as her pussy clamps down on my cock.

"That's my good girl." I grip her even tighter and jerk my hips up into her as her body goes limp. Within seconds, the orgasm explodes through my entire body, my nerve endings all firing, and I grip her tightly against me as I fill her with my cum. I push up into her gently a few times as I come down from the high and then wrap my arms around her, laying back onto the bed.

I'm still inside her as she relaxes her body on top of mine, her face pressing into my neck where it meets my shoulder. Her hair tickles my cheek. Her breathing steadies and I can feel her heartbeat against my chest.

"I love you."

She pushes up so she's looking down at me. Her caramel eyes alight. "I love you, Nate."

I exhale like I've been waiting my whole life to hear those words from her and I give her a smile before pulling her mouth down to mine.

Epilogue

Nate - One year later:

"Let's go, baby!" Norma's scream comes from behind me.

The pitch comes in and Will swings, sending a little dinger between the shortstop and left fielder. The team cheers for the lead off hit as Will stands safely on first but Norma's way louder than the rest of us. I look over to Elsi, her fingers threaded through the dugout fence, as she says something to Norma, who's sitting in the stands a few feet away, and then laughs.

Elsi looks unfairly sexy in our uniform. The team's emerald green shirt is fitted to her chest and is tucked into her baseball pants which show off her waist and perfect curves of her ass and legs. She wears the pants pulled up to her knees with black socks to complete the look. Her hair is in a ponytail pulled through the opening at the back of her plain black baseball hat.

This is my second year playing with the team though most of them have been playing together for years. Elsi, Will, and Frank all played and got me a spot on the team last year when I opted to move here permanently. It was an unexpected bonus of choosing to stay. I forgot how much I loved the sport until I got to our first practice and started warming up with my girl.

Elsi is *good*. Like, really good. She gets on base just about every time she's up to bat and she plays 3rd like a champion. I was surprised she didn't catch for the team but she said they needed a 3rd baseman when she started and now loves it too much to swap. She's one of only two girls on the team and everyone adores her. Because she's Elsi. And she's the best.

Harry hits a grounder to the 1st baseman and gets our first out. Then Natasha is up to bat and I'm on deck. Elsi comes over to stand next to me, cheering Natasha on.

I lean over to her, flicking the brim of her hat, and whisper in her ear. "I'm going to get on base," I assure her, "*then* if you hit me in, I'll fuck you nice and slow later. Just how you like it."

Her cheeks get pink, "I'm sure I can get you to fuck me regardless."

I laugh, "I don't think so." She's totally right, of course. I'll fuck her even if she strikes out every time and we lose by twenty runs. But that's far less fun than making this arrangement.

"Deal," she says with an eyebrow raised.

Natasha hits a nice pop fly over the right fielder's head, getting a double and sending Will home.

I grab my bat and walk to the batter's box. I live for this shit. I get myself positioned how I want and raise the bat, relaxing my muscles as I stare the pitcher down. He pulls his arm back and launches the ball at me. It goes too far outside and I don't swing.

"Ball," the umpire grunts.

I step out of the box, stretch my back, and then step back in. When the pitcher lets the ball fly, I know immediately that it's coming straight down the middle. I pick up my front foot, stepping as my arms start the familiar motion of my swing, my hips twist, and I feel the ball connect. And I'm running. The ball flies fast along the 3rd base line, past the infielder. The left fielder runs like mad to get to the ball as Natasha hustles from 2nd to 3rd. She stops there as I make the turn on 1st base. The left fielder only just reaches the ball and I don't slow down, going for the double. I reach the base easily before the shortstop has the ball next to me.

I hear my girl screaming for me.

The pitcher has the ball back in the circle as Elsi grabs her bat and walks to the plate. She looks out at me with narrowed eyes and gives me a sassy grin, shaking her head, annoyed that I was right and got on base. She gets in her stance, her perky little ass sticking out just slightly behind her. She looks so comfortable, so natural in the batter's box.

The count is two balls and one strike when she finally swings the bat, timing it perfectly and sending it ripping out beyond the center fielder. I run through

3rd base and make it home without any issues. I turn around to see her sprinting to 3rd base, trying to beat the throw. The ball comes in as she does and she drops into a picture perfect slide seconds before the 3rd baseman tags her with the ball in his glove. *Safe.*

Fuck, she's so hot.

She ends up scoring before the other team gets their three outs and she touches home and then runs to me, jumping into my arms. I catch her with a laugh and pat her ass affectionately.

"A deal's a deal, baby," she tells me and kisses my cheek before I drop her back to her feet. I'll happily fulfill that deal tonight.

We win the game, 13 to 8, and head down the street to the pub we always frequent after we play. Elsi grabs us beers from the bar and then sits down next to Norma. She reaches her hand out to rub Norma's belly, which is frankly gigantic. She's like 12 months pregnant or some shit. Due any second.

"Auntie Elsi is ready for you to come out, little man!" She sings to Norma's belly.

"Maybe he'll listen to you because he has not been listening to me," Norma groans, shifting uncomfortably in her seat.

"Oh, he's just so comfy," Elsi giggles as she grabs her beer to take a sip.

"So did you guys settle on your vacation plans?" Norma asks me and Els. We've been wanting to go on a trip but Elsi has so many damn places she wants to see, she couldn't figure out where to start. But I'll take that woman anywhere she wants to go.

"Yeah," I confirm and Elsi elaborates. "We're going to visit my parents first and then from there, we're going to the Grand Canyon. We rented one of those RVs so we can drive around the desert."

"No way!" Will's eyebrows raise, "That sounds badass."

Elsi runs with his enthusiasm and explains all of the things we're planning to do. We're not leaving for two months, mid September, but I know how excited she is. We're starting with two days at her parents. I already met them once last fall when we flew down to visit after Thanksgiving. They're really kind people, generous and loving, but they do harp on Elijah and the town a *lot*. Way more than I expected. Elijah was honestly kind of a jerk and though I won't tell Elsi, I don't hate only having to see him once or twice a year. The dude was very self important, dull as shit, and basically ignored Elsi's existence the whole time we were there despite her repeatedly trying to engage with him. But anyway, we're going to see her parents for a couple days and then flying into Arizona. We have a list of sights we want to see but I'm most looking forward to the Grand Canyon. She found a place where we can park the RV for a few days so we can do some hiking through there. It'll be awesome.

After our beers, we make our way home for dinner. Burgers on our balcony. We moved in together very shortly after my official transfer here last June. She loved my apartment so when Capulus Enterprises ended the lease, I applied to take it over. I flew back to California to settle a bunch of shit and ship everything here, like my car and the few pieces of furniture I was attached to. She was moved in by August.

My mother made a point to come visit at the end of summer, which I appreciated, and she and Elsi hit it off from the start. They talk to each other more than I've ever talked to my mom. Sometimes I'm a little resentful towards my mother about it, which Elsi completely understands, but overall, I'm just grateful that they get along. Elsi knows now what my relationship with my parents was like growing up. She's willing to be cordial with my mother but I know, like me, there is zero interest in a reunion with my father.

I finish grilling up the burgers and Elsi tops them with the mushrooms, onions, tomatoes, and pickles she cut up. She always cooks the onions and mushrooms down with garlic until their soft and fucking delicious. I could eat that alone by the spoonful, it's so good.

After we eat, I strip her of all her clothes in the living room, lay her on the carpet, and taste her pussy until she is writhing and throbbing underneath me.

"That's my girl," I say between kisses along her thigh. My fingers continue to swirl against her clit.

"*Please*, Nate," she begs and I smile against her skin. I take my time though, she can be patient. I push my fingers inside of her again and slowly pump in and out. I know she's still sensitive from her orgasm because she softly jerks against me. Sliding my fingers further back, I massage her tight little hole.

"When can I fuck your ass again?" I ask, my lips grazing her skin.

She arches her back with a moan as I slowly push one finger in. She's so willing. So goddamn perfect.

"Whenever you want," she coos, her voice dripping in pleasure.

"Mm," I hum, my cock leaking from her desire to please me. "Maybe next time."

When my cock slides into her, it isn't any less incredible than the first time. She feels so fucking good. She feels like mine. Her little fingers grip my arms as I grind into her slowly, as promised. She likes it when I give her slow, deep thrusts and when I'm as deep as I can get, I pause for just a second before moving again.

"You going to be a good girl and cum again? I want to feel you strangle me."

"*Yes,*" she whimpers and I shift her leg so I can push deeper.

Her lips are soft when I press mine against them and let my tongue slide lazily across hers. She breathes heavily into my mouth, getting close to another orgasm. Wanting to help her out, so she cums before I do, I slide a hand between us and rub my thumb against her clit.

"Nate-" she cuts off and moans hard, her head tilting back, her fingers digging into my skin. So beautiful.

Her pussy walls slam down on my cock and make me lightheaded with pleasure. "Fuck, you feel good." I pick up the pace slightly and thrust hard into her, her gasps and cries spurring me on until I feel the orgasm travel up my spine and I jerk, spilling inside of her. My heart is racing when I slow down and drop my body weight onto her. We lay in the silence like that for a long time.

When she randomly breathes out a little giggle, I push up onto my forearms to look down at her. I'm still inside of her. Her pretty hair is fanned out around her and her eyes are hooded with exhaustion but her smile is radiant and bright and just for me.

I can't believe she's mine. From that very first moment I saw her, I knew she was special. Sometimes I can't believe this past year has been *my* life. I never thought it could be like this. As I look down at her, I slide my fingers along her face and I feel my love for her pulsing deep in my soul.

"Marry me."

She stares back at me, her eyebrows raising marginally, her smile still wide on her face. "Is that a question?"

"Does it need to be? I have a whole speech rehearsed and I was going to wait until we were deep in the desert. I wanted to do it right and be this fancy, romantic guy but I can't wait one more second for my ring to be on your finger, baby. *Marry me.*"

"You have a ring?"

"Yeah, rolled up in my socks," I confess.

She glances towards the hallway, "When did you get a ring?"

"January."

"January?!" she borderline screeches in disbelief.

"I started looking in November, I think. Norma helped me. But I didn't find the right one until January."

"Norma helped you?" her voice cracks slightly and I can see her eyes start to water.

"Of course. I wouldn't dream of proposing without her permission. She's your soulmate after all," I tease.

She barks out a watery laugh, "I love you."

I press a soft kiss to her lips, "I love you too, Elsi. Marry me. Please."

"Yes."

I knew she'd say yes. I really did. But that doesn't stop my heart from hammering in my chest or the relief to wash through me. She pushes up to kiss me this time and I pour my love into it. My whole life has been leading to this moment with her. Knowing she'll be mine forever.

"Stay here," I say abruptly, planting another kiss to her mouth, and sliding out of her. Jesus, I proposed to the love of my life while my dick was inside her. That's probably normal, right?

She laughs as I stalk out of the living room, down the hall, to my sock drawer. I fumble through until I find the pair with the hard lump inside and rip it out.

When I get back to the living room, she's where I left her, but sitting up now with my shirt underneath her.

I kneel in front of her and feel like a little kid excitedly giving a gift to a loved one. I can't wait for her to see it. I hope she likes it. I hand the box to her and she takes it with an excited smile. When she lifts the lid, her smile drops to an open mouth and for one second I panic that she hates it.

"Nate..." she looks up at me as she lifts the ring from the box, "it's beautiful. It's perfect."

I smile at her and take the ring. She understands my intention and holds her left hand out for me. Gripping her fingers, I look up to watch her face as I slide the ring on. It's a simple design. Norma had suggested I keep it pretty traditional. So I went with a ring that has one large oval shaped diamond front and center with small circular diamonds going all the way around the band. It looks perfect on her finger. She holds her hand up, wiggling her fingers to see how it shines in the light, and then launches herself at me with tears in her eyes. I wrap my arms around her with a laugh and hold her close.

"I love it. I love you. Thank you."

She's going to be my *wife*.

"I love you too, Elsi. More than anything."

Acknowledgements

As always, I want to shout out to authors whose books have impacted my life, helped me through tough times, and inspired me daily. I find it hard to explain how important books have been to me since reading my first novel at 8 years old, but I know that I am who I am because of all the stories I have read. There's so much to learn from books. They let us enter worlds dreamt up by others, they teach us compassion, they create an escape. So again, thank you to all the authors, traditionally publish AND indie, who create worlds for all of us to climb into.

A big big thank you to anyone who read this book, or any of my others, even if it was just a few sentences. I always tell myself that I write these books for me. That it's okay that they're not viral and in the hands of millions. But it warms my heart that even one other person may pick it up and think "Hey, this might be good."

Thank you to mgk and fanfiction Draco Malfoy (of J.K. Rowling's wizarding world) for inspiring Nate. I know that there is some weird dislike of blonde male main characters in the romance world. But tall, fit, blonde men (especially those with tattoos) have been my weakness since I was like 12, so forgive me, people!

Nate's favorite poem, which is tattooed along his collarbone, is "Invictus" by William Ernest Henley. It is one of those poems that just kind of rewires your brain when you read it. The resilience and perseverance of the narrator is the kind of thing you hope to possess yourself, if the need ever arose. Anyway, read it. It's short and sweet and you'll find yourself thinking about it from time to time afterwards.

This book is dedicated to a dear friend. She was a loving wife and mother to two young kids. She was with me through some truly difficult times, always recommended the best wine, and was even my neighbor for a couple years. She was one of those friends who loved your children like they were her own. When she found something unbelievable, she would always scream "No way!" in this very distinct voice and I can still hear it in my memories. I know that's what she'd say if I handed her one of my books and I know that she would have been hugely supportive and absolutely loved all the spicy scenes. I miss you. I'll always miss you.

A shout out to my 3 kiddos, who ask me constantly what I'm doing on the laptop and who I constantly respond to with, "Oh, nothing." I know they know what's happening but I appreciate they're not pushing it. Maybe someday I'll tell them but I don't know if I'll ever let them read anything. Maybe when they're 30 or something. Regardless, I love you three more than anything.

A final thank you to my husband, who tries very hard to keep up with my writing despite reading not being something he enjoys. I appreciate the effort, babe! Thank you for all the help with my ideas and for working out logistics with me..hehe! I love you so much and I like you more than anyone in the universe.

About the author

Jamie O. Colt lives in the Northeast, USA – in the middle of nowhere – with her husband, three kiddos, and a bunch of animals. She spends her days teaching ELA to high school students and every other waking moment driving her kids to activities or cooking some kind of meal. In the very rare instances when she has a free second, she likes to read and write. Her favorite genres to consume are fantasy, sci-fi, and romance. She started writing novels because there were stories she wanted to read but couldn't find anywhere. Her goal is to write stories that are realistic with characters that are relatable, people you might actually meet in your life. Other than reading and writing, Jamie likes to always have a coffee in her hand, spend one-on-one time with Mr. Colt, and plan tons and tons of vacations.

Also by Jamie

Hold Me Tight

College romance

Another Round

Mixed martial arts sports romance

www.ingramcontent.com/pod-product-compliance
Lightning Source LLC
Chambersburg PA
CBHW022037240626
47154CB00007B/2444